C000205826

SHOOTING LESSONS

$HOOTING LESSON$

LENNY KLEINFELD

Published by Niaux-Noir Books

Copyright © 2019 by Lenny Kleinfeld

This book is a work of fiction. Names, characters, places and incidents are either products of the author's imagination or used fictitiously Any resemblance to actual events, locales or persons, living or dead, is entirely coincidental.

All rights reserved. No part of this publication can be reproduced or transmitted in any form or by any means, electronic or mechanical, without permission in writing from the author or publisher.

ISBN: 978-0-578-41359-4

Book design and typesetting by: Stewart A. Williams Design

For Sheldon Patinkin, 1945-2014
Writer, director, professor and loving uncle to
four decades of Chicago theater people.
He taught them the First Law of Chicago Esthetics:
"Better an asshole than a chickenshit."

Everybody gonna need
Some kind of ventilator

—THE TAO OF MICK AND KEITH

ONE

Ever since Bluetooth no one looks twice at a driver alone in a car who's deep in conversation with an invisible friend. Even if the friend is Shakespeare.

"'When I said I would die a bachelor, I did not think I should live til I were married. Here comes Beatrice—' well actually here comes Mitch," Kody Wallace corrected as a man standing at the curb waved at Kody's red Rav 4, which sported the world-famous Makro insignia on its windshield.

Mitch was nobody's Beatrice—fortyish, six-four, muscular, short blond hair, three days' stubble coating his square jaw. Windbreaker, work shirt, cargo khakis and for some reason Mitch was wearing thin leather gloves even though the temp was 54. Kody didn't waste time wondering about it; a guy wearing gloves on an unusually balmy autumn day didn't budge the needle on Kody's passenger weird-ometer.

He lowered the passenger-side window as he glided to a halt. "Mitch? I'm Kody."

The passenger nodded and reached for the rear door.

"More legroom up front," Kody offered.

"S'okay," Mitch said—in a casual, authoritative rumble of a voice Kody wanted to hear more of. Kody could—would—use that voice someday. Had to get this guy talking. Kody took a peek in the rearview. Mitch was looking out the side window. Erect posture, gloved hands resting on the tops of his thighs.

"Yeah, the gloves," Mitch rumbled. Now looking right at Kody.

"I wasn't... Fukkit, I'm busted. The gloves," Kody admitted, grinning.

"Know what never occurs to people? A dude my size, kinda hard-lookin', could be germophobic. Or even knows the word germophobic," Mitch added, sly.

Kody guessed, "So you get asked about the gloves like every day?"

"Not every." Mitch studied him for a moment. "So, Kody, what kinda work you really do?"

"Yeah, well… I'm the total Makro cliché: I'm an actor."

"You good at it?"

"I've got an Equity card… Tomorrow morning I've got a final call-back—lead role, down to me and one other—and it's a major theater, Chicago Shakes. Chicago Shakespeare Theatre, on Navy Pier?"

"Yeah, I been by there. What's the show?"

"*Much Ado About Nothing.* Shakespeare's best comedy. And Benedick's a great part… If I get this gig, it could lead to… I might have to give up my career as a Makro driver."

"Then why the hell you drivin' around instead of home rehearsing?"

"I'm rehearsing while I drive."

"Ain't it better to do that with other actors?"

"Which is why after work I'm gonna run lines with some friends. Then go home and try not to lay awake all night thinking about it."

"Good-lookin' dude like you, you don't have a girlfriend boyfriend whatever to help with that?"

"My girlfriend's in Minneapolis for her kid sister's confirmation." Kody sighed. "Great kid but she picked the wrong week to turn twelve."

"Hell yeah," Mitch agreed.

Kody glanced at the rearview. Mitch was also looking into the mirror, making eye contact with Kody and holding it. With an expression that was a strange blend of sympathetic and—hungry?

Was Mitch coming on to him? Kody returned his attention to the traffic.

Neither spoke again until Kody announced, "Here we are," as he pulled to the curb. "Have a great day." Kody turned to face Mitch. Said, in a carefully subdued imitation of Mitch's voice, "Been good talking to you."

Mitch gave him a small nod, saying, "Luck with the audition," and tried to hand him a twenty.

Fuck yeah he's hitting on me. "Thanks, but that's more than the fare."

"C'mon, buy yourself a coupla drinks, help ya sleep." Mitch continued to hold the twenty out, his arm rock steady. Body language a perfect fit with the voice.

"You can click on one of the tip options—how's this, rate me five stars, and if you want you can write a comment about how great I am."

Mitch promised, in that low rumble, "It'll be the best thing anybody ever said about you."

◆

When Kody knocked off work that evening the best thing anybody ever said about him still hadn't shown up. No way to tell if Mitch had been bullshitting, or just that Mitch was old enough to lack the instant-response imperative groomed into kids who've grown up digital.

◆

Kody got home close to midnight. As he walked up the stairs to his apartment he couldn't resist pulling out his phone to see if Mitch's—nope.

Get a fuckin' grip, Kody advised himself as he slowly, carefully opened the door to his apartment, *getting hung up on acting reviews is bad enough, now I'm gonna stress over driver reviews…*

"Katniss?" Their unusually affectionate, unusually dumb cat would rush right up to the door soon as she heard the key, which is why Kody always opened it gently—but she wasn't there. Kody closed the door and looked arou—

Katniss was splayed near the bedroom doorway, dead, fucking dead, Kody knew it before he knelt and touched her.

"Hey." That deep rumble—

Kody's head jerked upward—

Mitch emerged from the darkened bedroom, his gloved hand gripping a silenced gun aimed at Kody with that rock-steady arm.

"Kody Wallace died for his country," Mitch said and his gun clapped twice.

TWO

Turns out maybe Brooklyn was right," Doonie said, referring to Brooklyn McVay, the vic's distraught girlfriend, "there is nobody this whole fuckin' planet had a reason to pop Kody Wallace. Forget hire a pro shooter who charges money."

"We haven't interviewed the whole planet yet," Mark pointed out.

"We interviewed the whole part knew Wallace. My money's on Wallace was a mistake, contract shooter hit the wrong guy. An accident of God."

"Doon, it's been three days."

"All I'm sayin', if we do never clear this, I was the one predicted it was gonna be a dry hump." Doonie waved to their waitress to bring another round of Makers.

In the eight years since Mark Bergman made Homicide and was partnered with the semi-legendary John Dunegan, they'd been drinking Jack Daniels. When Mark switched to Makers Mark, Doonie gave Mark shit about how him being a Cubs fan was bad enough, he didn't have to go around drinking like one.

Then the JaneDoe thing happened. JaneDoe, a young artist who was the first and only woman Mark ever wanted to spend his life with, decisively informed Mark he was banned from her life, and moved to Europe.

Doonie took Mark to a blues club where they killed a bottle of Makers. Since then Doon kept ordering Makers, explaining he was only doing it because he was trying to cheer up a heartbroke friend.

Despite Doonie's noble sacrifice, the heartbroke friend wasn't buying Doonie's theory of the murder. Doon was right about the annoying lack of suspects. Nobody in Kody Wallace's family—or Brooklyn's—had motive to kill Kody, or knew anyone who might.

Neither did his friends and colleagues. The actor who'd been up against Wallace for the role of Benedick had a solid alibi for the time of the murder, and couldn't afford a skilled hit man.

Same with Wallace's day job. No problems with bosses or other Makro drivers. No known beefs with passengers—and Wallace didn't have a dashcam that might've recorded one. No accidents. No run-in with a taxi driver enraged at the ride-hail scum who were destroying his livelihood.

Kody Wallace had no rap sheet, no big debts, no significant bad habits, no insane exes. And yet he'd been given what looked like a pro sendoff.

The shooter had no trouble getting past the lock on Wallace's door. Picked a night Brooklyn was out of town. Fired two shots nobody heard; chest and head, .22 cal. Used a clean piece. Picked up his brass. Took nothing from Wallace's apartment. Left no gotcha forensics.

Which was why Mark wasn't buying Doonie's supposition: It assumed a pro this organized had an oops moment and killed the wrong guy.

Mark read every comment on Kody Wallace's driver page. Nothing but four- and five-star ratings.

Almost. Six months ago a passenger gave Kody a one-star rating and a one-word review: *Unexceptable.*

Mark and Doonie drove down to Hegewisch, Chicago's southern-most neighborhood, to knock on the door of a dilapidated clapboard cottage belonging to Wallace's one unsatisfied customer, Nancy Mittelhausen.

Mittelhausen was 82, frail, walked with a cane, and had dissed Wallace because she resented his gay hair and gay driving. They learned this from Mittelhausen's granddaughter, who was housesitting while Grandma was on a European tour with her church group.

Mark asked to see Grandma's itinerary. She'd been in Paris the night of the murder. Mark and Doonie called it a day and went to dinner.

◆

Paris. Mark ignored the reference until now, a hot meal and multiple bourbons into being off-duty. Paris was where JaneDoe was living. But the only time she'd returned one of Mark's calls it was to make clear what she needed was for him to stay out of her life. Totally. Said she'd let him know if that ever changed, and he'd better respect that. He did. No mystery why JaneDoe needed to get far away from him and Chicago.

"Excuse me," blurted a slightly inebriated young man walking by their booth as he jolted to a halt, with That Look on his face: he recognized Mark. "Sorry to, are you that cop—police officer, police officer—Detective, um, Mark Berkowitz?"

"Almost," Mark replied.

The slightly inebriated young man looked slightly confused.

"Bergman," Doonie clarified.

"You *are* you," the slightly inebriated young man exulted.

"And you are?"

"Stig, Stig Weston, this is so dope, like, an honor Detective—*Bergman.*"

"Good meeting you too, Mr. Weston."

"Stig call me Stig… So, uh, would it be okay to ask, um…" Stig struggled to work up the nerve to ask the *What's it like to kill four guys?* question. He failed, flailed and blurted, "Are you Jewish?"

"Nope."

"Oh—sorry sorry didn't mean to get personal. So, um—" Stig's eyes did a frantic dance, "—what religion are you?"

"None."

"Oh shit, sorry sorry, didn't mean—"

"Your drinks, gentlemen," the waitress announced, plunked down two fresh glasses, cleared the empties and left.

"Look, I apologize."

"Nah," Mark assured Stig, and shook his hand. "You're not gonna drive yourself home, right?"

"Sure… Uh, thanks."

Stig began to walk away, turned and started to ask—

"No selfies," Doonie growled.

Stig took a moment to process that alien concept, gave an unconvincing no-problem shrug and hurried into the men's room.

Doonie shot Mark a disconsolate look and waved to the waitress to bring the check.

"Relax," Mark counseled. "Don't gulp your dessert."

"Right now Stig's posting on Fuckchat while he's standin' there pissin.'"

"But this is the first time we've had to flee the scene of a bourbon in nearly two weeks." Mark raised his glass. "A new record."

Doonie gave Mark's glass a sarcastic clink.

"Don't worry, Doon, this celebrity cop shit is fading fast, soon it'll be gone. All I've gotta do is not shoot anybody."

THREE

Stan Vanderman, known to friends as the Silver Sidewinder and to the public as the Executive Vice President of the American Gun Association, had booked the penthouse suite atop Springfield's finest approximation of a posh hotel. Vanderman was in town to lobby the Minority Leader and Deputy Minority Leader of the Illinois General Assembly. The suite had been swept for bugs, there was security on the door, and the only other person at the meeting was a tall gangly baby-faced thirty-one-year old, who was sipping the ninety-year-old cognac the three oldsters were swilling.

"So what's this week's plan to sell more guns?" Minority Leader Charles Mason asked, prairie droll.

"Charlie," Vanderman sighed, D.C. innocent, "the AGA's sole mission is to protect the Second Amendment rights of Americans."

"Next you're gonna swear monkeys shit diamonds and I should let my daughter marry one," Mason predicted.

"*Let* her? Charlie, you'd insist on it," Deputy Leader Evie Burnett teased.

Mason and Vanderman laughed. The thirty-one-year old didn't; he was playing the inscrutable card. In fact he liked Evie Burnett. She was sharp, tough and in good enough shape to qualify as fuckable at fifty.

Mason drained his snifter and let Vanderman refill it. Mason gave the luxury lubricant a swirl and repeated, "So what's this week's plan to sell more guns?"

Vanderman answered, "Out of Illinois' one-point-five million licensed handgun owners, why have only ninety-one thousand bothered to apply for a Concealed Carry License?"

"Because that's how many people want one," Mason said.

"No, Charlie, every Illinois gun owner wants concealed carry. But they won't put up with getting screwed out of a four hundred dollar CCL fee, on top of paying for the mandatory fourteen hour training."

"Don't even think about easing the requirements for concealed carry," Mason warned.

"Not easing," Vanderman said. "Eliminating."

Mason blatted a dismissive snort.

"Stan," Evie Burnett wondered, "has it slipped your mind the Democrats control the Assembly, and the Senate?

"Nope."

"Ain't happening, Stan," Mason insisted. "Wouldn't even be able to flip the pliable suburban Dems. No way any of 'em's gonna vote to remove concealed carry requirements."

"There's always a way. We're gonna commit as much time and," Vanderman looked the politicians in the eye, "*resources* as it takes to make it happen." He paused to sip cognac.

Nicely played, the gangly young observer thought; after you mention money to pols, give them a moment to fantasize.

Evie wasn't in the mood. "Don't play dumb, Stan. You know the only way we got CCL passed was by including mandatory training. Over 80% of Illinois voters want to know the drunk on the next barstool with a gun tucked in his shorts was forced to hear a safety lecture. You're gonna change that how?"

"I unleash the Kraken," Vanderman explained, indicating the millennial.

Trey Fister gave his audience a moment to take in the edgy haircut, slim-fit Dolce & Gabbana suit and the super-confident smirk he wore as if it were a medal he'd won in the wunderkind wars.

Trey warmed his wundersmirk into a grin and aimed it at Evie. "Four hundred bucks plus mandatory training was the *price* Dems charged to vote for concealed carry, it wasn't the *reason*," Trey asserted, rising to his feet and pacing as he spoke, because that's what the unstoppable solitary genius did in every unstoppable solitary genius movie. "The *reason* is, Dems are human. Deep down, Chicago lakeshore libs want to know if push comes to shove they're free to pack a weapon. We're going to make them face the fact push has already obliterated shove. Chicago's murder epidemic is at three hundred a year and—"

"But damn near all of that's black on black or brown," Mason reminded the wunderkind.

"Which is why in the 'hood there's mad love for concealed carry," Trey reminded the pudgy old hack.

"But sweetie," Evie cooed, "that's got fuck-all to do with us converting that great big pile of middleclass white folks who actually vote."

"My point exactly," Trey enthused. "Illinois is averaging about seven hundred murders a year and 38% of those victims are white."

"But less than half of those whites are middleclass."

"Right, no one gives a shit about the dead spouse in a trailer-trash divorce. But that still gives us dozens of middleclass whites killed every year, and all they get is sixty seconds on local TV and a yawn on page nine. We're gonna fix that." Trey picked up his snifter, took a sip and set the snifter down slowly, to inject suspense before letting them hear the payoff. "In addition to a classic balls-to-the-wall AGA lobbying push, we're gonna post videos and TV commercials about every respectable solvent white—and a few respectable solvent ethnics—whose murders could've been prevented by concealed carry. We'll move fast, while the hurt's fresh—heard about that good-looking young actor in Chicago who got shot a few days ago? Threw this together on my laptop," Trey said, pulling a tiny remote from his pocket. "It'll be polished and on social media tomorrow, along with a 30-second TV commercial."

A video flared to life on the suite's 70-inch flatscreen.

A close-up photo of a young man, handsome, with an expressive, charming grin. A title fades in: **KODY WALLACE**. *Then another:* **AGE 25**. *Along with the titles is voiceover, by Trey Fister:*

"Kody Wallace... 25... Graduate of the Goodman School of Drama."

Graduation photo, flanked by beaming parents.

"Engaged."

Photo of Kody down on one knee, proposing to Brooklyn—in the Wrigley Field bleachers, surrounded by cheering friends and strangers.

"A talented young actor—" *montage of sexy Kody in various roles—*"who was up for the lead role in the next production at the Tony Award-winning Chicago Shakespeare Theatre."

Photo of Kody goofily mugging on the stairs in front of a gleaming three-story theater building on Navy Pier.

"But Kody didn't show up for his final audition."

Shot of Kody in front of the theater crossfades to news footage of a body bag on a gurney being rolled down the front walkway of Kody's building.

"The night before that audition, Kody Wallace walked into his apartment and confronted a burglar, who gunned Kody down."

EMTs load the body bag into the rear of an ambulance. Freeze on the image of the body bag half-in, half-out of the ambulance.

"We'll never know what might've happened if big-government red tape and steep fees didn't stand between us and our right to carry a firearm."

The body bag shot is replaced by the photo of Kody goofing in front of the Shakespeare Theatre.

"In a rational world, *every* Illinois handgun license would automatically include, with no cash penalty, the right to keep your firearm with you, *everywhere* you go."

The camera pushes in close on Kody's face:

"To be, or not to be."

The frame splits: Kody on one side, the body bag on the other.

"That's the question."

Fade up a title card:

EVERY LICENSE EVERYWHERE
Make your voice heard. Go to ELE.com

Vanderman gave the pols a triumphant, steely look. "One of these will appear every time any relatable citizen is murdered."

"That might sell some guns," Mason grudgingly allowed.

But Evie was intrigued. "The 'Every License Everywhere' thing, ELE... That works," Evie complimented Vanderman.

"Thank you," Trey murmured, modestly confirming that yes, I'm the one who came up with ELE. He snuck a glance at Vanderman, whose lips were just perceptibly tightening in anger. Hells yeah the Sidewinder planned to jack my credit. Never gonna happen the zombie speed you move, Sidewinder-bro.

"Trey," Mason asked, "your 'Everywhere.' You mean every school and church in Illinois, or every state in the country?"

"Both," Vanderman cut in. "Everywhere in Illinois—with a few reasonable exclusions like courtrooms and the State Assembly. It also means licenses in every state must include concealed carry. And a license issued by any state must be honored in every state."

Evie said, "So this is the opening shot in a national push."

Vanderman winked and—

"Exactly," Trey confirmed, beating Sidewinder-bro to the punch line. "No surprise some Southern states hand out licenses with free concealed carry. But the day Illinois—half Midwestern heartland, half world-class destination city Chicago—adopts it, that's the tipping point, free concealed carry goes serious mainstream. Goes inevitable. Which means the AGA's got your back all the way... and that I am gonna be here doing whatever it takes for as long as it takes," Trey vowed, aiming those last words at Evie, along with his subtlest intimate Tom Cruise grin. Just wide enough to flex the dimples.

Evie's expression didn't change... But she locked eyes and gave him a few seconds of *It's on.*

Boo-yah! Trey shoots, Trey scores. As always, bro.

FOUR

Five days in, the Kody Wallace investigation was showing the same amount of life as Kody Wallace. Mark could handle that; working homicide, your choice is to develop patience or ulcers. The problem with the case being stalled was that Mark couldn't use being busy as an excuse to cancel a charity date with one of the Mayor's heaviest donors, who'd bought Mark at a bachelor auction.

Four years ago Mark had been one of the Chicago PD's more visible and popular cops when he came out on the winning end of a shootout with a top-tier assassin, who'd murdered a beloved Chicago architect.

Six months ago, while hunting a serial killer nicknamed the Art Critic, Mark took down a gangster and two mercenaries who were trying to eliminate a witness. The four notches on Mark's gun, combined with Mark being single, smart and not ugly, put him on screens across America and beyond, which made him Superintendent of Police Gary Shook's favorite public relations toy. The Supe personally donated Mark to the bachelor auction, a fundraiser hosted by the wife of the Alderman who chaired the city's Budget Committee.

Mark was purchased by Bettina Dolan, whose family had been a power in Chicago's upscale real estate and politics since the 1920s.

Bettina paid top dollar for Mark because he'd make a dream escort at the Lyric Opera's toniest fundraiser. Being decades younger than Bettina was Mark's only resemblance to standard heiress arm candy. All of Bettina's friends and enemies would be panting for face time with the lethal local hero, and placing bets on whether Bettina would manage to coax Mark into her swag bag.

Mark checked his watch, sighed, "Okay," put his computer to sleep and stood up. "Time to face the tux."

"Poor guy," Doonie crooned, grinning. "Maybe you won't have to waste a whole night kissin' up to rich fucks. Maybe an hour in, you'll get a call, there's emergency murder developments need Det. Bergman's personal attention."

"Like that's gonna fool any woman over twelve. Let alone a woman of sixty-three who can ask the Mayor to please find out if I lied to her."

◆

Sitting there savoring extraordinary cuisine in an elaborately unreal setting, Mark thought, *My timing sucks.*

His fifteen minutes of fame were going to waste. Women were hitting on him almost every day, when Mark was, for the first time in his life, finding casual sex dull. A little depressing, even. At age thirty-five he'd finally managed to fall deeply in love. With a woman who promptly dumped him and moved four thousand miles away. Turned out Mark's favorite car radio sing-along back when he was age five—he liked shouting the lyric's funny hook—was funny because it was true. *Love stinks! Yeah, yeah.*

Still, Mark's ego and hormones were entertained by being flirted at by women wearing two years' worth of Mark's salary in clothing and jewelry, while sitting next to their husbands at one of the six tables on the Lyric Opera's stage, surrounded by the Renaissance castle splendor of a set from *Rigoletto*. Mark was the only diner who wasn't a six-figure donor and a current, former or potential member of the Board. Folks living at the private jet level of Chicago business, politics, arts, science and shopping.

They were miles more sophisticated than Stig Weston. A good seventy minutes went by before yeah, here we go, someone asked Mark about his work. Buckle your seatbelts, the conversation's begun its descent to its scheduled destination. *Tell us about killing four guys.*

Bettina was the reigning power at Mark's table. But the most alpha of the table's four male tycoons, the CEO of a global marketing strategies agency, was dominating the conversation. Mark knew it would be Most Alpha who popped the question.

Most Alpha was explaining how, when it came to dealing with corrupt megalomaniacal dictatorships, China was a piece of cake compared to FIFA. He basked in the chuckles that earned, then inquired, "So, Mark, how's business with you—any suspects yet for who killed that actor?"

Mark regretfully informed him, "It's an ongoing investigation, the only thing I can tell you is I can't tell you anything."

"Does that mean there aren't any leads?" Most Alpha wondered, hopefully. His young wife had been glowing at Mark more warmly than the other young wives.

"It means," Mark explained, "if I compromise a case by blabbing about it, I spend next year directing traffic at O'Hare."

"And I," Bettina instructed Most Alpha, "don't want to talk about murder while I'm eating."

"Quick before the next course arrives—have you seen that disgusting commercial the AGA put out using Kody Wallace," Most Alpha's young wife asked.

"Yeah," Mark said. *So have Kody's parents, who called, weeping, to vent about the commercial and ask if I'd made any progress.* "But I agree with Bettina: no talking murder, even between courses."

"This isn't about murder, it's politics," Mrs. Most Alpha protested with a charming pout. "Does the AGA really think exploiting a victim isn't going to backfire?"

"Backfire!?" her husband barked. "That commercial kills. The more brazen it is the more it reinforces their brand with their inbred demo. You know that," Most Alpha scolded. "And the more disgusting it is the better it scares normal people—who are more concerned about ending up like Kody Wallace than they are about his corpse being used as a prop." Most Alpha aimed a predatory grin at Mark. "And the longer it takes to find the killer, the more powerful the AGA's disgusting message will get… Shit," Most Alpha sighed, giving Mark a sadistic parody of a sympathetic look. "I am never again gonna bitch about having to deal with FIFA."

"Sure you will," Mark predicted.

Bettina chuckled, then one of the Less Alphas did too.

Most Alpha's cheeks flushed hot red and the rest of him froze. He gave Mark a sour smirk that, if this were a bar, would be an invitation to step outside. Mark, amused, held Most Alpha's gaze. Most Alpha lowered his eyes.

Mrs. Most Alpha beamed at Mark. "I knew you two would get along. Mark, you absolutely have to join us for the opening night of *Rosenkavalier.*"

"Too late dear, I've already invited him," Bettina lied, and under the table pressed her leg against Mark's.

His phone rang. Doonie.

"Excuse me," Mark apologized to his dinner companions, and walked into the wings.

"Told you not to call, asshole. But thanks, I needed a breather."

"Fuck that, you're leaving."

"Fuck me, I can't."

"Kaz and Kimmie caught a case. Gunshot, two taps, no brass. And the vic drives for Makro."

FIVE

The vic's residence was near Lincoln Square, so Mark went alone. It'd take Doonie too long to drive that far north from his place in Beverly.

Mark called from the car to let Kazurinsky and Kimbrough know he was on his way. They'd just finished interviewing the family. Kimmie gave him the tour.

"David Gold, 47. Former reporter for the Trib, got bounced a few years ago during the paper's annual downsizing. Gold couldn't find another reporter job. But he's a widower with a son at Northwestern, so they move in with Gold's older brother, while Gold freelances articles, and teaches journalism at Columbia College and drives a Makro, so he can keep his kid in a good school.

"Last night as usual Gold gets home around eleven-thirty, changes and walks eight blocks to a twenty-four hour gym. Gym staff confirmed Gold worked out and left about twelve-thirty. Never shows up home. Doesn't answer calls or texts. His brother, Nate, walks up and down Gold's route; nothing. Then he checks Gold's car—it's there, but somebody broke into it and stole the dashcam. So Nate calls the cops, they tell him it takes twenty-four hours before this turns from a missing camera into a missing person. 'Call the hospitals in your area.' Nate does; Dave's not there.

"Tonight a little after dark a driver sees a coyote trot across the street and into an alley. Driver pulls into the alley, gets out looking to Instagram some urban wildlife footage. Spots the coyote's tail sticking out behind a dumpster, starts shooting video and moves closer— the coyote whips out from behind the dumpster, bloody muzzle, snarling…" Kimmie's voice trailed off.

" 'Stay the fuck away from my meal,'" Mark said, so she wouldn't have to.

"Uh-huh. The family's looking forward to meeting you."

◆

"Thank you for agreeing to go over this again. And—" touching his tuxedo, "—my apologies for the inappropriate attire," Mark told the relatives of the murdered and partly eaten victim.

David Gold's wet-eyed brother Nate and sister-in-law Cheryl were huddled on a large couch, along with Gold's elderly parents. The mother slouched against the father, weeping softly. The old man stroked her hair, but he was far away, slowly bobbing his head and chanting under his breath, a whispery dazed Kaddish.

David Gold's 19-year-old son Danny stood leaning against a wall. He was the definition of sullen. Five-eight, thickset, pear-shaped, with unruly curly hair and large, expressive dark brown eyes that were staring coldly at the floor, wanting to kill that distressed hardwood for murdering his dad.

Mark asked, "Did Mr. Gold know Kody Wallace? Do you know if they ever met, had any connection, anything in common other than driving for Makro?"

Nate gave his head a weary shake. "No. Not that I knew. Danny?" he asked his nephew.

Danny shrugged, eyes fixed on the floor.

Mark asked him, "Did your father have any hassles with taxi drivers? A hostile passenger?"

Another shrug.

Mark looked at Nate, who shook his head.

"Dave got along with everybody," Cheryl volunteered. "Everybody," she emphasized, bewildered.

Gold's father stopped chanting and whispered something in Mark's direction.

"Sir?" Mark gently coaxed.

The old man asked, "You think the same person killed my Davey?"

"I don't know," Mark said. "When Kody Wallace was killed, did

Dave say anything?"

"Just how terrible it was," Cheryl said.

"Dave hated that AGA commercial," Nate added. "But he never said a word about Makro."

"I did," Danny announced, hard. He transferred his death glare from the floor to Mark. "I said Dad, Wallace drove for Makro. Dad said Wallace got shot at home, not while he was driving, far as we know this had nothing to do with Makro. I said why don't you stop driving until we do know? He said life's too short to waste it worrying. And now, now Dad, who was a Makro driver like Wallace, has also been shot, also while he wasn't driving, and here you are, pretending you're not sure as fuck they're connected. It is all *connected*... Northwestern tuition got bumped up again this year." His voice going quavery, distraught with guilt.

Cheryl rose to go to her nephew—

"Don't," Danny ordered, and his aunt sank back down. He returned his attention to Mark. "I'm glad you're the one working this case. I want you to be the cop who finds this guy. And shoots him. Will you do that?"

Cheryl gasped and Nate hissed "Danny!"

The grandmother sat up straight and gave Mark an imploring look. Hoping he'd say yes.

"Danny," Mark said. He went to Danny and offered him a business card. Said, "Any time."

Danny glowered at the card, grabbed it, stomped out and a few seconds later a bedroom door slammed shut.

Mark gave another card to Nate, thanked the family for speaking to him and promised to keep them informed.

The grandmother treated Mark to a scowl of contempt for him not being man enough to do what was necessary for her slaughtered son and shattered grandson.

SIX

Mark headed to the office, calling Doonie to fill him in as he drove.

"*Behind* the dumpster?" Doonie mused.

"He wanted the body found. If he puts it in the dumpster a garbage truck might run off with it."

"Or he couldamaybe beeninna hurry," Doonie said, slurring a little. "Or he just ain't big enough to hoista body that high."

"This guy's a planner. Scoped the best place to catch them alone—knew Wallace's girlfriend was out of town, knew Gold walked to the gym every night."

"Yeah. But the shooter musta cased 'em *after* he rode with 'em—you don't get to pick what driver Makro sends, so he's just whacking whatever lucky Makro shows up—wait, howzeee find out their last names an' 'ddresses—shit, the license plates."

"Probably. I'll run the drivers' logs, see if there's a passenger who rode with both of 'em."

"I'm on my way."

"For what? If there's anything worth putting your shoes back on, I'll let you know. My love to Phyl."

"I'll do that," Doonie said, without protest. Which meant Doonie agreed with Mark about him sounding far enough into the booze tonight that if he insisted on joining Mark—all the way up at Area 3 HQ on Belmont and Western—Phyl would've insisted Doonie take a Makro.

◆

Mark already had Kody Wallace's passenger list and had no trouble acquiring David Gold's despite the hour. In just over a decade

Makro had swollen from a one-city startup into a global behemoth that kept its security op staffed with live humans 24/7.

Mark ran a search.

Wallace and Gold had exactly one passenger in common, who'd taken exactly one ride with each.

Mitchell Saad.

SEVEN

Y ou two are turning into serial killer magnets," Lt. Husak complained, complimented, commiserated.

"It gets worse," Mark promised.

"Always," Husak agreed.

"Our Mitchell Saad is a deep thinker. He shot Wallace the same day he rode with him, but shot Gold two days after the ride. Used a different gun for each hit. Not only didn't leave forensics, there's no POD footage." Police Observation Devices, bureaucratic Latin for surveillance cameras. "On both rides Saad got picked up and dropped off at places where we have no coverage—and there's no private security cams."

"But we do got video of the real Mitchell Saad," Doonie said. "In Albuquerque, where Saad is a fuckin' judge. Who was in his fuckin' courtroom both times fake Mitchell Saad was ridin' in a Makro, and home in bed both times fake Mitch whacked a driver. Also, Judge Saad's real surprised to hear he has a Makro account."

"Identity theft," Husak surmised.

"Uh-huh," Mark said. "IT couldn't backtrack the account's email address, bounced through too many servers in Southeast Asia and the Balkans. The phone number's a burner no longer in service. And the only things the shooter bought with Saad's credit card were his two Makro rides."

"Did you tell Makro to flag the account and notify us the instant Mitchell Saad books another ride?" Husak asked.

"And also to warn their drivers not to pick him up," Doonie confirmed.

"Not that it matters," Mark said. "Shooter knows this identity's burned. He won't use it again. Or the same email, or the same phone."

"So if he thinks like you," Husak said, "he's got a whole stockpile of hacked IDs."

"Buy 'em wholesale on the web," Doonie shrugged.

Mark nodded. "The shooter opened the Saad account two weeks before he booked the first ride. I asked Makro for a list of everyone who's opened an account but hasn't booked a ride. Their security guy promised he'd get back to me—soon as management and legal sign off on it."

Husak flashed a sour grin. "They're gonna risk the lives of their staff rather than give us those names."

"Customer privacy, sacred third rail of e-commerce. Though letting a bunch of your drivers get killed might be almost as bad for your brand. Hell of a dilemma."

"Tell me you already requested a subpoena."

"Carrie Eli should be putting it in front of a judge any minute. But even if he signs it…"

Husak gave a meditative grunt. "Who knows, maybe Makro will play nice—no company wants the kinda shitstorm they're in—you watched any a this?" Husak picked a remote off his desk and turned on the TV.

The media had been in serial killer heat since news of Gold's murder broke. The perp had been dubbed the Makro Killer, which inspired a deluge of speculation and memes about whether that moniker wasn't only his job description, it was a prediction about what he'd do to the Makro empire.

CNN was playing clips of two Chicago Makro drivers who said they were going on hiatus until the Makro Killer was found, or maybe forever.

Live in the studio, the anchor said anecdotal evidence indicated "dozens" of Makro drivers in Chicago were doing the same, and so were an "unknown number" around the country. Makro claimed it was only a "handful." Rival ride-hail apps claimed they were getting "hundreds" of applications from Makro drivers.

The anchor was joined by a financial reporter. Makro's stock had plunged 9%, so far. The anchor asked the financial reporter to guess what kind of long-term damage—the anchor interrupted herself—breaking news.

A senior VP from Makro was about to make a statement.

Husak gave Mark and Doonie a bleak approximation of a faintly hopeful look.

Mark didn't get swept up in his boss's microscopic optimism, because Makro's CEO wasn't making the announcement himself. Wasn't gonna take a chance his career might get haunted by tape of him bullshitting while Makro burned.

The sacrificial VP issued grave condolences to the grieving families and promised Makro would do everything it could to aid them during this difficult time. Said Makro was cooperating to the fullest with the police—

Husak snorted, muted the sound and laid a blast of evil eye on the lying son of a bitch. "Where we at on motive?"

Mark ran it down.

Taxi companies hated Makro but killing Makro wouldn't save taxis. To do that they'd have to kill the internet.

It was other ride-hail apps who'd gobble market share if someone slew the 900-pound gorilla. Detectives were running background on all of them.

Makro's security guy said no rival firm had ever gotten physical. There had been threats from laid-off taxi drivers, rejected Makro drivers, unhappy customers, and the usual Twitter he-men trying to convince themselves that making anonymous threats was the same as having a sex life.

The security guy claimed not one threat had been carried out, and 99% weren't even close to credible. But he was "unable" to let the cops see that elite 1% of credible threats—

"Until management and legal," Husak guessed.

Mark's text alert rang. He read it, and told Husak, "Carrie's got our paper."

"Shove that subpoena far up their ass as it'll go," Husak ordered, wearily. "Bet you five bucks it bumps into their lawyer before it's half-way in."

EIGHT

Oh fuck I'm good," Trey murmured to Trey.

99% percent of gun rights messaging is produced by Neanderthals who keep banging the *Ayatollah Pelosi's Gonna Take Away Yer Guns* drum, with *Hitler Loved Gun Control* rim shots and *So Do Rapists* cowbell. Same old same old scary monster riffs, preaching to the already lost their shit choir.

But *my* shit, look at this! This is for *real*, bro, this one's gonna gut *everybody*, libtards included, Trey exulted as he fine-tuned the timing of the VO with the closing visuals of the 30-second spot:

A freeze-frame from the dumpster video: The bloody-muzzled coyote snarling at the camera.

"And like always, the killer's bullets tore into more than just the victim."

Cut to a happy family photo of 10-year-old Danny Gold flanked by his smiling parents.

"Nine years ago Danny Gold lost his mother to cancer."

Mom fades to black, leaving Danny and David.

"Now he's lost his father, ambushed while walking home late at night, unarmed."

David fades to black, leaving little Danny alone in the center of a mostly black frame.

Mothuhfuckuh! Yes! But… maybe needs a visual topper? Maybe morph happy ten-year-old Danny into bereaved nineteen-year-old Danny. And add a VO tag line as we bring up the ELE logo at the end.

Or is it great like it is? Just leave it on kiddie Danny with that dorky, unsuspecting grin, let it hang there in silence for a beat, then fade up the ELE?

Shit, let's look at both ways—worth the effort bro, this one's gonna be a classic, gonna be taught in universi-titties, yo! Straightup *knew* this campaign was gonna rock, but damn—this spot is Godzilla sick, this shit's cooler th—

Trey's phone intruded. The ringtone was *Crawling King Snake.* Stan Vanderman. Micromanaging asshole, interrupting The Master on a roll.

Trey punched himself in the chest and put on a happy voice.

"Hey, Stan."

"Yeah. How's it going?"

"Could literally not be better."

"So you finished Gupta?"

"No but I'm an inch away from finishing Gold, which is—"

"Goddamn it! Gupta's been dead thirty-one hours! I told you finish him before you do Gold!"

"I was two-thirds through Gupta when Gold broke—I'll finish Gupta's video tomorrow, promise, but—"

"Fuck you fuck your promise, this can't only be Chicago, we've got to show it's happening statewide."

"You're right, and a businessman in Carbondale getting brained with a baseball bat is perfect—and he'll still be perfect tomorrow. Stan, I'm sitting here cutting the world champion campaign commercial— Gold's a gift from God, it's a sin not to unwrap it! Heartbreaking family story, *plus* now it's a serial killer, which means a quantum bump in eyeballs and clicks, *plus* it's Serial Killer Versus Makro. *Makro!* Every second that goes by we're missing out on the mega-retweets and news cycle domination we can get with a Makro Killer video." Silence from Vanderbro. "Stan—two hours. Just gimme—"

"The way it works you little shit, you state your case and get my approval before you proceed to jerk off."

"My bad. Won't happen again."

"Good," Vanderman muttered, making it a threat. With that established, he relaxed into his version of human. "You're right about how the serial killer factor gooses the heat."

"And it'll get hotter every time he scores," Trey gloated.

"If he stays busy—and the cops don't nail him."

"He'll keep going, guys like that can't help themselves. And it sounds like the cops aren't getting anywhere. I got a feeling the Makro Killer's smarter than they are," Trey said. "But y'know what adds even more heat? The lead detective is that stud cop Mark Bergman—I mean Jesus, four years ago he takes out that assassin who murdered that major architect, and this year the Art Critic thing, where Bergman blows away a hit man in the middle of the fucking Art Institute, then puts down two more in that firefight in the woods? Bergman's the all-time AGA poster child, bro. I wanna reach out, we gotta get him in our corner."

"Take your head out of your ass, Trey—most big city cops, even the ones who like to shoot perps—"

"—are big into gun control, they think nobody should be legal to carry except them and their families. But those same cops vote Republican and... you never know 'til you ask."

"You're gonna stay the fuck away from Bergman—and anybody or anything else that could bring any blowback on this campaign," Vanderman snarled. "That's a fucking order, genius boy."

Trey took a breath.

"Yes sir. Heard. Totally." And you're gonna totally pay for talking to me like that, reptile boy. "Please, Stan, can I have your permission—let me lock down this asskicker and deliver it to you tonight."

"Can't wait," Vanderbro grumbled and hung up.

"Me neither," Trey confided to the empty phone.

NINE

When Makro announced it would refuse to comply with the subpoena, Mark suggested to Lt. Husak it was better to lob one PR grenade than to curse the darkness. Husak agreed. So did Superintendent Shook, whose new hobby was finding ways to leverage Det. Bergman's celebrity.

◆

Det. Bergman was too busy to give a full interview but consented to answer a few questions from Chicago's most prominent investigative journalist, Marina Karrel. She had high cred, large audiences in both print and TV, and was the go-to choice for national networks when they needed an authoritative analysis of the city's latest sins.

◆

"What's your response to Makro's statement this morning that the subpoena is a fishing expedition, demanding access to sensitive data that's not relevant to your investigation?"

"I'd say Makro's expertise in determining what's relevant to a homicide investigation is a lot like my expertise in writing algorithms to determine surge pricing."

Karrel exerted her immense professionalism to suppress almost all of a grin. "What kind of data did you request?"

"I can't reveal that."

"Isn't that the exact same thing Makro is saying to you?"

"What I'm refusing to reveal protects the investigation. What Makro's refusing to reveal might be something we could use to protect Makro's drivers."

Marina Karrel's report went viral seconds after it aired. Every **Breaking News!** chyron and social media post was headlined with some variation of HERO COP SAYS MAKRO REFUSES TO PROTECT ITS DRIVERS.

In the next half-hour 41% of Makro's remaining Chicago-area drivers logged out. Some posted vows to stop driving until Makro cooperated with the police. Many more vowed to stay out until the Makro Killer was caught.

In solidarity with the drivers, tens of thousands of customers boycotted Makro, worldwide. The company's already depressed stock jumped off a cliff.

◆

A funny thing happened on the way to the Richard J. Daley Center.

An hour and nine minutes after Mark's interview aired, one of Makro's pinstripe SWAT teams got out of a Makro Tux town car and headed across Daley Plaza toward the court building, where a judge they owned—better, rented on an as-needed basis—was going to grant them a stay on the subpoena. The lawyers were striding past the famous massive Picasso sculpture of a nonspecific beast when the lead attorney's cell rang.

She put the phone to her ear. She slowed down. She stopped. Her two associates stopped. She ended the call, muttered, "Makro caved," did an about-face and retreated, trailed by her associates, the younger one summoning a new Tux on his phone as he hurried to catch up. They arrived at the curb and waited.

For about five seconds. Then the angry lead attorney hailed a cab.

Some days the celebrity cop shit did have its uses.

TEN

And some days that usefulness stalled at the five yard line.

The subpoena ordered Makro to provide data on any customers who, like "Mitchell Saad," had opened an account but not used it.

The overwhelming majority of Makro's new customers booked their first ride within thirty seconds to thirty minutes after registering. That left a mere 33,018 customers whose accounts remained suspiciously virginal.

Citing its core mission—customer privacy—Makro claimed it complied with the subpoena by sending the cops a list of the virgin account-holders' names. Only the names. No contact info. No account numbers. When what the cops needed, fast as possible, was to contact all 33,018 to find out which if any were unaware there was a Makro account using their name and credit card, so those accounts could be flagged.

When Mark told Husak the bad news, Husak frowned. "Didn't the subpoena specify turning over all the account data?"

"Of course it did, Carrie wrote it," Mark said. "Makro's contesting the validity of those demands, and claiming they're moot, because the company is contacting all those customers, which they claim they can do faster than we can. And their security guy swears—" Mark's phone vibrated—the caller was Nate Gold. Mark let it go to voicemail. "The security guy swears if any account comes up bogus he's gonna notify us 'within seconds'."

"That would be in their best interest," Husak noted, dourly, meaning that was why Makro would never do it.

Mark's text alert went off. Nate Gold again, unable to wait for

Mark to return his call:

Have you seen the video?

◆

Mark sat at his desk. Doonie stood behind him, watching.

The David Gold video was the featured item on the AGA home page.

Mark clicked.

When it was over, Doonie muttered, "Cute," turning the word into an ancient Celtic curse. "Coffee?"

Mark nodded. Doonie went to score some caffeine and give Mark some privacy.

◆

"Hello, Detective, thank, uh, thank you for calling back, sorry if this interrupts um, any…" Nate tailed off, too stricken to slog his way to the end of the sentence and too bitter to give a fuck.

"You're not interrupting."

"I spoke to my lawyer. He's writing a letter to the AGA demanding they stop using Dave and Danny's images, and also, also to cancel the whole damn campaign, stop tormenting the families just for—politics."

"Good."

"But my lawyer says we shouldn't sue. He says their use of Dave and Danny's images they got off the web, that's legal. But, but emotional damages, what it's doing to us… The lawyer says yes, there we have a case, and no, we shouldn't sue. Says the AGA has deep pockets and is litigious as shit and they'll, they'll bankrupt… But that's not what I'm calling about," Nate revealed, and fell silent.

Mark quietly asked, "How's Danny?"

"He…" Nate swallowed hard. "Danny likes the video."

"Nate, that's understandable. When you get slammed by this kind of shock, you grab for whatever's gonna help…" Ahhh, shit. "Danny wants a gun."

"Can you come talk to him?"

Doonie plunked a coffee on Mark's desk and plunked himself into the chair at his own desk, which faced Mark's. "So?"

"Danny's got his heart set on buying a piece on the street so he can feel safe, and maybe shoot anyone who pisses him off. Uncle Nate asked if I'd stop by tonight and give Danny the talk about the birds and the bullets."

"The Makro Killer!" a young detective waving a phone shouted across the bullpen at Mark and Doonie. "The Makro Killer's holding a driver hostage!"

Mark looked at Doonie. Said, "No he's not."

ELEVEN

During Mark and Doonie's sirens and lights dash up to Edison Park, Husak phoned them the scant info available about the situation and the suspect, Chris Shakeley. The cops had established a perimeter and a hostage negotiator was already chatting with Shakeley. By the time Mark and Doonie arrived at the site—a weary brown brick bungalow with an even wearier brown lawn—they were cautiously optimistic about not having to waste the whole afternoon on this.

When they entered the comm van the negotiator, Sgt. Erik Regensberger, was on the phone with Shakeley. Regensberger motioned for Mark and Doonie to be silent, and told his phone pal, "Hang on a sec—Detective Bergman has arrived. Chris, I gotta get off the phone a coupla minutes, bring Bergman up to speed. Call you right back. Okay?... Thanks."

Detective Bergman has arrived? Mark and Doonie shared a moment of silent mourning over the sudden death of their optimism.

Regensberger hung up, said a quick "Hey Doon," then informed Mark, "The Makro Killer will only surrender to you."

"Okay. But he's not him."

"He says he is. How we sure he isn't?"

"One, he didn't kill the driver. Two, he's an idiot." No arguing that; Chris Shakeley used his own account to book a ride to his own home, where he took driver Willie Marlow hostage and marched Willie into the house at gunpoint, in front of witnesses.

"Or he's the Makro Killer and he's seriously nuts," Regensberger dutifully theorized, meeting his operational obligation to keep an open mind.

Text alerts went off. All three cops pulled out their phones and read the update on Shakeley: failed NFL wannabe, failed Marine wannabe, failed reality-TV wannabe, failed bouncer, failed Makro driver applicant, successful meth scorer.

Mark looked at Regensberger, silently asking if he still believed this fuckup could've staged those two hits.

"Makro rejected him, he's got motive," Regensberger pointed out.

The secure line to the suspect rang.

Regensberger handed Mark a water bottle, explaining, "He's talkative," then put the call on speaker. "Chris, hi—"

"Yeah-yeah-yeah where the fuck izzy? Don't fuck d-didda-don't fuck with me or Willie's brains are gonna get shot in the head, swear ta God—fucking Bergman there OR NOT?!?!" A nervous avalanche of words from a tight dry throat, raspy as radio static.

"Yes. This is Detective Mark Bergman. And I'm not here to fuck with you."

"Better not cause you do it's Willie's brains y'know? Can I call you Mark?"

"Sure. All right if I call you Chris?"

"Yeah-yeah—No!—H-how do I know this-this is you really?"

"My voice. I'm guessing you've heard it on TV. Probably more than once. Sorry."

"Okay-okay. 'Kay. I do recog—yeah."

"Good. So how about this: You come outside, let Willie go and I personally take you into cust—"

"'Kay 'kay 'kay, here's what we're gonna what you're gonna do, first we get the uh media-media, you let the cameras come right near here then Mark you're-you're gonna strip, *strip to your shorts* and raise your hands walk to the house and stop until I say come inna house then-then-then you walk-walk in SLOW, slow… And then I'll tell ya what we're gonna do. Next after that."

"Yeah," Mark murmured thoughtfully, "but Chris, I think there's an even better way we can—"

"DON'T YOU FUCKING FUCK WITH ME!! MARK!!"

"I'm not, this is a professional point I wanna make. Consider, this is the first time you and I meet, face to face. That's a big moment. If we do it indoors, there's no cameras, nobody sees it."

No reply. Only the sound of short choppy not quite hyperventilation.

"Do we really want to throw that away?" Mark wondered.

"Mmmmmmmmmmmmmmmmmmmmmmm—" a buzz like contemplative guitar feedback, "—mmmmmmmmmmmmmmmmmm-mmmokay. 'Kay! Ca-call me when the cameras are, and don't fuck with me gun's gonna stay on Willie's brains so you-you just call me when."

"Deal. Now you know how this works. I give you something, you give me something. I need to know Willie's brains are still working. Just put the phone to his mouth so he can tell me, and I guarantee, network news cameras."

An affirmative grunt. Then a ripping-tearing sound, accompanied by a sharp cry. Regensberger made a sympathetic grimace. Doonie grinned and silently mouthed, "Duct tape."

"Willie? This is Detective Bergman. How you doing?"

A moan, then Willie managed, "I umm, ahh… yeah. Yeah."

"So didda-don't fuck with me!" Chris, suddenly back. "You call me when the cameras—you *strip to your shorts* and you tell the TV we go live or-or-or!"

"Got it."

"Chris—" Willie's voice, in the background, "—I uh, I gotta go to the bathroom again. I'm sorry, Chri—"

The cops heard a slap, then an "Mmff" as the duct tape was reapplied, then the line went dead.

"Not bad," Regensberger complimented Mark.

"If he insists on me going out there in my undies, I'm gonna tell him to go ahead and shoot Willie," Mark warned.

TWELVE

Two cameramen were escorted through the outer perimeter and joined the array of cops ringing Chateau Shakeley.

Mark rang up the lord of the manor.

Lord Shakeley's phone rang. And rang. And rang. And rang. And rang. And rang. And rang. And—

"I changed my mind I changed my mind," Chris blurted as he picked up, "and you-you better not fuck with me—Mark you there? Mark?"

"Yeah it's me. So Chris, what's the new plan?"

"You-you-you only gotta take off your jacket nothing else, a-a-a guy in his shorts is gonna make this into some fucking comedy a comedy."

"Good point."

"But NO VEST! I ga-gotta be able to see you're not packing, so, awright, let's do this I'm comin' out right-right now—"

"No! Chris hang on a minute—I gotta tell the guys it's on. You can't pop out and surprise them, we don't want any accidents. Take a breath, get Willie on his feet, and I'll call ya right back."

◆

They stood behind the van, where Chris couldn't see them.

Mark took his jacket off and handed it to Doonie. Then his gun.

Regensberger handed Mark a cell phone.

Doonie offered Mark a tactical vest. "Shut the fuck up and put it on."

Mark gave him a fond, "Thanks, Mom," then used the phone. "Chris, this is Mark, I'm on my way."

Mark entered the yard and stopped far from the front door, hoping that would entice Chris to come down the front steps into the yard, where snipers on the sides would have cleaner angles. "I'm here, can you see me?"

An affirmative grunt and the line went dead. Mark, the other cops, and millions of viewers on six continents, and passengers on airliners with premium wi-fi, and a Pakistani astronaut aboard the International Space Station stared with rapt, life-and-death intensity at a closeup of Chris Shakeley's weathered, cracked, peeling, rock-salt-stained front door.

The door took its own sweet time soaking up the attention before reluctantly swinging open, and… After a while…

Willie and Chris inched into view, Chris clutching Willie from behind, jamming a gun into the underside of Willie's jaw. Willie was five-five. Chris was six-two and scrunching down to shield as much of himself as possible behind Willie, so their movement was a series of slow jerky lurches.

They stopped on the concrete doorstep, which was for the best. If they tried to lurch down the crumbling concrete steps to the yard they were a good bet to take a pratfall Willie might not survive.

Chris saw Mark. His twitchy-eyed scowl softened into a delighted child's grin, then he screamed, "Hands in the air air, turn round slow don't fuck with me me!"

Mark raised his arms and did a slow 360, pausing to show the handcuffs clipped to his waistband. "We cool?"

"Yeah fine put your arms down—slow slow slow!"

As Mark lowered his arms slow slow slow, Chris noticed—

"The fuck!? The fuck!? *Two* cameras??!! ONLY TUH-TUH TWO????!!!!"

"It's a pool feed! Chris, we're live, everywhere," Mark promised.

Chris yelled to a cameramen, "That that true?!!"

The cameraman gave Chris a thumbs-up.

Chris returned his attention to Mark. "Cameras cameras I want ca-cameras live at my trial every every every fucking m-minute."

"Well yeah, that's the only way CNN does it."

"And… a Dream Team! At least three lawyers three! All A-List!"

"After this? No problem."

"You can guarantee GUARANTEE IT???"

Mark turned and gave Doonie a questioning *Can we do that?* look.

Doonie mulled it a moment, then gave Mark a solemn nod. Mark turned and passed the solemn nod to Chris. "Guaranteed."

Chris' head twitched as he tossed the decision around inside his skull.

The twitching slowed. He took a deep breath. Looked Mark in the eye. Said, "All right. All right. Take out the cuffs."

Mark unclipped the cuffs.

"All all right. Let's, yeah. Okay. S-so so here's what how we do it. I'm gonna shoot Willie drop my gun then then you cuff m—"

"No! That's not our deal!" Mark bellowed, and dropped the handcuffs.

"Don't fuh-fuck—YOU PICK PICK THOSE UP!!"

"You break the deal, I don't cuff you," Mark growled. "Nobody cuffs you. Chris there are snipers painting you. Shoot Willie you're dead before he hits the ground."

Chris went crimson. Until a solution hit him. "Yuh-yuh-YOU," he cackled at Mark. "I'm gonna gonna be the man who kill killed *you*."

"Impossible."

"What the f—*Whysit?!*"

"Chris, by the time you pull the gun out from under Willie's jaw and point it at me there'd be a couple of bullets in you. Even if you get a shot off you got no time to aim. And I'd be moving. You'd miss. That's not a cool death."

Chris ground his teeth. Began to pant, a sharp enraged huffing… An idea blossomed and Chris broke out a sly sneer. "A gun! Suh-somebody body throw him a gun gun! NOW!"

"Nope," Mark told him. "You don't get to have me shoot you."

"Don't don't you fuh-fuck with me, YOU SHOOT ME! Or I, I, I, I shoot Willie!"

"Chris we've been over that—you pop Willie and you get shot by some totally anonymous cop—those snipers are wearing balaclavas, they're literally faceless. And Chris, we know you're not the Makro Killer. So after all this effort, you'd end up a nobody shot by a nobody."

Chris stopped panting, twitching, vibrating. Dead still. Suspended animation.

Mark gently reminded him, "We made a good deal. Let's stick to it."

Chris came back to the world. Looked Mark in the eye.

Chris slowly, gradually moved the gun out from under Willie's jaw, keeping the muzzle pointed straight up, aiming at the sky. Released his grip on Willie.

Willie looked at Chris. Asked through the duct tape, "Rmm I?"

Chris gave a resigned grunt.

Willie cautiously went down the first step. Then the second. Started walking slowly toward Mark, then accelerated into a panicked dash to the promised land.

Chris remained motionless, gun pointed at the sky, eyes locked on Mark's.

"Good man," Mark complimented him. "Now you very slowly lower your gun and lay it down."

Chris kept the gun pointed at the sky.

Mark kept selling. "You lay it down, then I cuff you and we walk out of here together, right past those cameras. We get in my car and drive away." He gave Chris a conspiratorial grin. "With the whole world dying to know what the hell we're talking about in that car."

Chris whimpered.

His face contorted in gargoyle anguish.

He whispered something desperately important and inaudible.

"Sorry…?" Mark coaxed.

"I didn't have have the balls to shoot Willie. I… I, I, I AM THE ONE ONE WHO ALWAYS FUH-FUCKS WITH ME!" Chris screamed and jammed the muzzle under his own jaw—

"STOP! Wait! There's something—I didn't tell you the best part! I was saving it for when it was just us, in private!"

Chris, keeping the gun pressed into his jaw, muttered a suspicious, "Yeah?"

"Chris… Do you know what percentage of my audience is women between eighteen and thirty?"

"No."

"Sixty-one-point-six-three percent. You got any idea what that means?"

Chris didn't.

"Guess what your fan mail's gonna be like. Guess who's gonna be on your visitor list."

"You you can't *guarantee-eee* that."

"Yes I can. What celebrity convict *doesn't* have women writing to him and visiting him? Name one. Just one. Huh?"

Chris shrugged, stumped. But didn't lower the gun.

"And Chris… unlike most of those guys, you're not going away for life. When you get out you'll still be young enough."

Chris lowered the gun. Tossed it aside.

Cops started to surge forward—Mark waved for them to stop.

Chris stepped into the yard. Sank to his knees. Laid face down.

Det. Mark Bergman cuffed Chris, helped him to his feet. Put his arm around Chris and walked him right past those cameras.

Doonie opened the rear door of their car.

Mark put Chris in the back seat.

Doonie closed the car door. Handed Mark his gun, his coat, and informed him, "You're doin' a fuckin' shitty job of gettin' less famous. I'll drive."

THIRTEEN

Trey's got all kinds of young energy and velocity but shit rhythm, this feels less like being humped than being rattled by an unbalanced jackhammer, Deputy Minority Leader Edie Burnett thought as Trey lobbied her.

Trey accelerated into even faster-harder hammering and Edie was about to stop him but—*OH, uhn-uhn-uhn-n-nnnnn*—Trey hit a groove, smooth frenzy at a speed none of Edie's age-appropriate usuals could manage.

An alert sounded on Trey's phone—which, while he and Edie were urgently pulling each other's clothes off, he'd taken care to place on the night table.

Trey jolted to a halt and Edie saw a yearning to look at the phone flit across Trey's face before he blurted an apologetic "Shit!" and hurriedly reached across the bed to silence the phone—he had to stretch a millimeter too far and he popped out of Edie. Trey swatted his phone into submission, whispered a cute "Sorry," eased back into Edie and resumed, slowly. And then even slower.

Trey stopped. Said, "I gotta."

"I know."

Trey read the alert, grabbed the remote and turned on the TV. There was breaking news about the Makro Killer.

Oh my, Edie thought, Trey's set a Makro Killer alert that's more important than sex. What a truly adorable level of commitment.

The story for which Trey stopped in mid-fuck: A man claiming to be the Makro Killer had taken a driver hostage.

Trey frowned at the TV.

"What?" Edie asked.

"Hostage… Doesn't seem like something he'd do," Trey murmured, eyes glued to the screen.

The alleged Makro Killer, Chris Shakeley, and his hostage were barricaded in Shakeley's home—breaking news!—Shakeley's offered to surrender, but only to Det. Mark Bergman.

Edie and Trey watched Bergman enter the yard and wait. Trey tensed as the camera stared at the bungalow's dilapidated front door. It didn't open. Trey barely breathed, riveted to the grimy door that suddenly was the most important thing in his life.

Edie needed to take a leak but no way was she gonna stop watching Trey watching TV. This was so terrific compared to making between-fucks small talk with her usuals.

The door finally opened. Killer and hostage inched into view. Shakeley screeched instructions at Bergman.

Trey relaxed. Took his first real breath in a while.

He felt Edie's eyes on him. Said, "I don't think that's the Makro Killer."

"Why?"

"Don't see those murders being the work of some strung-out tweaker asshole. Do you?"

Edie gave a noncommittal shrug.

They watched in silence, except for gasping at the moments Shakeley threatened to kill the hostage. Then Bergman. Then himself.

When Bergman finally seduced Shakeley into surrendering, using the dream of prison groupies, Trey gave one sharp laugh and shook his head in admiration.

"Yeah," Edie agreed. "That cop's not just some idiot who keeps getting into shoot-outs. He's one goddamn sharp idiot."

"Uh-huh," Trey murmured, with a delighted smirk. "Though I'll a bet you a million he didn't catch the Makro Killer just now," Trey said, and rolled on top of Edie, and his dick swelled to combat-ready status as he gave her a long, deep kiss, and Edie laughed in his mouth.

"Hey!" Trey protested.

Edie grabbed his hard-on. "You're happy because the Makro Killer can keep murdering people."

"So are you," Trey declared, and proved it by treating Edie to eighteen minutes of rhythmically challenged but acceptable humping.

Leaving the TV on as CNN ran replays and analysis.

FOURTEEN

Not bad, Det. Hotshit," Rudy conceded. He raised a contemptuous toast with his beer can and drained it as he watched Bergman cuff Shakeley. "But I am the one and only goddamn bona fide hotter than shit Makro Killer."

Rudy popped another Coors Light. Tasted like carbonated Saran Wrap, but he'd reached the age where his weight was never again gonna watch itself. Life's one fucking tragedy after the other.

Tragedy, and insults.

On top of that piece of shit meth freak tries to pass himself off as me, he does such a crappy job he couldn't fool a standard-issue meatball cop, forget this Bergman bitch. Star of the Chicago P-fucking-D, those upright high-standard bastards who wouldn't even let young Rudy into their training camp for a tryout. Well how you like me now, ladies? Made my debut at Number Seven on the FBI charts. And be movin' up fast, you watch. Which you will, standin' there with your CPD thumbs up your asses.

Rudy poured himself a shot of Anejo. Took a sip, savored it. Went to chug the rest, but stopped.

Get real. You know what you just saw.

This Bergman is deep freezer frosty. Cold enough to mess with my chances?

Am I still okay sticking with the plan?

Well…

Fuck yeah.

More than fuck yeah.

I'm gonna use Det. Hotshit to upgrade the plan.

FIFTEEN

Mark never made it to Nate Gold's apartment to have that talk with Danny. Celebrity fever killed his day.

Mark and Doonie tried to deliver Chris Shakeley to the 16th District house and get back to work.

The desk sergeant, a lifer named Tim Mula who'd been in Doonie's cadet class, told them, "This isn't the scene commander's collar, it's yours." Delivered it with don't-bitch-at-me-about-it firmness, but not without sympathy.

"Orders from on high," Mark said, letting Mula know he wasn't blaming the messenger.

Mula gave a little nod.

Doonie looked at Mark. "So now we gotta interrogate a guy we know ain't our guy," Doonie said, blaming Mark and enjoying it.

Mark asked Mula, "And then?"

"When you're done with Shakeley, you gotta go straight Downtown, do a presser." Mula added, with a tiny grin, "That was a good bust. And good TV."

"Thanks," Mark said. Welcome to the age of police work as a career on camera. Body cams, dashboard cams, security cams, phone cams, news choppers with aerial cams, reality TV crews with Steadicams.

Mark and Doonie took Shakeley to an interrogation room where their session was recorded by two evidence cams.

It wasn't good TV. The babbling tweaker was deep into fantasizing about what stardom would be like, and aggressively disinterested in discussing trivia like kidnapping, attempted murder and not being the Makro Killer. Mark and Doonie were finally beginning to drag some details out of Shakeley when the meth crash hit and he fragmented into a jumble of fried ganglia and synapses deeply unhappy about being trapped in Shakeley's body.

Shakeley went to the hospital. Mark and Doonie went downtown.

◆

As usual the press avail began late and ran long. As usual the bulk of the questions were for Mark. The initial batch demanded a second-by-second, move-by-move dissection of the entire event. Then reporters asked six versions of "What makes you certain Shakeley isn't the Makro Killer," that being the story they really really wished they were writing.

Then began the hunt for the Meaningful Personal Details. "Have you spoken with Willie Marlow since saving his life? Do women 18 to 30 really make up sixty-one-point-three percent of your fan base? Where can we access that data?"

Later, when Mark finally finished the arrest report, he phoned Nate Gold to apologize for not showing up, and to ask how Danny was doing.

Nate told him no apology necessary, they'd watched the whole thing. As for Danny… "Danny's out with friends and not responding to messages."

SIXTEEN

Mark tossed his snail mail on the kitchen table, tossed his jacket over a chair and yawned, unable to decide what next, bourbon or toothpaste. He put off the decision by opening two emails he hadn't had time to look at.

One was from a publisher who'd contacted Mark before. Today's message was a gush about how incredible this morning's thing was, how incredibly brassy Mark's balls were, how incredibly relieved people were when he didn't get those inspirational balls blown off and how incredibly great their memoir would be. The other email was from a British TV network imploring Mark to please not make any movie or TV deal until he'd spoken to them, citing the unmatchable list of award-winning detective series they'd produced.

Mark moved the messages into his Offers folder, poured himself a sizeable drink and turned on the TV. It was tuned to TCM. King Kong was beating the crap out of a subway car, frustrated because his missing girlfriend wasn't one of the tiny humans inside it. Love stinks.

Just because it was a bad idea, Mark Googled JaneDoe. Found a recent BBC interview.

It began with a recap of JaneDoe's amazing year. She'd been getting some local notice for her crazy elaborate sci-fi costumes—an idea as old as those crazy elaborate Renaissance suits of armor—you can wear it, or stand it up in the drawing room and call it sculpture. JaneDoe's were whimsical, satirical, sneaky-serious eyegrabbers, their own kind of beautiful. Like her.

When she got anointed prime suspect in the Art Critic murders, her sales went ballistic. When it turned out she was an unfairly accused innocent, sales went exponential. JaneDoe was offered gallery shows in Europe, and accepted them all.

Mark paused the video and poured himself a modest refill. Career considerations hadn't been the only thing driving JaneDoe's decision to change continents. There was also her second affair with Mark.

The first had ended four years ago. The second ignited when Det. Bergman showed up at JaneDoe's door to question her about her relationship with one of the Art Critic's victims.

Then a hotshot FBI profiler declared JaneDoe was, to a scientific near-certainty, their serial killer.

Mark didn't recuse himself. He kept the relationship secret so he could remain lead dog on the investigation. JaneDoe was being railroaded. Couldn't let that happen.

Success, sort of. JaneDoe was cleared. But she was enraged when she found out the FBI had been bugging her apartment, phones and devices. She got even more enraged when she learned Mark knew she was being audio-raped and hadn't warned her. His pragmatic reasons for that didn't impress her. JaneDoe also made it clear she wasn't built for living with a guy who repeatedly almost got killed at work but refused to change jobs.

Mark finished his drink and resumed watching the video.

The recap ended with JaneDoe getting swept up in the continent's celebrity jet stream, hanging out with the brilliant, talented, sophisticated, wealthy, powerful, connected, famous, attractive elite. Which was what the interviewer was panting to hear about.

"How would you describe it, this rapid transition from life as a little-known artist in Chicago to life in Europe's cultural-social glam lane?"

"Fun so far," JaneDoe replied, with that enigmatic, sultry surly Cheshire cannabis grin she was so good at.

SEVENTEEN

The next morning Mark went in early, to make sure he'd be there when Makro called with the requested information about their new accounts.

This time the caller wasn't Mark's usual contact. It was Evan Sturgiss, Makro's top number one global worldwide chief senior security chief.

"Every one of the new but unused accounts opened in the past six months is legit. We've double-checked those results. Which I think indicates the Mak—" Sturgiss almost violated company policy by saying Makro Killer, "—the murderer has changed his MO again. He hit Wallace the same night as the ride, he hit Gold three days after the ride."

"Uh-huh."

"Next time, to keep ahead of us, he'll have to make an even bigger change," Sturgiss amiably suggested. "Just to throw an idea out there—now that he's got everybody fixated on Makro, got all the other ride-hails convinced they're not targets, his safest move would be to hit a driver from one of those apps. Just a theory, but—you think it's possible?"

So that's why the personal call from the Grand Poobah. "I see the MK making a simpler change in his MO. He can use another stolen ID to open a Makro account, but this time not wait before using it— just book a death ride the instant the account's approved," Mark said, refusing to answer the *You think it's possible?* question. If Mark had said anything resembling Yes or even Maybe, there'd be a leak saying the police believe the killer is done with Makro and is targeting those other companies.

"Hunh," Sturgiss commented, unable to mask his displeasure at his question being dodged, combined with his displeasure about the request he knew Mark was about to make.

"The most effective thing for Makro to do," Mark declared, "both for the safety of your drivers and to not blow a chance to catch this bastard, would be to hold off on activating any new account until we confirm it isn't a stolen identity."

After a brief silence, Sturgiss said, "I disagree." Which was a lie. "But I'll communicate your request." Which was true. "I'll get back to you soon as there's a decision." Which was gonna be Fuck Off.

No chance Makro was going to turn itself into the only ride-hail whose new customers weren't able to register, be approved and sitting in a moving vehicle within minutes.

If one of those new customers turned out to be the Makro Killer, well, that was a price the company was willing to let some unlucky driver pay.

EIGHTEEN

Two days after Mark's conversation with Evan Sturgiss there was a definite change in the Makro Killer's MO.

Kody Wallace and Dave Gold had been killed five days apart.

On the fifth day after the hit on Gold there were four murders in Chicago. Two were gang-related, one was domestic, and one was a five-year-old using Mom's cute pink superlight .22 to silence his annoying one-year-old brother.

Not a dead Makro driver in the bunch.

◆

Makro also changed its MO, though only in Cook County. It lowered the price of rides, and raised the driver's cut from 50 to 70%, in order to lure back enough drivers to meet the—*C'mawn, God*—surge in demand.

God and a statistically significant number of passengers answered Makro's prayer. Cheaper fares and the fact the Makro Killer didn't shoot passengers was a winning combination.

The number of drivers who returned to work was negligible. At first. Each day that went by without the Makro Killer returning to work, more drivers decided to roll the dice for that 20% bonus.

Mark finally had time to call Nate Gold to re-schedule that talk with Danny.

"Thank you but, um, Danny doesn't want to talk to you—which I think is no longer a problem, because—he had some bad days, but he's settled down, pulling it together. He woke up yesterday like his old self—a slightly depressed version, but—the gun obsession, *gone.* Hasn't said a word about guns since then."

"Uh-huh… Nate, have you searched Danny's room?"

There was a guilty-sounding silence.

Nate whispered, "Yes. Nothing there. No weapon, any kind. And, Danny's stopped talking about the murder at all—I wish he'd go to grief counseling, but he's working through it his own way, and he's definitely gotten past the insane initial shock part. Which is—it's pretty damn mature of him. Dontcha think?"

"Yeah. I do." Incredibly damn mature, considering maturity wasn't Danny's long suit. "In the meantime, Nate, if there's anything you need to talk about, call me."

"Thank you. I'll uh, I won't unless it's absolutely—I don't want to interrupt your work."

"Not a problem."

◆

Not a problem at all. The investigation had stalled. So had the Makro Killer.

No Makro driver was murdered in the ten days following Dave Gold's death.

Or on the eleventh day. Or the twelfth, thirteenth or fourteenth.

◆

"Two weeks," Doonie mused, and took a contemplative sip of bourbon. "We think he's done or just throwing a changeup?"

"Changeup," Mark voted.

They looked at each other.

Broke out mordant grins. Drank a wordless toast to the truth: They were 99% relieved no one else had been killed, and 1% impatient for their perp to get back to work so they'd get another crack at him.

NINETEEN

Two weeks! Where the hell's my Makro Killer, Trey fretted, staring at the screen but not seeing it, unable to concentrate on his newest video—an okay murder but it was downstate, had nothing like the Makro Killer's worldwide buzz—which was fading, thanks to his fucking endless pause... Trey was tempted to—No! Control yourself, do the job, this has to be on the air tomorrow.

A female professor at UI had been raped and strangled by a colleague because she got tenure and he didn't. Heaven-sent proof of the need for concealed carry on campus, except it happened in her home, fifteen miles off campus.

Screw that. Genius makes its own reality.

Every shot of the victim-professor and of the strangler-professor would show them on campus. Trey found enough suitable images of both so he could assemble a montage, alternating shots of her on campus, then him on campus, ending with a shot of the two of them together on campus—gave the impression the strangler's montage had stalked and murdered the victim's montage on the campus, where she should've been allowed to carry a gun.

Trey resumed editing, trying to nail the montage rhythm. Needed to gradually accelerate the pace to maximize the effect... Shit. *Accelerating the pace to maximize the effect was what the Makro Killer should be doing.*

And there went Trey's concentration. Replaced by clouds of indecision, intermittent frustrations and a sixty percent chance of dismal funk.

A text alert went off. Trey' spirits went up.

It was from Danny Gold:

3:30 works. Where?

The kid had emailed Trey's website fours days ago. Said he was down with the ELE campaign and wanted to help.

Trey experienced a surge of elation followed by a healthy dose of caution. He spent a few days verifying the email was really Danny Gold. Even then, Trey couldn't be sure Danny wasn't playing him; most family members of the murder victims were pissed off about the ELE campaign.

Trey emailed a request for Danny's cell number. Danny sent it immediately, along with a warning for Trey not to call until Danny signaled he was someplace private, explaining, IT'S VITAL MY FAMILY NOT KNOW ABOUT THIS. Danny specified a time when he'd be alone and it'd be safe for Trey to call.

Trey called, using a burner with a blocked number. They had a brief, insanely promising talk. Danny was angry as shit and desperate to hit back. Volunteered to appear in a video.

Trey wanted to vet Danny in person. Suggested tomorrow at 3:30. If Danny turned out to be for real, this was going to be so… But only if the Makro Killer resumed scoring. The way to max out the shock and awe of Danny Gold's appearance would be to have Danny show up in the next MK video. Whenever the fuck that finally was.

Trey began to reply to Danny—

A text alert went off on Trey's other burner. Heart pounding, Trey entered the lock code and opened the text.

It was photo of Det. Bergman.

Rudy sent him a photo of Bergman.

WHAT THE FUCK? Rudy's been holding fire just because Bergman's working the MK case? Oh shit—does this mean Rudy's backing out, running the fuck away?

Trey typed **What the hell?** Shortened that to **?** and sent it.

Rudy made him wait a couple of minutes before replying:

Sixty?!? What the fuck is that supposed to... Ah shit. Sixty thousand. It means Rudy wants sixty thousand.

Fucking Rudy insists on total operational silence, no communication unless it's a life or death situation—then he contacts me *to demand a raise*? A huge one, son of a bitch wants his fee *doubled*. My good ol' bro, that ungrateful prick, *knows* every dollar is comin' out of my own pocket...

And that's why Rudy let me dangle this last two weeks, showed me how it'd feel to see my project go down the crapper... Fuck Bergman, fear of Bergman isn't Rudy's reason, it's his excuse—a goddamn fig leaf, so Rudy, that backstabbing turdfucker, can pretend this isn't pure scumbag extortion and...

And, welcome to the fucking world.

Get real.

Trey crunched numbers. Determined his absolute max.

Texted:

40

Trey propped the burner against his computer. Glared at the burner, gave his balls a defiant tug aimed at the burner. The burner went to sleep.

A text alert.

Trey raised his middle finger. Used it to open the text:

Trey shoots, Trey scores. As always, bro. Boo-fuckin' yah.

Trey deleted the Rudy texts, sent Danny Gold the location for tomorrow's meet, sat down and edited the shit out of that strangled professor montage.

TWENTY

Never occurs to people a dude my size, kinda hard-lookin', could be germophobic. Or even knows the word germophobic," Rudy said, with a small conspiratorial grin.

Roz unleashed a hearty, delighted chuckle. She was a sturdy woman, late thirties, bland round face, no makeup, super-tight butch haircut. She was light-skinned Latina, no accent, no ink or piercings and was wearing a wedding ring. Even so, Rudy wasn't sure a bulky plain-faced old-school dyke could squeeze into Trey's parameters for "middleclass relatability."

Roz gave him a twinkly grin via the rearview and said, "As the saying goes, *Fronti nulla fides.*"

"That Latin?" Rudy asked, pleased; Roz's stock just went up.

"Uh-huh. 'Put no faith in appearances.' Apparently people have been making that mistake for at least two thousand years."

"For sure." Rudy went quiet for a moment. "Like… My wife—she wasn't what you'd call a looker. Roly-poly little thing. But she was… the best."

Roz gently inquired, "Was?"

"Botched-up surgery… sepsis."

"I'm so sorry."

"Thanks. I'm doing okay… But, my daughter, she, uh…" Rudy caught himself, changed to a sunnier gear. "How'd you come by the Latin?"

"Parochial school, college and seminary."

"You're a nun?"

"I was. Until I decided to get married. To Sister Clara." That hearty chuckle again.

A warm smile from the big man. "So it's going good?"

Roz nodded. "Clara's apprenticed to a pastry chef and I'm six months from taking the huge awful test to be anointed a psychologist."

Rudy gave her a thumbs-up. College grad, nun, married, almost a shrink. Relatable.

Rudy kept Roz talking about psychology and pastries. It was getting dark as they neared the destination, southwest of Midway Airport, in a bleak industrial neighborhood. They drove past a parking lot jammed with cement-trucks, a railroad depot where acres of structural steel beams were stacked, a vast junkyard where massive machines crushed dead cars into scrap-metal sandwiches.

Roz looked around, checked the GPS, then looked at Rudy. "Where are we going?"

"To where my daughter left my car last night."

"So, she's really mad at you?" Roz guessed, indicating the surroundings.

"Not last night. She asked if she could borrow the car so her and a coupla friends could visit another girl who moved to Justice last year. I said yes."

"So how did…?"

"She kept our deal about if she ever got too loaded to drive, she would pull over and call me."

"Good kid. And she trusts you."

"Yeah. Thing is—normally I'd take a Makro down here, get in my car and drive the kids home, but—she calls a half-hour after I took a Vicodin—back pain, wouldn't wish it on my worst… So I sent a Makro to pick 'em up. Not the best way to prove she can count on Dad."

"Oh yes it is, it's exactly what a good Dad—what?—she parked it *here*?" Roz asked as she approached Rudy's SUV, which was parked beneath freight tracks. "Why'd she stop in an underpass—an unlit underpass?"

"Why you think," Rudy said, with a resigned Dad sigh.

Roz gave Rudy a wry glance in the rearview as she pulled to a halt behind his white Cherokee. "Your car's gonna smell like pot."

"I like you," Rudy confided, then shot twice through the back of her seat, reached forward and unbuckled Roz's seatbelt, yanked her flat across the front passenger seat so she couldn't be seen, put a kill shot in her head, took the key out of the ignition, grabbed her phone and dashcam, shoved them in his pocket, collected his shell casings, got out, locked the car, got in the Cherokee, took the battery out of Roz's phone and drove away, forty thousand ahead of where he'd been a minute ago.

TWENTY-ONE

Mark got a call.

"My name is Clara Cahill. My wife Roz Espinosa is a Makro driver. She didn't come home last night which has never happened before, she isn't returning calls texts or mail, and the locator app on her phone is switched off. I called Makro but they won't tell me what time her last fare was or what the destination was. I know you're thinking this is just another cheating spouse story and I pray to God you're right, but I know you're not."

"I'll find out," Mark promised.

◈

WBEZ broke into its broadcast of The Takeaway.

"The Chicago Police Department has just confirmed the so-called Makro Killer has struck again. The victim's name is being withheld until the family has been notified."

"Her name is Roz Espinosa," the victim's family told her kitchen radio. Clara turned it off and began to wail softly, but before tears could come a wave of nausea sloshed through her and she doubled up, arms gripped tight across her stomach. The biliousness ebbed and Clara straightened up. She went to the stove and hefted the kettle; not enough water. She filled the kettle, put it on the burner. She was still standing there, motionless, gripping the kettle's handle, staring at nothing, when however many minutes later the intercom rang.

Clara buzzed the detectives into the building. She went to her front door, unlocked it and waited, gripping the doorknob. She heard elevator doors open. Men's footsteps coming down the hall and stopping. Three light, considerate taps on her door.

Clara slowly opened it.

There they were. The middle-aged one who could pass for one of her uncles. Hefty powerful body gone halfway to seed, thinning sandy hair worn as carelessly as everything else he had on, broad cheeks laced with broken capillaries from the drinking. A bruiser. Who'd just knocked so tactfully on her door, the way Roz would've done.

And the other one. Him. Who'd done and survived those things. Who was regarding her with an expression that combined compassion with pragmatic alertness, a rare quality, one which Roz also… Oh God. I'm going to go through the rest of my life with anything that's good reminding me of Roz.

"Clara Cahill?" Bergman asked, softly.

Clara gestured for the cops to come in.

They did. She closed the door and turned to face them, her hand still gripping the doorknob. She gestured for them to go to the living room. They read her face and obeyed.

It took a minute, but Clara forced herself to let go of the doorknob that was the only thing keeping the earth from opening up and swallowing her.

◆

Mark had been impressed by the organized, determined force with which Clara Cahill marched through what she had to say on the phone that morning, defeating the sickening fear that had compelled her to make the call.

Now she couldn't manage more than a dull monotone as Mark and Doonie tortured her gently as possible with the necessary questions. When Clara gave up on mumbling and answered two questions in a row with downcast eyes and hopeless shrugs, Mark wrapped it up.

"Thank you. Ms. Cahill, is there someone who can come over and be with you? If you want I'll call them, just tell me who."

Cahill slowly raised her head and looked at—into—Mark. Her voice was firm and bitterly precise. "Know what the truly hard part is? Uniquely, despicably hard? I don't get to grieve. I get to grieve while I sit here waiting, knowing the American Gun Association is going to take a big fat dump on my sweet Roz. You want to make a call for me? Call the AGA and tell them, *Don't do that*."

TWENTY-TWO

The prick had made some changes in his MO.

This time there was a two-and-a-half week pause between kills.

This time he didn't show up at the driver's home. He killed the driver at the end of the ride, in the car.

This time it was a woman.

This time he didn't use a stolen ID to open a new account, which was what Makro and the cops were watching for. He hacked an existing account. It belonged to B.J. Zacek, an intern at Stroger Hospital who'd been twelve hours into working a 20-hour shift at the time of the murder.

But this time a Police Observation Device observed something. Roz Espinosa's blue Prius drove past a POD that caught one blurry glimpse of the MK. The tech's unblurring app had no trouble enhancing it into a crystal clear portrait of the back right corner of her passenger's head.

The Makro Killer was Caucasian. Blond hair trimmed tight, at least on the sides; the top of his head was out of frame. The rear view of the outer edge of his right ear displayed no distinguishing features. The back of his neck was covered by the upturned collar of a tan windbreaker.

Forensic analysis of the image confirmed Mark's eyeball analysis: the MK was over six feet tall and had a big head.

And this time he might've left forensics. The most probable scenario was the MK had Espinosa drive him to where he'd parked a getaway vehicle. The TV stars—Doonie's name for crime scene techs—lifted some tire tracks. Tread marks found directly in front of Espinosa's car were from Kumho tires used on SUVs and pickups.

"We ordered two scans of the footage from every camera in a three-mile radius," Mark told Husak, who'd stopped at Mark and Doonie's desks for an update. "One starting twenty-four hours before the murder, to get screen caps of every vehicle driving toward the underpass—special attention to SUVs and pickups. And then, starting from the time of the hit, we're looking at every vehicle heading away from the underpass, see if we get a match."

"Even we do get a match," Husak pointed out, "doesn't mean the vehicle belongs to the MK. Hell, maybe he never parked a car down there—he coulda had an accomplice, drives in and picks him up after he shoots Espinosa. Or he coulda just walked."

"Yeah," Doonie agreed, "but this is finally some kind of any progress. Feel like I just took my first good shit in two weeks."

"The Bowels of Delphi," Mark gravely assured his Lieutenant.

As it was spoken, so it came to pass.

The cameras caught two SUVs that were headed toward, and then away from the underpass within the critical time frame.

One was a twelve-year-old Toyota 4Runner wearing a big plastic Domino's Pizza warning on its roof. Illinois plates. The driver was twenty years old, five-four, one-hundred-eighteen pounds, Ethiopian, undocumented and the happiest man in Chicago when the cops convinced him they didn't give a shit about that.

The other SUV was a 2011 white Cherokee. No view of the driver; tinted windows.

"And…" Doonie informed Husak, as if this were the clincher, "Arizona plates."

"So?" Husak shrugged.

Doonie grinned. "The plates came up stolen."

"Put out a bulletin—cops only," Husak specified, on the zero-percent chance Mark and Doonie forgot that on a case this viral, the decision to go public about a vehicle that wasn't yet confirmed as the MK's was above everybody's pay grade except the Supe's.

"The bulletin should be for *any* 2011 white Cherokee," Mark said, "even if it isn't wearing those Arizona plates."

"Shit," Doonie agreed. "The fucker uses a new gun on every job, so maybe plates too."

Husak nodded at Mark. "Good call."

"Thanks. But, thing is, this guy might not settle for switching the plates. He might've ditched the Cherokee and be driving something else by now."

Husak raised a skeptical eyebrow. "Expensive."

"Yeah," Mark said. "So is buying a pile of stolen IDs and using a different gun for each hit."

Doonie stared at Mark. "You ain't gonna let me enjoy my magic bowels are ya."

"Maybe he'll keep driving the Cherokee," Mark said. "But so far he's anticipated what we'd learn from each kill, and he's had a plan—and enough cash—to shift gears. He's mapped what he's gonna do and how we're gonna respond. This thing is… scripted."

TWENTY-THREE

Roz Espinosa, just like Kody Wallace, and just like my Dad, did not have a gun—fuck!—I mean, was unarmed, *un-armed*," Danny scolded himself. "Sorry," he told Trey, who was operating a tripod-mounted camera.

"Chill, bro." Trey flashed a sly smirk. "Talking to camera's like sex, nobody does it great their first time, you feel me?"

"Yeah," Danny acknowledged, unconsoled. He was Generation Smartphone, life is what you do so you have something to upload. Being on camera was a natural bodily function. But today it's weird. Soon as the little red light goes on, brain-freeze. He gets this amazing chance at the only thing that matters, and he turns shaky little bitch. "This time word for word," Danny swore.

"Boo-yah!" Trey returned his attention to the camera. "Rolling. Danny Gold, Take Four… Just relax and whenever you're ready."

Danny stared at the floor, concentrating. Raised his head, looked into the lens and told it, "Roz Espinosa, just like Kody Wallace, and just like my Dad, was unarmed. They never had a chance." Danny took a small pause, as Trey had instructed. "My Dad deserved a chance."

Word for word, but it sucked. All stiff, like it's fourth grade and he's reading a book report.

"Cut," Trey said, too kindly, confirming Danny's assessment of how shit he sounded.

Danny muttered, "Let's do some more takes."

"Let's do some beer." Trey shut down the lights and waved for Danny to follow him out of the apartment's second bedroom, in which he'd set up a studio.

Trey pulled a six-pack and guac from the fridge and grunted for Danny to grab the half-finished bag of chips that was sitting on the breakfast bar.

They settled into newish leather furniture around a newish coffee table. It was a furnished unit in a shiny newish Streeterville tower designed for short-term corporate rentals. It had great views of the river, the lake, Navy Pier. Danny resisted asking how much the rent was. He'd embarrassed himself enough in front of Trey Fister—who wasn't the lowlife right-wing propaganda thug Danny until recently assumed him to be. The guy Dad called Video Vermin. *"Video Vermin strikes again."* Yeah, well, one more thing Dad was wrong about.

Danny and Trey spent the first beer talking sports, video games, women and which Chicago beers does Danny think Trey should try.

Trey started to hand Danny a second bottle but stopped. "Truth bro, can you handle it?"

"Fuck yeah."

"Can't have you sounding like a drunk-ass punk."

"Fuck no, we cannot and will not," Danny agreed, with fierce certainty and crisp diction.

"My man," Trey complimented, with an approving grin. Pleasantly surprised. Impressed. Not like Danny's family, friends and shrink, who look at him like he's something to worry about.

They clinked bottles and swigged.

Danny belched, a mortar-blast. He instinctively covered his mouth—

"L'chaim," Trey grinned, raising his bottle.

Danny replied, "Praise Jesus."

Clink, swig.

Danny's neck and shoulder muscles unclenched, tension he hadn't noticed was there until it was gone. Danny grinned at his beer to keep himself from grinning at Trey.

"Sup, my man?" Trey wondered.

"Nothing, just thinking… That it's true, about you I mean, you really still do everything yourself, the writing, shooting, editing."

"You don't like my shit?" Trey mock-protested.

"No it's great, I was just—" Danny gestured at their surroundings. "These days you could afford a crew. If you want."

"But I don't want."

"Got it… Awesome."

"By which you mean, 'Trey, why the fuck don't you let grunts do the grunt work?' "

Danny laugh-snorted, nodded, swigged again, belched again.

"Coupla solid reasons, bro. One: I know exactly what I want. I don't have to explain myself, or listen to expert opinion how it could be better. Trey Fister don't have no time to waste—especially on this project, which has gotta be rapid response every time we lose another good man." Trey raised his bottle and took a swig in Dave Gold's honor.

Danny did the same. Asked, "What's the second reason?"

"Preserving the ecology, mothafuckah. Trey Fister the one-man show is the best way to make the best videos, and the longer I keep being Trey Fister the one-man show the more it builds my brand, and the bigger the Trey Fister brand gets the higher the Trey Fister fee gets… And Trey Fister ain't gonna pollute that by pissing away his natural fees on unnatural expenses, is he?"

Danny grinned. "What natural expenses does he piss them away on?"

"I don't," Trey insisted, for real. "Never. I… put it to good use."

"What kind of good?"

Trey replied, carefully, "Trouble is, bro… If I answer that question, tell you where my money goes and who it supports… It would destroy my magnificently constructed image as a ruthless bastard who don't give a shit about nothin' except getting whatever footage I need." Trey grinned. "Can't let that happen, can we?"

Danny shook his head, smiling. "Nuh-uh."

"So I can trust you to never say a word about my secret soft-hearted do-gooder shit?"

"Forever," Danny vowed.

"Then let's get back to work and nail this fucker."

"Boo-yah," Danny agreed. Meaning it. Feeling it. Feeling right.

His real self again. Ready to rock.

He took his position and looked into the camera like he owned it.

Trey, watching Danny's face in the viewfinder, murmured a stoked *"My man."*

"Roz Espinosa, just like Kody Wallace, and just like my Dad, was unarmed," Danny said, as if telling his best friend a truth he must accept. "They never have a—not *have!*—hadda—*fuck*—HAD A— never had a fucking chance just keep fucking rolling, I'm doing this, I'm doing it."

Danny ran his lines at high speed to make sure he had the words straight and his mouth remembered what it felt like to say them. For Dad. For Dad.

And to not humiliate himself in front of Trey.

Danny stood up straighter than he ever had. Spoke a little slower to make sure it came out right.

"Roz Espinosa, just like Kody Wallace, and just like my Dad, was unarmed. They. Never. Had. A. chance." He took the small pause. "My Dad deserves…" a lump blossomed in Danny's throat, "yeah he *deserves…*" and his eyes filled and he turned away from the camera and stomped on the floor, twice, because it was starting to tilt out from under him—

"Hey, it's okay," Trey's voice, soothing—

"It's not fucking okay!" Danny snarled, turning to face Trey. "*It's not.*"

"It will be, bro. Just chill—"

"No! Get back behind the camera! Get behind the fucking camera!"

"First—"

"NOW!!!"

Trey's eyes narrowed, as if he was deciding where to punch Danny other than in the face. He decided to get back behind the camera.

Danny glared at the lens, gave it a small disgusted sneer and let it rip. "You—all of you—think the important thing Roz Espinoza and Kody Wallace and my Dad had in common was they all drove for Makro. Wrong. The important thing they had in common is not one of them owned a gun… Why? Why is that? Why did my Dad not have a chance?"

Danny stared into the lens, waiting for an answer… Then the air went out of him. Danny rubbed his face and muttered, "Okay, okay." He raised his head, stricken, and told Trey, "I just… I'll do it till I get it right—your script, every word exactly like you wrote."

"No you won't," Trey declared. "From now on you'll do it your way. Every time."

Danny frowned, uncertain he'd heard what he just heard. " 'Every time?' "

"My man, from now on you are the face and voice of ELE… You cool with that?" Trey asked with a confident smirk.

TWENTY-FOUR

The day began with sprinkles of cold rain and a deluge of bogus tips about the Makro Killer. Makro, inspired by the new plunge in ridership and stock price inflicted by Dead Driver Number Three, announced a $250,000 reward.

"I can match that," Lt. Husak told his squad. "First one a you comes up with a solid lead, I'll put ya in for a quarter-million dollar bonus."

◆

Mark and Doonie accessed the registrations of every white 2011 Cherokee in the country, along with the owners' DLs. Sorted for males 5-9 to 6-4 with blond hair.

Started with Illinois, because most serials work at home. And Arizona, because that's where the plates where stolen. And they checked auto thefts, in case the rest of the vehicle was stolen too.

◆

There were eleven qualifying blond males in Illinois. Three were in Cook County.

The eight out-of-town blonds were just plain dull.

Local Blond Number One had committed a DUI involving the vehicular homicide of a fire hydrant.

Local Blond Number Two had a sheet dotted with D&D, misdemeanor assault and resisting arrest. Decades ago. He was now 56, confined to a wheelchair and driving a modified white 2011 Cherokee with hand controls.

Local Blond Number Three had potential. At 19 Nelson Miller did a six-month bit for arson. At 23 an ex-girlfriend was granted a restraining order. At 28 his new ex-girlfriend got one too. At 33 he was busted for possession of an illegally modified AK-47. He was now 36 and living with his parents in Berwyn.

Nothing suggested Miller had the MK's smarts and self-control. But the Cherokee, the gun lust and the home address spitting distance from Chicago demanded a look-see.

◆

Mark and Doonie found Nelson Miller at his day job as a telemarketer for PrideCare America. PrideCare's legally registered charities legally solicited funds to allegedly support the families of troops deployed abroad. Also the families of disabled vets, injured police and firefighters, and pretty much anyone else who suffered or died wearing a uniform. But 92% of the money PrideCare collected stayed at PrideCare. Operating expenses.

Miller began seething the moment the cops tore him away from his patriotic charity work; he got paid on a strict commission basis. Miller did somehow manage to contain his rage, which was kind of a shame because he was a guy you want to punch in the face and send to his room without dinner. Worse, he was a guy you couldn't bust for being the MK.

Miller was hard at work at the charity factory the evening Kody Wallace was murdered. When Dave Gold was killed, Miller was at his part-time night job manning the shoe counter at a bowling alley. When Roz Espinosa died, Miller was at a bar with a couple of guys he'd met earlier that evening at a court-mandated anger management class.

◆

The next morning reports came in from the FBI, and police departments in the other forty-nine states; from sea to shining sea there wasn't one blond male owner of a white Cherokee you could cast in the role of Makro Killer .

A citywide sweep of PODs footage scored zero. No new sightings of the Cherokee since Espinosa's murder.

Detectives investigating the boilerplate on Roz Espinosa—was there anyone with motive, did Espinosa have any connection with the other two victims besides driving for Makro—came up empty.

Mark and Doonie looked at each other. Silently asked, *Got any idea what the fuck we do next?*

Doonie glanced at his watch. *Is 11 AM too early to go grab a drink?*

Mark's computer beeped. *Yes.*

TWENTY-FIVE

It wasn't an auto theft. It was a vehicle in a missing person alert.

Seven months ago 48-year-old white female Vanora Yard and her white 2011 Cherokee disappeared from Phelpton, California. Yard was last seen with an unidentified white male, described by a witness as 40ish, burly, with black hair. It was not known if they left town together.

Mark did some homework.

Phelpton was in the Sierra foothills 120 miles northeast of Sacramento. Population 3,801. 81.2% white, 13.7% Hispanic, 3.8% Hmong, 1.3% African-American. Saw some gold rush action in the 1850s. These days the economy centered on farming, ranching and mining the wallets of tourists.

The missing person alert had been issued by the Sheriff's office, which according to the national police registry consisted of Sheriff Dan Abbott and three deputies.

Vanora Yard's social media accounts were still open. Families maintain them in hopes the missing person will post something, and so anyone who's seen her will have a way to make contact.

Yard's FaceBook bio: **An American Girl. Hell, THE American Girl.**

Works at **Independent Businesswoman**

Status **Unmarried**

Nothing else. No mention of what Yard's independent business might be.

Her photos showed a tall, handsome woman who looked her age but favored the wide-eyed mock-innocent flirty grin of a high school heartbreaker. Strawberry blonde hair worn long, strands styled to cascade down in front and come to rest where they'd draw attention to how buxom she was, on the off chance anyone had missed them.

In most of the photos Yard was alone. In the others she was in a group at a social event. No shots of just her with someone who might be a significant other.

Nobody in the group shots was a 40ish burly guy with black, or blond, hair. Neither was anybody in the headshots of Yard's 117 Friends.

There were pictures of Yard posing with a gun or at a range firing one. Mostly handguns. A few assault rifles. And, at a gun show, her flashing a bad-girl scowl as she pointed a fat WWII water-cooled machine gun at the camera.

Yard's posts indicated she was fond of Tom Petty, state's rights, Cabo San Lucas, the Second Amendment, spa weekends, deporting illegal immigrants, Adele, the death penalty and freedom.

Her Twitter account was more of the same. Plus she'd commented in a couple of threads linked to militia groups in northern California and Idaho.

❖

"Not a problem, I'm shootin' you the case file right now," Sheriff Abbott told Mark. His tone was laid-back but not enough to mask a background whir of constant calculation.

"Thanks. Has there been anything new—no hit off her credit cards?"

"Not a one—but unless someone finds a set of remains I wouldn't jump to conclusions. Vanora can get by fine without VISA. Men like to take care of her."

"For seven months?"

"First time Vanora ran off she was gone two years, been married and divorced by the time she came home."

"Where'd she run off to?"

"Idaho."

"She go alone?"

"No, some young buck swept her off her feet. But the next two marriages were older fellas who had a dollar."

"When she ran off that first time, was it the same way as this—without telling anybody and never contacting anyone?"

"No, she stayed in touch with her sister and friends."

"Her media profile says Independent Businesswoman. What business was she in?"

Abbott chuckled. "Vanora and her sister inherited their mother's little shop. Sells mainly greeting cards and crafting supplies, but also scented candles, bath salts, local jewelry, whatever girly stuff is popular this week. But Vanora sold her share to her sister—Vanora ain't much for retail. She liked it better being the prettiest waitress in tourist bars and restaurants. Made enough to get by while she got better at marrying. Vanora's eighty-year-old third husband left her enough to live on, and also invest in her sister's shop—spiffed the place up, and started carrying cool sunglasses, hypoallergenic sun block, stuff that ain't necessary, at a price only a tourist's gonna pay," Abbott explained.

"Yeah we got that too. It's why North Michigan Avenue is the Miracle Mile. Did you ever meet the young buck, her first husband?"

"Nope... What kind of connection you think Vanora has to the Makro Killer investigation?"

"Probably none. At this point I can't go into detail. You know the drill."

There was a five-second silence as Abbott's calculations kicked into overdrive. "Sure do. So you don't have to ask me to keep this confidential."

"Thank you, Sheriff. I have just one more question."

"No problem."

"While we've been talking I gave the file a quick look. It doesn't name the witness who saw the burly unidentified male with black hair."

Another chuckle. "Ah, Detective... It was Vanora's older sister, Kalinda—nice lady, but you'd just be wastin' your time there. Kallie's a drinker, on top of being kinda nuts and kinda creative with the truth. If she comes up with some new detail it won't be something you can trust."

Mark thanked Sheriff Abbott, ended the call, located Kalinda Yard's contact info, picked up his phone—

"Ah shit," Doonie sighed, staring at his computer. It was a quiet, heartfelt ah shit, not Doonie's usual.

Mark asked, "What?"

"AGA's video on Roz Espinosa is out," Doonie said, giving Mark a sympathetic look and swiveling his monitor for Mark to see.

Wasn't any shittier than the first two videos. And then it was.

Danny Gold.

Who I never talked to because I was busy talking down a speed freak who needed to be on TV.

"You had no fuckin' choice," Doonie said, reading Mark's silence verbatim.

TWENTY-SIX

Clara Cahill and her father-in-law Raul were at a funeral parlor pricing caskets when their phones blew up.

"I'm sorry," Clara apologized to Raul, gave him a quick hug and left. Watching that thing for the first time any way but alone was unthinkable.

◆

Clara had watched the Wallace and Gold videos too many times, studied them, analyzed them. She hoped learning what to expect in Roz's video would inoculate her.

Clara didn't cry when, as expected, the video opened with a montage of sweet Roz photos. Unexpectedly, it showed their wedding picture. Clara had assumed this ammosexual propaganda would avoid mentioning Roz was a lesbian. Forget a married one. But seeing herself exploited along with Roz in an attempt to lure LGBTQs into the gun tent didn't make Clara cry. It just made her angrier, stronger—*Oh God!*

The shock of seeing Danny Gold. The realization the little shit was collaborating—

Clara's anger at Danny swiftly decayed into guilt that she'd let herself blame him. When the video ended her eyes were wet and she was whispering, "You poor boy, you poor boy."

All that pain... Exploiting the dead was—but this, using, doing this to a child in such agony... Clara saw Danny years from now, when he realized what he'd done and that he'd never be able to undo it.

Clara let the tears spill until she got fed up with them and rubbed them the hell off her cheeks.

Something must be done. Something... must.

Clara picked up a framed wedding photo of her and Roz, the one which for the past two days she'd been carrying around the apartment with her. The one they'd posted on FaceBook seconds after it was taken. The one the AGA's slimeball auteur, that Trey Fister, found and used.

Clara held the photo up so she and Roz were eye to eye.

"I'll send lawyers. I'll use the media... But if that doesn't work I *will* find something that does," Clara promised Roz.

TWENTY-SEVEN

Okay, back to work. Mark bookmarked the video starring the son of a murder victim, and phoned the sister of a possible murder victim.

Kalinda Yard's line rang once and went to voicemail. Mark spoke slowly and repeated his name and number, to give her time to pick up in case she was screening calls. Nope.

He emailed and texted. He'd give her ten minutes before he called again.

He wondered why Sheriff Abbott tried to talk him out of talking to Kalinda.

He replayed Danny's video. The kid was on fire, devastated and devastating. Made it the kind of commercial that can define an election. Free concealed carry for everybody, here we come. Gun peddlers gonna goose their profits, Doonie and me gonna goose our stats.

Mark's phone rang.

Kalinda Yard introduced herself and asked how she could help him. She didn't ask what she'd be helping with.

Kalinda's voice matched her FaceBook photos: An older, thicker, plainer, wearier but warmer version of her sister. Kalinda's answers were calm, clear and relevant to what Mark asked. No rambling, no confusion. No discernible sign she'd been drinking. And no discernible distress over the fact Mark's questions were about her missing sister's possible connection to the Makro Killer.

"Where did you get this glimpse of the man?"

"Vanora asked me to swing by after work and drop off samples of cosmetics she was thinking might sell. But when I got there Van only opened the door a few inches. She wasn't wearing anything. Behind her this dude was walking away—I only saw part of the side of his face—his hair was black and very short, buzzcut."

"Natural black or dyed?"

"Mmm, I'm gonna say dyed."

"Any resemblance to Vanora's first husband?"

"God no. Tony was a short pudgy rooster, nasty little militia nut up in Idaho. This dude was big, had muscles—he wasn't wearing a shirt."

"Any tattoos?"

"Nuh-uh. At least not on the parts I saw."

"How tall?"

"Maybe six-three?"

"Did you see or speak to your sister after that?"

"Once. She called next morning to apologize for not letting me in, but mainly to giggle and tell me not to take it personal if she didn't answer calls or texts the next couple days."

"Did she say anything about him?"

"No, and I asked. Wouldn't even tell his name, said he was a man serious about his privacy."

"Uh-huh," Mark agreed. "Do you remember the name of the militia her first husband was in?"

"The Sovereign Swords."

"They still exist?"

"Last I heard. Van was still in touch with her ex—Tony Mower, I'll send you his contact info. The last time Van went up there it was for a Sovereign Swords Fourth of July ceremony. That was five—no, six years ago."

"Thank you, Ms. Yard, I appreciate your taking the time to speak to me."

"Why wouldn't I? If you have more questions, need any documents, just call. And, Detective—I assume it's best if I keep this conversation to myself?"

"You've got that exactly right." No shit; if this woman was drunk, she was an even more functional drunk than Doonie. "Ms. Yard, is there a reason Sheriff Abbott might not want me to talk to you?"

"Oh yes, totally. When your call went to voicemail it was because I was on the phone with Dan Abbott. Dan was trying to convince me to not speak to you at all, to email you that I was too upset to discuss Vanora. Dan said Makro is offering a two-hundred-fifty-thousand dollar reward for information leading to the arrest of the Makro Killer, which he'd split 50-50 if I stonewalled you, and gave him time to try to dig up who that beefy guy was."

"Huh," Mark said, and waited.

"Well, truth be told, it's not like I couldn't use the money. I'm still paying off debts my ex-husband ran up, and I'm putting our son through college."

"And yet you called me back."

"Well, while maybe there's a chance this guy turns out to be the Makro Killer, there's no chance Dan Abbott is capable to get off his dumb lazy ass long enough to track down the guy's real name. But you'll get after it. And even if you don't find him, you might find Van... Even if that turns out bad, I think knowing would be better than going through more months, years, of wondering, 'Alive or dead?'... You know?"

"Yeah." Living in that kind of prolonged uncertainty about a loved one was living in an impossible spin cycle of optimism and dread. Gets to a point where a funeral is a relief.

Also, if Vanora was dead, it'd be a big help for Kalinda to inherit now, instead of waiting the five years before a court can declare a missing relative legally deceased.

Mark didn't blame Kalinda for wanting that. He knew how hard it was for a single parent to raise a kid. He'd watched his mother raise two after his father walked out.

TWENTY-EIGHT

Mark contacted Agent Carlson, his FBI liaison. Agent Carlson agreed Vanora Yard's missing white Cherokee and her vacationing at a Club Paramilitary in Idaho made her worth a look.

"We'll get right on it."

"Thanks," Mark said. "In the meantime can I see your file on the Sovereign Swords—not the summary, the unredacted intelligence porn."

"I doubt it, but I'll ask. And I'll contact the agent who covers these patriots, find out if he knows any who match the MK's description."

◆

Mark settled for reading the Sovereign Swords website.

Their *Declaratum Of Sovereign Principia* said, in exactly 1,776 words: The federal government was not legal. State's rights were legal but state government was mostly not. The Sovereign Swords were legal. And asskickers. "Every Sword is a fully trained CRM (Combat Ready Militiaman) prepared to sacrifice his life—but even more prepared to sacrifice the lives of any Tyrants foolish enough to violate Our Freedom."

The group's founder and author of the *Declaratum* was Clayton Mower, whose son Tony had inherited the family militia business. The only names and faces on the site were Clayton's and Tony's. There was no mention or photo of Tony's first wife, Vanora Yard. There were stills and videos of heavily armed camo-clad Swords fondling or firing their weapons, but they all wore ski masks. Two also wore cowboy hats. The combination of Stetson and ski mask was impressively creepy. Tony Mower was missing a trick by not ordering all his troops to go with that look.

Mower's effectiveness as a commanding officer may have been impaired by the amount of time he spent maintaining the group's social media profile and running the Sovereign Swords merch store.

There were Sovereign Swords baseball and fatigue caps, t-shirts for the whole family, tank tops for the ladies, coffee mugs, stickers, pins and armbands. The priciest items were a series of Combat Ready training videos.

Every item was decorated with a the group's name and logo: The letters SS, floating on a diamond-shaped field of camo. The letters were in a sci-fi Gothic font. Each S was outlined in silver. The broad interior of each S was filled with red, white and blue stripes. Third Reich gone Fourth of July.

Mark scrolled through the group's FaceBook and Twitter feeds, then Tony Mower's personal pages. Just the usual everyday networking: Trading tactical tips and conspiracy updates. Cheering the good guys, jeering the Mud guys, Islamobeards, libtards, Zios, women, butt-fuckers, rug-munchers and science. Nothing useful; the indictable communications would be in private chat rooms, on encrypted Deep Fringe apps.

Mark examined the photos. None of the masked men was a reasonable facsimile of 6-4 and burly.

Mark ran Mower's name. Tony had a sheet. Couple of youthful D&Ds, and seven years ago a domestic disturbance resulting in a misdemeanor assault charge, dropped when Mower's (second) wife changed her story.

Mark Googled. A regional weekly noted the Swords' annual blanket and toy drives for military families. A daily paper and a TV station in Boise ran brief reports about heavily armed Swords attempting to block a farm foreclosure, attempting to disrupt county board hearings, and attempting to intimidate National Park rangers by tailing them as they made their rounds.

There was only one Swords-related bust. A man got caught stealing a tractor while wearing an SS T-shirt under his sweatshirt. He denied he was a Sovereign Sword, claimed the T-shirt was a Secret

Santa gift from his church's Christmas potluck.

Agent Carlson called back.

"The Sovereign Swords file has IDs and photos for most current and former members. No one matches the MK's description."

"Have—"

"Yes I spoke to our Idaho agent. He doesn't recall any Sword who fits—but he's going to check with a source who used to be in the group. But first the agent has to track down the source—the guy's batshit paranoid, lives way off the grid, and he's pissed off at us because he's sure we don't pay him as much as we pay black and Muslim snitches."

TWENTY-NINE

anny kept his side of the gun deal. He was beginning to wonder when Trey would get around to keeping his.

At their first meeting Trey had one demand. "We can't work together unless you swear you won't get a handgun. Not until you're twenty-one."

"But, why?"

"You get caught with an illegal weapon, your cred is fucked. And I'm the asshole who trusted you. And the AGA are the assholes who trusted me."

"It's… I can drive and vote and go fight and die in the military but in Illinois I can't own a gun until twenty-one? That's. Not. Fair."

"No, it's the law. For now. So for now we gots to do what we gots to do, bro… But can't own one don't mean can't use one. I will take you to a range where you'll fire some bitchin' weapons. Deal?"

They shook on it. And that was the last time Trey said anything about Danny getting to pull a trigger.

Until this morning.

The three days since Danny's video dropped had been amazing. Full spectrum news coverage, with heated arguments between talking heads over The Meaning Of Danny Gold's Statement. Thousands of social media battles about whether Danny was a hero or a victim or a vengeful emotional cripple, a chubby nerd or a semi-hot chubby nerd. 186,077 Twitter followers, and more every minute. A surge in support for ELE and a call from Executive Vice President Stan Vanderman, thanking Danny and telling him his courage and honesty were resonating across America.

Danny also got sympathetic and/or angry calls and texts from his friends, saying they understood he was hurting but how could you turn yourself into a tool for those evil bastards? You hate them. Your Dad hated them. You're betraying your Dad.

Danny texted **Doing what I need to**, then blocked them all.

Reporters desperate to get at Danny staked out his uncle's apartment and prowled the Northwestern campus. The AGA moved Danny into a studio apartment in Trey's building.

Danny and Trey's voicemails were flooded with requests for a Danny Gold interview. Trey was against it, said it was important Danny not get overexposed. But after days of nonstop phone/email/ Twitter clog Danny suggested maybe he should do just one interview, to y'know feed the beast so it'd go away.

Trey shook his head. "You can't control an interview. The liberal media will make you look like a confused child, make you sound like you didn't mean it—they got the skills, bro, those bitches are sharks. And yeah, Fox will guarantee you a super-friendly. But their viewers are already on our side. It's indies and libs we need to win over—if you give Fox an exclusive you're handing our target audience an excuse to write you off. Danny Gold, just another wingnut. If the only place people can see you is in our videos, you control the message, bro. You make yourself the face who got ELE passed... Okay enough of this fucking business shit. We got an appointment to sling some lead."

Danny's eyes widened.

Trey smirked. "Worried I forgot?"

THIRTY

It was over an hour's drive, out past Barrington. All Trey would tell him was that it was a facility with indoor and outdoor ranges.

It also had a wall and a gate. Valet parking for the members' six-figure cars and Trey's rental Corolla. A large main building with a pool, a fitness center, a restaurant, a bar and a gunsmith. Two indoor ranges, one for handguns, one for long guns. Outdoor ranges for target shooting and skeet. It called itself a hunt club, which as far as Danny could tell meant a country club with fun instead of golf.

The pretty woman behind the registration desk recognized Danny, gave him a warm-sad grin and welcomed him by name. Two club members walking past paused, nodded and gave Danny the warm-sad grin.

A shooting instructor—ex-Ranger, ex-sniper—escorted Danny and Trey to a weapons room, where he selected a 9mm Sig, demonstrated how to strip and reassemble it, and briefed Danny on safe handling.

They went to the pistol range where during forty minutes of world-class tutelage Danny's aim improved from nonexistent to not awful. Every shot, the bang, the recoil, the cordite perfume and just holding the damn gun, the way it lived in his hand, felt so fucking right. And so much more. Target shooting is about stillness. Slowing the breath. Concentrating, mind emptied of everything except what you're doing: focusing on the impossibility of making your arm completely still. Being relaxed and ready for that microsecond when the gun sight crosses that tiny bull's-eye. Blowing the shit out of those pieces of paper was the first peaceful, empty-minded moment Danny experienced since two cops had knocked on the door and delivered the news about what they found in an alley two blocks down.

As Danny left the pistol range three people recognized him, introduced themselves, shook his hand and flashed the warm-sad. More of the club's members did the same while Danny, Trey and the instructor were taking a coffee break before heading off to introduce Danny to an AR-15.

That shit was beyond words.

When Danny finally, reluctantly returned the weapon to the instructor, the ex-Ranger grinned, said, "You're gonna be a good shot," and on behalf of the club handed Danny a guest pass good for a year, with unlimited lessons—"So get your ass out here at least once a week."

Danny stammered his thanks. As the instructor walked away Danny tried to thank Trey but all he could manage was a look of undying gratitude.

"I gave my word, bro," Trey said. "And my new word is: Lunchtime."

Fuck yeah. Danny was starving.

They took an elevator to the Founder's Lounge, a wood-paneled retreat with an antique bar and upholstered leather booths. Trey led Danny to a corner booth where yet another surprise was waiting. Stan Vanderman.

Danny devoured a filet mignon that was the best steak of his life, and sampled Trey's bison burger, and Stan's venison. Both were firsts for Danny, as was the Phelps Insignia cabernet. But Vanderman allowed him only one glass.

"At nineteen that's as much daytime drinking as you should be doing," Vanderman ruled. He gave Danny a grin that was nothing like sad or warm, just all business. "Also, you and I are about to have a very important discussion. If you keep making videos for—"

"Not *if*," Danny objected.

An approving nod from Vanderman. "There's something else—something more. We're launching an organization called Youth For ELE—Second Amendment supporters between the ages of eighteen and twenty, who can vote for Every License Everywhere, even if they're not allowed to apply for a license. Their participation won't only strengthen the ELE campai—"

"It'll automatically build a group that'll push to lower the age—ah shit this is so—I'm in," Danny declared. "Whatever I can do."

"What we envision is you being the YFE's President—wait, hear me out. In addition to organizing people your own age, you'd have tremendous impact in one-on-one meetings with legislators. And this year's AGA convention will be in Chicago. We'd like you to address that convention. Obviously we're talking about a full-time—a more than full-time job. So you'll have a contract and commensurate compensation. Now you can talk."

"Thank you… Thank you. Yes."

"Don't decide now. Slow down, think this through. You're nineteen, sophomore year. As much as we'd like to have you on board, I'm loathe to interrupt your education. And you should be too. You need to give this careful consideration—"

"I need a gap year. I'm in. Let's shake on it."

Vanderman studied him for a moment. Gave Danny an approving grin and shook Danny's hand. Said nothing. Just picked up the bottle of Insignia and began to refill Danny's glass

A tweener girl and a woman who was clearly her mother approached the booth, gazing at Danny.

The girl apologized, "Excuse me… Mr. Gold, but, I just…" She gave Danny an embarrassed, touchingly sincere warm-sad grin.

The mother put a comforting arm around her. "I hope you'll forgive us for intruding on your meal, but my daughter—and I—"

"You're not intruding," Danny said, rising to his feet. "You're being incredibly kind. Thank you," he told the girl, and asked her name.

The girl whispered her name and asked if she could hug him. He hugged her. And the mother.

The girl asked if she could take a selfie. Danny did one with her, another with both of them.

Vanderman and Trey exchanged a voraciously pleased look.

The girl asked if she could also have an autograph.

Danny hesitated, frowned. "I… It's just… There's something, the autograph thing feels too—celebrity. Y'know?... I'm doing this for my Dad. Y'know?"

The girl, mortified, moaned, "I'm so sorry, I shouldn't have..." and the tears came. Danny gathered her in for another hug.

Vanderman looked on with a benign grin, which he maintained as he leaned close to Trey and hissed, "He has *got to* do autographs at the convention."

"He will," Trey smirked, amused the Silver Sidewinder was still underestimating Trey Fister's powers.

An alert sounded on Trey's phone. He read it, and, with a pleased smirk, informed Vanderman, "The minister of the largest, most liberal Unitarian church in Winnebago County, married, three children, killed in a carjacking. Sorry to eat and run but me and President Gold gotta get back to work."

THIRTY-ONE

After promising Roz she'd do something about the AGA video, Clara placed their wedding photo next to her laptop. .

Clara went to the AGA home page. She turned the wedding photo face-down and watched the Roz video two more times.

Clara closed the browser, stood Roz upright and began writing.

◆

Clara read her statement live on Chicago's highest rated evening news show.

The segment opened with a Marina Karrell backgrounder on Clara and Roz, illustrated with photos of them as young novitiates together, as nuns working together in the community, as newlyweds at their wedding, ending with a recent selfie of Clara and Roz leaning against their new Prius the day they bought it. The image faded from the selfie to a freeze-frame of a news report showing the Prius surrounded by crime scene tape in the underpass, with a chyron announcing **Makro Killer Strikes Again**.

That image faded to black. Then the AGA video played.

Clara's turn. She looked into the camera, took a breath, and delivered her statement. "My wife, Roz Espinoza, would forgive the man who shot her. That's who she was." Clara offered poignant examples of Roz's warmth, kindness, generosity, wit and achievements. Then she recited the section of the autopsy report describing Roz' gunshot wounds. "For her body to be torn apart like that, for her to suffer and die in such a brutal manner, is an atrocity almost beyond bearing. But to then see Roz, who believed in gun control and was adamantly opposed to the AGA's policies, have her murder exploited and her memory defiled in an attempt to popularize those policies, is more shameful than words can say. And also a recurring torment, to all who loved her, every time that video is shown. I respectfully request the AGA remove all references to Roz Espinoza from their advertising. I respectfully request anyone who agrees with me to do the same... My wife's murder is not a marketing tool."

Marina Karrell asked Clara, "Your statement never mentions legal action. If the AGA doesn't honor your request, would you consider taking them to court?"

"Yes."

"And if that doesn't work?"

"God will," Clara said, her face cold as any stone.

❖

Clara's video played on every news outlet. Racked up hundred of thousands of views, retweets, shares.

The AGA received tens of thousands of requests/demands/threats. It released a statement expressing sympathy for Clara Cahill and undying devotion to the First Amendment as well as the Second.

Clara's email and social media accounts were inundated with fervent declarations of admiration and support, and counter-inundated with rabid trolling that puked on her politics, motives, looks, sanity and Catholic atheism, accused her of being a traitor Muslim whore who used the Constitution as toilet paper, and the alt-right diagnostic consensus was she'd die from cancer of the cunt.

Claramania ruled for twenty-two hours. Then Kanye complained about something and the digital opinion party danced over there.

❖

Clara didn't wait to see whether her plea to the AGA would work. Soon as she got off the air her phone lit up with offers of assistance from attorneys. Most were transparent hucksters looking to get on TV.

Clara began contacting reputable law firms.

She spent a week going to meetings, at which the lawyers advised her not to sue. It was a near certainty she'd lose; it was an absolute certainty the AGA would drag the case out and run Clara's expenses into the high six figures. Or more.

No major firm offered to take on the AGA pro bono. No medium-sized firm or lone wolf could afford to.

Clara asked what it would cost to file a suit and keep it going for at least six months, during which she could solicit support. The estimates varied from ninety to three hundred thousand dollars.

Clara launched a GoFundMe. It stalled at seventeen thousand.

Kody Wallace's and David Gold's families made modest pledges. Neither family was interested in joining Clara's suit or subjecting themselves to the public shitstorm it would bring. Both families were still raw with grieving. The Golds were also in agony about Danny, who'd severed contact with them.

Clara appealed to liberal foundations and PACs. All of them sympathized. The PACs declined to fritter away their resources funding a doomed lawsuit. The foundations required voluminous grant applications and months to assess them.

Clara received a call from Wendy Stinson, president of a national organization run by parents of school massacre victims, which lobbied for gun control. Clara's heart leapt.

Stinson asked if Clara would be willing to write an endorsement the organization could use in a fundraising email.

Clara's heart sank. "Yes. Of course."

"Thank you. I can't tell you how much we appreciate you doing this."

"Well... can a percentage of what the email raises go to my GoFundMe?"

A brief, sticky silence.

"If—if it were up to me... But our charter forbids expenditures not directly related to the enactment of gun control statutes. Our donors trust that's where their money will go." Stinson sighed. "If you want to—reconsider—your participation in our fundraiser, I understand, entirely."

Clara closed her eyes. Said, "What length should the endorsement be and how soon do you need it?"

◆

Clara went to her computer. There was an email from GoFundMe;

Stinson had donated fifty dollars. Clara stared at the computer for a few minutes, swallowed hard, and began to compose her endorsement—

An alert chimed.

There was a new AGA video, about a Unitarian minister who'd been killed in Winnebago County. Danny Gold narrated it. At the end Gold announced the launch of Youth For ELE. "Because even if the law says we're too young to own a handgun, we're not too young to vote to do something about that."

Clara looked at the YFE's website. It was slick, inventive, engaging. Expensive.

It gave links to chapters that had already been launched in Chicago and Springfield. It promised chapters would be established nationwide within thirty to sixty days, and the YFE was ready to help you organize your own.

There was a donations page. For the next four weeks there was a *$1.01 SPECIAL: a YFE t-shirt for ANY donation over one dollar!*

An offer that would lose money, not raise it. The AGA had cash to burn.

Clara took the wedding photo into the bedroom and placed her and Roz on the nightstand.

Clara left the bedroom, closing the door behind her. She went to the hall closet and fetched a bottle from a carton at the back of the closet.

It was a wedding present six nuns had chipped in on. A vintage Port which Roz and Clara were forbidden to open until their tenth anniversary.

She uncorked it.

THIRTY-TWO

Nine days after Roz Espinoza's death the only positive development was the Makro Killer hadn't murdered another driver yet. Mark and Doonie were parked at their desks like two heaps of wasted taxpayer dollars. Until Mark received an urgent tip, from the PR department.

It was a link to that morning's *Chicago Hots & Nots*, a clickbait gossip segment on a local TV morning talk show, delivered by a droll young woman wearing large bright orange intellectual geekster glasses.

"Today's final Hots & Nots: Two Chicagoans who earlier this year became media sensations launched by the Art Critic serial killer case.

"Chicago Hot: In the six months since she was exonerated as the suspect in that investigation, artist JaneDoe has rocketed to success, while rocking the glam expat life in Paris. Last night JaneDoe attended the opening of a new production at the Paris Opera and her date was the scorching hot—in every sense of the word—young French filmmaker Didier Corsu. JaneDoe and Didier claim they're just friends. We'll see if that turns out to mean the same thing in French as it does in English.

"Chicago Not: Chicago's hunky hero Det. Mark Bergman is leading the investigation into the Makro killings that have terrified the city and trashed Makro's popularity. So far Det. Bergman's been stuck on the launch pad, unable to come up with a single lead. Now a source close to the investigation says there have been rumblings about replacing him. But no decision has been made—yet."

"A source close to my fat pimply ass," Doonie grumbled. "This leak's from Makro. They're tryin' to make this into Bergman the fuckup to distract people from thinkin' about Makro the death car. The Supe ain't benching you."

"Not unless my Q score tanks," Mark said, looking at his computer, where the *Chicago Hots & Nots* segment closed with its trademark split-screen image. *The Hot*, JaneDoe and Didier Corsu at the opera. *The Not*, Mark holding up a pair of empty handcuffs, in Chris Shakeley's dismal front yard.

"So, ah, you seen any movies by this Diddly Corsooo?" Doonie asked.

"Two. Both good," Mark lamented. His cell rang—Agent Carlson.

"Your guy's name is Rudy. No last name but there are some details."

❖

When Mark got off the phone he and Doonie went to Husak's office so Mark could brief them both.

"Rudy's blond, burly, the right height and age. The snitch said Rudy has a wide nose and a two-three inch scar along the jawline on his left cheek. But no photos, Rudy was camera shy."

"They putting the snitch with a sketch artist?" Husak asked.

"Soon as they can. The snitch is dickering over price, location, procedure—he'll only work with the artist through an encrypted video link, with his face blacked out and his voice distorted."

"He watches too much TV."

"Who doesn't? Here's what we got: Seven years ago the snitch met Rudy at a Sovereign Swords training camp. Rudy—if that's his real name—came in to teach infantry tactics. And also tips about law enforcement—how to handle a cop, how to work the system. Rudy told them he's ex-military—Army, but wouldn't say which branch or where he served. And also ex-cop—said he worked for a number of departments. Again, Rudy refused to name them. Which our paranoid snitch took as proof Rudy was the real deal."

"Let's hope he's right," Husak said, with his usual mournful optimism.

"Not so far—the FBI's militia files show nothing about a Rudy working as a freelance drill sergeant. They're checking the employment records of police and sheriff's departments in Idaho and the adjoining states, and also Arizona. I told them to add Illinois, since here's where the MK decided to put on his show. And I asked if they could get the Defense Department to send us the records of every white male first-or-last-name Rudy or Rudolph over six feet tall who served in the military the last twenty-five years."

◆

While waiting on the FBI and DoD, Mark checked with another source.

"No, you're not interrupting," Kalinda Yard assured Mark. "What can I help you with?"

"You said your sister went to Idaho for a Fourth of July event, five or six years ago."

"Yes."

"Could it have been seven years ago?"

"Of course it could. Vanora's drifted in and out of my life, over and over, since forever. So, far as specific dates, y'know?"

"Yeah. Did Vanora ever mention—in connection with Idaho or anyplace else—a man named Rudy?"

"Rudy? Mmm, sorry, not ringing any bells."

"Ever mention a man with a scar on his jaw?"

"Never."

"Did Vanora ever show you pictures from that July Fourth?" Rudy didn't like be photographed but Vanora lived for it, and you never know.

Kalinda took a moment. "No. Not that I remember. Sorry."

"The report said Vanora had a laptop that disappeared along with her. Did she also have a desktop?"

"Yes. And I have the keys to Van's house. I'll go right after I close up. But if it's urgent I can go right now."

Silence from Mark.

"Detective? Detective are y—"

"Yes—sorry—thank you Kalinda, if you find anything let me know, okay?" Mark said, rattling it off, distracted.

"You sound—did something just happen?"

"Yes. Sorry, I gotta go."

The Makro Killer possibly named Rudy had scored again. And changed the rules again. Made his first kill outside the city. Forty miles west, in Oswego; the vic was a Makro driver who'd bet his life Chicago was the only market the Makro Killer was targeting.

THIRTY-THREE

State Senator Nadine Detmer (D) favored an assault rifle ban, stricter handgun control and the AGA rotting in hell, but she agreed to meet with Danny. Which Trey had predicted. Said Detmer would take the meeting because she and Danny had something in common. Her son had been killed by a sniper in Fallujah.

They flew down to Springfield and took a cab to the Capitol Building. When they arrived at Detmer's office, Trey told Danny he'd wait in the hallway. "The Senator thinks I'm the Devil and you're my victim. She'll try to save you."

◆

Senator Detmer was a slim silver-haired patrician with crisp diction and no trace of the *you poor wounded puppy* warm-sad smile. Danny liked her right away.

"Thank you for taking the time to see me, Senator."

"Not at all. I'm pleased to have this unexpected chance to make your acquaintance," Detmer replied. "May I ask who suggested you contact me?"

"Trey Fister."

"Ah."

"Senator, Trey's not manipulating me. He never—I was the one who called him. I'm doing this for my father."

"I know."

"I'm not crazy. And I'm not stupid."

"Me neither. Fister told you I'd take a meeting with you because of my son. He was right. You're getting this chance to lobby me to vote for ELE because I'm getting this chance to lobby you to step back, take a long deep breath, look at what you're doing and why you're doing it—and what the consequences will be, for yourself, and for all the people you're doing such a powerful job of persuading."

"I think the consequences will be good ones. So I'm going to keep working for Every License Everywhere."

"And I'm going to vote against it… Turns out neither one of us is any good at lobbying," Detmer noted, approvingly.

Danny grinned. "That's okay. I mean I like ELE but my own bottom line—all I ask is that you think about voting to make concealed carry free. Lots of people can't afford it—I think they deserve as much of a chance as people who can."

"And I think more people carrying will just make things worse."

"Senator… My Dad was walking home alone, unarmed. Maybe a gun would've have saved him, maybe not. But now we'll never know."

"My son was firing an M2HB fifty-caliber machine gun when he died."

"He died fighting… I wish my Dad could have had that."

After a moment Detmer quietly said, "I know." After another moment she added, "I'll think about it… But don't get your hopes up… But do call me any time you want to talk about anything except politics. I mean it."

"I know."

Out in the hallway Trey was absorbed in his phone but pocketed it when he spotted Danny. "How'd it go?"

"Okay, personally, I mean, she's cool. But far as changing her vote?" Danny shrugged. "On ELE, never… She said she'd think about free concealed carry but told me not to get my hopes up."

"She said she'd think about free concealed carry?"

"But not to get my hopes up. She ain't gonna change her mind."

"Bro, you got Nadine Detmer to say out loud she'd think about free concealed carry," Trey said, giving Danny his most delighted smirk. Then announced, "C'mon, we gotta get to the airport," and headed for the elevator.

Danny hurried to catch up. "I thought we were gonna see a couple more Assemblymen and Senators if there was time."

"There isn't. First plane back to Chicago. Got work to do, bro."

"Ah shit, there's been another?"

"Not just another. It's the MK again," Trey said, quietly exhilarated, giving Danny a significant look.

Trey's exhilaration was contagious—Makro Killer murders drew a ton more attention. Danny kinda hated himself a little bit for getting stoked about another driver, like his Dad, getting… But every time another Makro driver died, it gave Danny's response a ton more force. So, complicated shit.

Trey gave Danny's shoulder a reassuring squeeze. Like he was reading Danny's troubled mind. Like an older brother could.

THIRTY-FOUR

The murder scene in Oswego was no help at all. Nothing in it got Mark and Doonie any closer to the MK. Just rubbed their noses in how far ahead of them he still was.

It was his first hit outside Chicago. And, after killing Roz Espinoza in her car, the MK reverted to his original MO, killing the driver at his residence. But this time the MK also suffocated the vic's 76-year-old mother, who inconveniently shared the home where the MK waited for him.

Now the MK had every Makro driver in the country wondering if their town was next, and do I really wanna tell Mom I love Makro so much I'm gonna risk her life in order to keep working for them.

The company doubled the reward to half a mil, and offered drivers a hundred dollar bonus for every ten rides they booked.

◆

Mark got an email from Kalinda apologizing for taking so long, but Van had literally thousands of pictures of herself, some on the computer and others on a half-dozen thumb drives she kept in a silk pouch in her desk.

Kalinda sent every photo taken in Idaho and anyplace that looked like it. A couple were kind of embarrassing so she was trusting Mark not to show those around.

147 shots were taken at Sovereign Swords events. Mark scrutinized every male. No winners.

The only glimpse of a possible Rudy was in one of the kind of embarrassing shots. Vanora was sitting in bed, propped against the pillows, wearing only a pair of aviator shades and holding an enormous handgun, a .44 magnum Ruger Redhawk with a seven-and-a-half inch barrel, against one of her copious breasts. The other breast was cupped by a man's hand. A large, muscular, hairy hand. The hair was blond.

Mark checked the data. The photo was taken on July 5th, seven years ago. When the FBI snitch met Rudy.

So now they not only had a shot of the back of the right side of the Makro Killer's head, they had a shot of the back of his left hand, maybe.

◆

The next day Agent Carlson called with the results of the FBI's search of police employment files. Nationwide, there was only one Rudy or Rudolph who almost qualified. He was a working cop in Oregon who was a dead ringer for the MK's age, military service and physical description, except for being Samoan.

"There are some records we couldn't get our hands on," Agent Carlson cautioned. "A handful of shitkicker PDs, the same ones that refuse to list current personnel in the national registry, told us to fuck off."

"But in a good way," Mark said, "out of deep respect for state's rights."

That, and a deep desire to keep the Feds from finding out what kind of goons you've been handing a badge, a gun and a taxpayer-funded salary.

◆

Two days later the Pentagon delivered a list of Rudy/Rudolphs who matched the MK's profile.

There were three. One was dead, one was in a Louisiana VA hospital and one was a SEAL, who'd been and was still otherwise engaged, far, far away.

THIRTY-FIVE

know, from what so many people have written to me, and about me, a lot of you think I'm going nuts from pain and anger. What I think is, all that pain and anger has made me—forced me—to think clearer than ever. But hey, they got their opinion and I got mine… What's not an opinion, what's a *fact* is the Makro Killer has now killed four people. Four. What's a *fact* is he's no longer only murdering inside Chicago. What's a *fact* is the police have not arrested him, not identified him and far as we know not made any progress… So tell me again why Illinois is still making it so hard for its citizens, for us, to defend ourselves? Tell me that. Tell me."

Trey held the shot of Danny staring into the camera, silently demanding an answer, for six long, uncomfortable seconds before fading to black and fading up the logo:

EVERY LICENSE EVERYWHERE
Make your voice heard. Go to ELE.com

Danny's "Tell Me" video won even more clicks and coverage even faster than the previous ones. Tell Me became a hashtag, memes, T-shirts, tats, a hook in two country music singles and an audience chant at GOP campaign events.

After #TellMe, in five Democratic Assembly districts where support for ELE had never touched 40%, the favorables now ranged from 43 to 48%. In one Democratic Senate district, approval poked its persuasive nose across the magic line: 50.3%.

Democratic legislators denied rumors they'd begun quietly polling about how a vote for ELE would play with donors and constituents.

THIRTY-SIX

It arrived like a miracle. A brief call from out of the blue, and suddenly that million pounds of frustration, that crushing helplessness, disappeared.

Dev Kwelty called Clara Cahill from his plane, said he was going to be in Chicago for a few hours and asked to meet her.

Clara hung up the phone and sank to her knees. Dev Kwelty was the 28-year-old tech billionaire who'd created the Whatever Matters Foundation, to which Clara had applied for funding but never heard back from. Until now.

From Kwelty. Personally.

◆

A town car delivered Clara to a security-gated section of the garage beneath one of the city's iconic skyscrapers. A well-dressed NFL-size young man escorted her to a private elevator.

When the elevator doors opened Dev Kwelty was there to greet her, wearing an exquisitely tailored black sport coat, lead-singer-grade skinny jeans and a logo T-shirt from a soccer franchise he'd purchased earlier that week.

He was honored to meet her, sorry for dragging her up here on such short notice for a much shorter meeting than he'd hoped, but his schedule was a nine-headed monster, and call him Dev.

"Call me Clara."

Dev escorted her to a living room where they settled into fantastically comfortable chairs.

Dev beamed. "I have to tell you, Clara... I admire you so—that interview you gave, was so powerful, so dignified, so *polite*. And so, just—lucid and on point, Clara... You rising to that, so soon after... I mean that took balls—sorry, *courage*, and—No, I need to testify: Clara Cahill, you got a king-size pair of titanium *huevos*."

"*Muchas gracias*," Clara murmured, trying not to betray how her heart was soaring.

"So I have full faith and confidence you're going to persevere, even though... the Foundation won't be awarding the grant you requested. My opinion of the AGA is the same as yours, but even if you had the most killer lawyers in the world, it'd be years before you set foot in a courtroom, and the ELE vote is coming in a matter of months. And the reality is, even if you took this to trial tomorrow, you'd lose—and the Whatever Matters Foundation, like everything I do, is laser-targeted on actions with the strongest calculable chance of a positive outcome. *Positive outcome.* That's the only—"

"*Why!?!*" Clara yelled, glaring. "Why did you make me come here?"

"Out of respect."

Carla's glare went murderous.

Dev sighed, puzzled by Clara's inability to grasp the obvious. "I assumed the rejection would be easier to process if you got to access it from me, personally."

❖

Clara declined a ride home in the town car. She needed to walk. And walk.

She walked past a branch of her bank. Stopped. Stared at it for a minute. Went in, withdrew a bundle of cash and went shopping.

THIRTY-SEVEN

Mark gave Husak's door a token knock, then he and Doonie barged in.

Husak was on the phone. He gestured sharply for them to be quiet. The quickest move Mark had ever seen from his cosmically laconic boss.

"Excuse me, I need a moment. Be right back," Husak promised the caller. He covered the mouthpiece and gave the intruders a *this better be fucking important* look.

Mark held up his cell. "Agent Carlson. His paranoid snitch came through, we've got a sketch of Rudy."

Husak guiltily apologized to his caller, "Sorry, Mom. Gonna have to call you back."

Shit. It'd been over a week since Mark visited his mother. Not that she was aware of time any more, or was certain who Mark was. Lately, neither did Mark. He put Agent Carlson on speakerphone and forwarded Husak the email Agent Carlson had just sent. Husak clicked on it and the sketch appeared on a wall-mounted flatscreen.

It was a shrewd thug face. Broad features on a big skull coated with buzz-cut blond hair, as the snitch had originally described. Pale blue eyes, as he'd described. Wide nose with a bulbous tip, as he'd described. But the jaw he'd described as clean-shaven was wearing a thick blond goatee.

"When did Rudy grow the beard?" Mark asked.

Agent Carlson said, "The snitch says he held back on the beard in case he needed a bargaining chip. If we didn't meet his price he was going to warn us his previous description of Rudy had an unspecified flaw."

"How about this version," Mark wondered.

"This one's a thousand percent accurate, he swears it on his Momma's bible."

"Does Momma know he's the one who stole her Bible?" Mark muttered. "Still, I vote we go public with this sketch."

"I agree," Agent Carlson replied, in a careful, neutral way. "But it's not up to me."

Mark and Doonie looked at Husak.

Husak said, "Same here, Agent Carlson. Thank you for the good work."

Husak ended the call and looked at Mark and Doonie, waiting to see if they were going to waste time protesting.

Mark knew Husak agreed with them. Even if the sketch was flawed it was worth putting it out, so at least there'd be a chance someone would recognize Rudy—and it'd warn Makro drivers to speed past any customer who looked anything like Rudy.

Normally the decision to release the sketch would be Husak's to make.

This case was under a global media microscope. The source of the sketch was a paranoid hermit who kept his own face obscured and his voice distorted.

The lords of the CPD and the FBI would need a moment to weigh the embarrassment of releasing a sketch that might be a con job, versus the embarrassment of another driver getting shot in the head while they refused to release a sketch that might be accurate.

Mark said, "Please tell your mother I apologize for the interruption."

"She'll like that," Husak replied.

Mama Husak was a fan. She'd recently sent Mark a batch of homemade pierogi after she saw him on TV and thought he looked a little thin.

◆

As they returned to their desks, Doonie asked Mark, "If you were bonin' Husak's Mom you'd tell me, right?"

"Not right away," Mark murmured, as he picked up a remote and unmuted the sound on the bullpen video screen, which was tuned to a news channel. It was showing Danny Gold's new AGA video, featuring the latest Makro victim.

"What's a *fact* is the police have not arrested him, not identified him and far as we know not made any progress," Danny mourned/accused.

No fair, Danny. We have a possible person of interest and a possibly reliable sketch of him we might possibly show you, possibly today.

Danny's video was being shown as an introduction to a profile of Trey Fister, recapping a career that began when Fister was a college kid in Oregon who made a splash with videos pranking campus liberals. Fister splashed onto the national stage with attack videos pranking an abortion clinic, and an immigrant resettlement agency, and an elderly gay climatologist with leukemia who'd won a Nobel for a definitive study of global warming.

Fister, carrying a hidden camera and disguised as a sympathetic supporter, lured each into discussing false accusations that had been leveled at them. Fister edited the conversations to sound as if the clinic was harvesting baby organs, the immigrant resettlement was a cover for human trafficking, and the elderly climatologist was falsifying Arctic ice sheet melt-rates while suffering from purely psychosomatic leukemia.

Fister parlayed his lib-smiting notoriety into more profitable work making campaign commercials and "documentaries" for hard-right interest groups, culminating with his current gig with the six-million-pound gorilla of political intimidation, the AGA.

The gestalt-changing success of Fister's ELE campaign was propelling him back into the spotlight, as the mastermind behind the murder-victim videos and the Youth For ELE movement. Both of which starred Danny Gold. Who was conspicuously shunning the spotlight.

The reporter asked about that.

"Since Mr. Gold is already going public, making videos and speaking at YFE rallies, all to honor his father, a journalist—why won't he speak to the press?"

"Danny's on a mission. He's totally committed to saying what he needs to say, exactly the way he wants to say it. So he's decided to not give interviews, to make sure his words can't be twisted to fit the media's agenda."

"And this way you hog all the fuckin' publicity," Doonie complimented Fister.

"Good," Mark said. "He's the one it'll bite in the ass."

"Downtown said yes," Husak announced, striding up behind them. "And the Supe lit a fire under it. Sketch went out a minute ago."

Mark and Doonie traded a mildly impressed look.

The three cops stared at the newscast and waited.

The reporter was asking Fister, "Given your filmmaking talent—will it always be politics for you, or do you ever think about, see yourself going Hollywood? Directing movies?"

Fister shrugged and smirked, aiming for modest and reticent but hitting smug and coy—

A *Breaking News* banner ran across the bottom of the screen: **POLICE RELEASE SKETCH OF PERSON OF INTEREST IN MAKRO KILLER INVESTIGATION.**

The taped interview froze in mid-smirk, and Fister's face was replaced by Rudy's.

THIRTY-EIGHT

Trey hosted an intimate viewing party for the broadcast of the longest-ever cable news profile of Trey Fister. An entire segment, from commercial-break to commercial-break, filled with pure Fisterness.

The original guest list was limited to Betsy and Liberty, two of Trey's most dedicated groupies. The list expanded when, during the taping of the interview, Trey was asked about Danny's decision to boycott the press. Trey couldn't risk letting Danny watch that part all alone in his room, getting jealous.

Trey had a private chat with Liberty, then invited Danny.

Trey ordered pizzas, popped champagne and fired up a blunt of Colorado's finest, putting everybody in the proper mood. And putting Liberty in the proper spot on the couch, next to Danny.

The dangerous moment arrived. On the TV the reporter wondered why Danny Gold, the son of a journalist, who's on a crusade inspired by and in honor of his slain father, was refusing to speak to his father's colleagues.

On the couch Danny's brow furrowed.

The brow remained furrowed as on TV Trey extolled Danny's commitment, explaining Danny was boycotting interviews "to make sure his words can't be twisted to fit the media's agenda."

Liberty gave Danny's plump thigh an approving, empathetic squeeze. And left her hand there. Danny's brow unfurrowed and his eyes left the TV. Liberty was bathing him in an adoring gaze, moved by Danny's nobility and lusting to prove it. Gazing at him as if he were... sexy. Liberty gave him a crinkly grin, laid her head on his shoulder and resumed watching TV. Danny resumed looking at the TV, but the expression on Danny's face said he wasn't seeing anything except the porn romance in his head.

Boo-yah up the wazoo-yah! Just too easy, Trey congratulated himself, and got back to enjoying the show. *Damn I am hot onscreen. Hotter at thirty-one than I was at twenty-one. And even more the smartest guy in the room. Maybe the planet. Yeah! Shit shit shit this is all gonna go exactly the way I—hey! Focus, bro, here comes the best part.*

"Do you ever think about, see yourself going Hollywood? Directing movies?"

Betsy gave an excited whoop and raised her glass so sharply the quarter-inch of champagne at the bottom sloshed out. Liberty and Danny grinned at Trey, and Danny gave him a thumbs-up.

Trey did a mock-modest shrug-smirk and resumed watching his interview, fantasizing about what he wished he was free to be confiding to his acolytes. *Directing a coupla hit movies would be cool, but Trey Daddy ain't spending his life answering to Hollywood libtard Jews—or New Hollywood commie Chink billionaires, yo! Or to the AGA, or fucking anee-bod-ee. Trey Daddy's goin' all the way to President Daddy, sickest dude who ever set up and threw down in the White Hou—THE FUCK?!*

A crawler at the bottom of the screen was silently screaming **POLICE ANNOUNCE PERSON OF INTEREST IN MAKRO KILLER INVESTIGATION.**

The tape froze on a close-up of future Oscar-winning director and POTUS Trey Fister, then there was a hard cut to a Wanted bulletin featuring a sketch of—

CHRIST!

—as a voiceover reporter announced, "Police have just released this sketch of a Makro Killer suspect—person of interest—who is possibly named Rudy."

THEY KNOW HIS NAME!

Danny leaned forward sharply, his whole being focused on the killer.

"Awright! They got him!" Betsy exclaimed.

"Not yet but this means they will," Liberty purred.

On TV the reporter said, "Short blond hair, six-foot-four, thickly built—"

Trey's stomach slid down into his ankles—

"—and possibly having a military or law enforcement background, or both. Also possible ties to a white supremacist militia in Idaho."

Trey's stomach bounced up into his throat.

A photo of a coy middle-aged blond appeared next to the sketch of Rudy.

"The suspect may be traveling with this woman, Vanora Yard. The suspect may also be driving a white 2011 Jeep Cherokee." The photo of Vanora Yard was replaced by a brief shot of her Cherokee, then the sketch of Rudy filled the screen. "Police regard the suspect as armed and dangerous. Anyone spotting this man should not approach or follow him. Just contact the police, immediately."

Danny pulled out his phone, downloaded Rudy's sketch and glared at it; the image on the TV was a yard across but this one was *his*.

Liberty put an arm around Danny, and this time her gaze glowed with sincere compassionate lust.

"Are you okay?" Betsy asked Trey, who seemed hypnotized by the news, dead still, like maybe he forgot how to breathe.

Trey's smirk reflex kicked in. He nailed Betsy with a pitying one, amused at the notion he might ever not be okay. "More champagne in the fridge," Trey advised Betsy. She hurried off to liberate it. Trey resumed watching the Rudy disaster, making sure to keep his expression cool and his body in an elegant slouch, giving no hint of the shriekfest in his brain or the gymnastics in his digestive tract.

They got Rudy's name, his face—but only his old pre-surgery face, with the beard, his old eyes and the fat nose. But all that shit they have on Rudy's background was true—they only coulda got that from somebody who knew Rudy—which means oh God he might also know me! Stop! Fuck this, fuck who dimed Rudy! The one thing I gotta do RIGHT NOW is—

"This cork hates me," Betsy sighed and handed Trey a bottle.

—call off the final Makro kill! Trey uncorked the champagne and

returned the bottle to Betsy, who began pouring refills. *Gotta throw these fuckers outta here so I can call Rudy—NO! Fuck fuck fuck can't risk any contact now, if the cops are closing in on Rudy they could grab his phones—or fucking walk in while he's on the phone with me—*

"Here's to the Makro Killer getting busted," Betsy toasted.

"Getting his brains blown out resisting arrest," Danny corrected.

"Let's drink to that," Trey agreed. *Better Rudy's dead than alive to cut a deal and give me up... But that's not good as the cops never busting him—I have to warn him—wait, calm the fuck—Rudy's got this! He's gonna see the news, he'll know not to do that last hit—That it's over, time to get gone... Do I message him and make sure?... Stop it, stop, this is Rudy not some fucking bitch. Rudy ain't gonna put his ass in a sling. Second Rudy sees that sketch, he's outta here... But what if he's not?*

"Boo, no fair," Betsy scolded the TV, on which a PhD meteorologist dressed like she worked for an escort service was cooing at a high pressure front. "They're not gonna show the rest of your interview! Bum-murr!"

"Worse things could happen," Trey murmured, smirkless.

THIRTY-NINE

*M*otherfuck. Now what? Do I take out the final target, or get my ass straight to Latvia?

Rudy muted the sound but left the tube on, in case the cops added another layer to the shit sandwich.

Rudy had prepared for the possibility the Cherokee would get blown. The house had a two-car garage, in which he'd pre-positioned a second vehicle. He'd stash Vanora's suddenly famous Cherokee in there and switch to an invisible blue Civic. By the time anybody discovered the SUV, he would've aced the final kill and disappeared.

If he did the final kill.

Shit. The Cherokee, no game-changer. But his face on TV? Even though the face the cops got was from before he lost the goatee and had the eyes and nose done, it was close enough—especially when paired with the name Rudy. Some fuckwad who knew him would go for the reward. Yeah. That's gonna happen. The risk on doin' this hit just went to a whole other level.

But did it go unacceptable?

Fuck. Only a fool bothers to find out the answer to that one. Especially if his extraction plan's good to go. Had a new identity with good paper. Had Wulf, a first-rate smuggler gonna ship him express to Latvia, where a hardass nationalist group was eager to shelter an American brother packin' sick skills.

Which I goddamn do. Skills to take down my target and walk away clean, no matter what those CPD bitches got.

What's un-fucking-acceptable is leaving that last forty grand on the table. Ain't like I won't need it.

And ain't like I'm ever getting another shot at fucking the CPD up the ass with no grease—and their FBI girlfriends. You bitches are gettin' all giddy, 'cause once you find out who I am it's just a matter of time till you find out where I am... True that.

Rudy plucked a can of beer out of a plastic bag next to him on the couch, popped it and chugged half.

Also true I could still whack this target right under your noses, leave you holding your dicks and crying for Mommy.

Rudy finished his beer.

Unless... I guess wrong about how long before you show up. He crumpled the can, belched, and accepted reality.

He turned the TV off. Went to the kitchen, where his laptop was sleeping on the table. He looked down at the laptop.

Decided to have a shot of tequila.

No—a margarita. Not gonna see any of those the next coupla years in some cabin deep in some fucking medieval Baltic forest. No Mex food at all. Fuckin' Latvia. He poured tequila, triple sec and lime juice into the blender.

I've won. Killed four, in their home court. Payback with interest. And a fuckin' cherry on top—today, the day they get lucky and ID me, I turn ghost and I'm gone.

He turned the blender on. Put ice in a glass. Turned the blender off.

But fuck... If they got me in their sights and I nail another target <u>anyway</u>... Now that is me taking one epic Viking dump on the CPD. On their goddamn Pretty Boy Bergman.

Rudy poured himself a margarita. Drank it standing by the kitchen counter. Went to pour another. Stopped.

Fuck.

Rudy put the pitcher back on the blender, went to his laptop and sent Wulf an encrypted message:

Tempo

Meaning Rudy was ready to head for the homeland.

He watched the screen and waited. And waited. Wondered if

recent events had spooked Wulf, and he was never gonna hear back from him.

The laptop chimed.

Upbeat. But only if double. You understand.

Rudy did. Wulf was still game but only at twice the price.

Shit. There was no other escape route. Gotta pay whatever that prick feels like charging.

Yes

Wulf replied:

W?

Meaning when would Rudy arrive?

Tomorrow. He could be at Wulf's safe house in Cleveland by tomorrow.

Rudy typed **Tomorr**—stopped, stared. Erased it. Typed:

Within week

Because, fuck the risk, now I cannot afford to pass up that forty grand.

Rudy gazed at the unsent message.

Bullshit. Even with the extra forty, it won't add up to lifetime money. If you run this risk, that ain't why.

"I like it better this way," Rudy admitted. He hit SEND.

FORTY

Minutes after the sketch of the Makro Killer aired, sightings of Rudy and/or the white Cherokee began to stream in. The FBI bumped Rudy up to Number Three on their Most Wanted list, and the stream became a river. Makro upped their reward to a million dollars, and the river became a flood. People from Tallahassee to Juneau had a quiet suspicious neighbor who was the spitting image of that Makro Killer face. An astonishing seventy-two percent of these Rudy lookalikes also drove a white Cherokee that was absolutely a 2011, you could tell because that model had that, uh, thing, on it that year.

Ninety-nine percent of these suspiciously quiet neighbors turned out to be men who looked somewhere between a little and nothing like Rudy, and drove a black Durango, a silver Camry or a red Vespa.

The Vermont highway patrol did pull over a white Cherokee, in which they found five barrels of premium grade maple syrup heisted from a Canadian warehouse.

The CPD and FBI were nowhere near that successful. They hustled their butts off running down anything resembling a plausible tip from anywhere within a fifty mile radius of Chicago. After five days of around-the-clock grinding they had no Rudy, no Cherokee, not a drop of maple syrup and no idea about what next.

◆

"At least Rudy ain't killed another Makro since we put out his sketch," Doonie said, raised his glass and drained it in one long pull.

"Taste it, don't waste it," Mark counseled, taking a philosophical sip of his own bourbon-rocks. "Even if he's done killing, he can't stay holed up forever." *Just like JaneDoe can't stay mad at me forever?* Mark chugged the rest of his drink. Asked, "What's happening with Phyl and the kids?"

"They're all being extra fuckin' nice to me," Doonie reported, glum.

"Ah jeez," Mark commiserated.

Their waiter arrived and presented a bottle. "The 2009 Malbec."

Mark nodded. The waiter uncorked the wine and poured a taste. Mark sipped, told him it was fine. The waiter filled their glasses. "Enjoy."

"Every time," Doonie assured him. As the waiter walked away, Doonie asked Mark, "I had this one before?"

"No. It's from Argentina, so it goes great with steak—that's the only thing they eat."

"And first time since Thursday we're not eatin' in the fuckin' car."

They drank to that, and Mark's phone rang. He answered. Listened. Said, "Put her through."

Doonie gave Mark a skeptical look and poured himself more wine.

"Hello, Mrs. Sheff. This is Detective Bergman, thank you for calling. I understand your husband may have some information?"

"Yes, he does—we would've called sooner, but Morgan—my husband—was having heart surgery the day your Wanted notice came out. The doctor said the operation went well, but—there were complications… Morgan just stopped breathing. They brought him back but he was four days in the ICU. Today they moved him to a regular room, we were watching the news and there was a mention of how there was still no progress in the Makro Killer, and they showed the sketch, and Morgan recognized Rudy—from before I met Morgan, I never heard of Rudy till just now or I would've called right away."

"Of course. Is it possible to speak to your husband?"

"Yes, he insists on it, which is why I insisted on being the one to contact you. Morgan's doctor says to keep the call brief as possible, and, you know, low-key."

"I understand."

Mark heard Mrs. Sheff whisper a stern "Three minutes!" as she handed the phone to her husband.

A painkilled, Valiumed, but determined voice said, "Hi. Morgan Sheff."

"Mark Bergman. How you doing?"

"Like uh, hit by a bus and carved like a turkey."

"We'll keep it short," Mark promised. "How did you know him, and how certain are you this is the same guy?"

Doonie locked eyes with Mark while Mark listened to Sheff's reply.

"Got it," Mark told Sheff, repeating, for Doonie's sake, "You were cops together, and he broke your jaw."

The waiter returned and placed sizzling steaks in front of them, followed by platters of homemade fries with lemon aoli, and crispy brussels sprouts with cilantro, mint and scallions. The waiter asked Doonie, "Is there anything else I can get you?"

"Yeah," Doonie grumped. "Doggie bags."

FORTY-ONE

Soon as they were in the car Mark told Doonie what couldn't be said in the restaurant: "Guntars Markuss Rudzutaka."

"So everyone but his Mom called him Rudy," Doonie nodded, and started the engine.

"Nope," Mark said, carefully typing the name into the computer. "Sheff says he wanted to be called Guntars."

"Serial killer, no fuckin' doubt about it," Doonie ruled.

Rudzutaka was in an Illinois police database. Mark pulled up an eighteen-year-old personnel file from the police department in Marion, a small city at the far Southern end of the state.

"Just like Sheff said, Rudy—Guntars—was on the Marion PD, for about a minute." Mark studied a photo of Guntars as a rosy-cheeked hostile twenty-four-year-old. "Sheff said our sketch was only a vague approximation—he wouldn't have recognized it without the name Rudy."

"What'd Sheff say when you asked why Guntars broke his jaw?"

"Later. Sheff said Rudzutaka wasn't from Marion, he was from 'someplace near' Chicago." Mark gestured at the file on the computer. "Palatine."

A northwest suburb.

◆

Lt. Husak deserted a family dinner and hurried back to work. Mark began briefing Husak as he walked in the door.

"The Palatine address was his parent's house. Both are deceased and the house changed hands three times since then," Mark informed him. "Guntars does have a younger brother, Ansis Jevgenijs

Rudzutaka, who graduates from Palatine High, and then—nothing. Gone. Like he got Raptured."

"That name and we can't find him?" Husak mourned.

"Kaz and Kimmie are working it."

"Meantime we just had the best thirty minutes of this investigation," Doonie promised.

"Lemme take my fuckin' coat off," Husak said. "And bring that," Husak ordered, indicating the three-and-a-half French fries on a plastic plate on Doonie's desk.

They followed Husak into his office. Doonie put the fries and what was left of the aioli dip on the Lieutenant's desk and confided, "Marion wasn't Rudzutaka's first crack at gettin' on the job."

"Uh-huh," Husak grunted, dipping a cold fry in congealed aioli.

"Five years before, when he was twenty," Doonie grinned, "Rudzutaka got it in his head to join the CPD."

Husak paused the fry he'd been about to put his mouth.

"Rudzutaka passed the exam," Mark explained, "but washed out on the psych profile—multiple indicators for borderline personality disorder."

"So now maybe we've got motive," Husak said and bit off the top half of the fry.

"One that's fuckin' nothin' to do with Makro," Doonie said.

"Or it could be Rudzutaka does have motive for going after Makro, and getting rejected by the CPD might only explain why he's doing it in Chicago," Mark cautioned. "Here's what we know for sure. After the Department tells Rudzutaka to fuck off and find a good therapist, he enlists in the Army. Where his police dream comes true, almost: Rudzutaka becomes an MP. But doesn't get to play cop. They make him a prison guard, at a correctional facility in Fort Lewis, Washington."

"Which is right across the street from Idaho," Doonie pointed out.

"Rudzutaka's MP scorecard shows one commendation for uncovering a drug smuggling ring, two reprimands for excessive force on prisoners, and one accusation of sexual assault on a female MP. Three days later she withdraws the complaint. But right after that, Rudzutaka, with seven months to go on his enlistment, is granted a

General Discharge."

"Instead of the OTH he deserved," Husak muttered.

Mark nodded. A General discharge was a step below an Honorable, but had no taint—unlike an Other Than Honorable. An OTH would've made Rudzutaka unemployable as a cop.

"Rudzutaka applies to the Marion PD. He's accepted, does their Academy, gets sworn in. Then, on his first and only day as a probie, Rudzutaka sucker-punches his training officer, breaks his jaw."

"Why?" Husak asked, openly curious. Rare, for him.

"Sheff and Rudzutaka roll up on a teenager, African-American, getting high behind a 7-11. Rudzutaka's out the car before it stops, slams the kid against a wall and whacks the joint out of his mouth. The kid says something, Rudzutaka starts slapping, Sheff runs up yelling at him to stop, Rudzutaka doesn't, Sheff pulls him off the kid and orders him to get in the car. Sheff gives the kid a choice, get busted for possession and resisting, or shut up go home and ice your cheek. Sheff gets back in the car, Rudzutaka sits there staring straight ahead, ignoring him. Sheff puts the key in the ignition and Rudzutaka's fist hits his face."

"Talk about too fuckin' sensitive," Doonie mused.

"We know where he's been between then and now?" Husak asked.

Mark shook his head. "The FBI's checking regional and local databanks. If Rudzutaka was a gypsy, something might turn up. Or not."

There was no compulsory registry of decertified cops. Most departments did share data, but some defined that as Big Brother invading their privacy. Most departments did thorough background checks. But some, especially smaller ones, didn't bother. Their Number One requirement was that the applicant had graduated from a certified academy, so there'd be no training costs. And from sea to shining sea there were image-conscious departments, of every size, with a deeply ingrained habit of allowing fuck-ups to resign instead of firing them. The result, thousands of gypsy cops floating from one out-of-the-way badge to another.

Mark glanced at his watch. "Any second now we and the Feebs will release Rudzutaka's name and his age twenty-four picture, along with the computer's best guess of what he looks like at forty-one."

"We located the brother!" Kimbrough, rushing in, triumphantly waving a sheet of paper. "When he was nineteen," Kimmie read, carefully working her way through the obstacle course of syllables, "An-sis Jev-genijs Rud-zu-taka... legally changed his name to John Roberts." Kimmie grinned. "John Roberts lives in Albany Park."

A neighborhood ten minutes from where they were standing.

FORTY-TWO

Props to the Silver Sidewinder. Old Stan Vanderbro don't stint when it comes to romancing a target.

It was just the three of them—Stan, Trey and Danny—sharing a weapons-grade business dinner in a 27th-floor Chicago hotel suite with night-time glamor views; a platoon of gleaming sculptural skyscrapers posing along both banks of the river, connected by the circa-1918 bare-girder sinews of the Michigan Avenue Bridge, while in the distance Navy Pier's giant Ferris wheel pulsed out megawatt party colors, their reflections doing a psychedelic shimmy across the busy surface of the lake.

The meal came from the hotel's Michelin-starred restaurant. The compliments were from what there was of Vanderman's heart.

They were meeting to finalize the details of Danny's role at the AGA convention, nine days off. Between his viral videos and the way his tragic charisma was attracting fervent recruits to Youth For ELE, Danny had become the face of the campaign. The proof was in the polling. Among ticketholders to the convention Danny Gold was the speaker they'd most like to meet.

The meal was leisurely and convivial, with Stan asking Danny about his childhood and his father, and seeking Danny's opinion on a wide range of heavy national issues. When they were halfway through the main course and their second bottle of LaTour, Stan told Danny they wanted to slot him in the convention's penultimate spot: final speaker before the president of the AGA delivered the closing address. Would Danny be okay with that?

Danny would.

Stan praised the draft of Danny's speech. But that wasn't all. The Vanderbro gave his blessing for Danny to improvise; speaking from his orphaned heart was what made Danny Gold golden.

It wasn't until they'd demolished an insanely labor-intensive molecular-minimalist-meets-Viennese-baroque dessert, and were burnishing the glow with coffee and Dow's 1980 Vintage Port, that Stan brought up a vital but touchy matter, the only one where Stan had worries about how Danny would reply.

Danny wrestled with it. Issued a quiet, grim, determined declaration: "I'm sorry. I can't sign autographs."

"I understand—and admire—your concerns," Stan commiserated, "but this is about acknowledging the great respect and affection people have for you. It's not about celebrity."

"Yes it is."

"Danny… I get it. You won't have to wade into the crowd, in front of the cameras, looking like a movie star. All I'm asking, as a personal favor, is that backstage, in private—maybe just for the children of our most—"

"In public I refuse to give autographs to real people but in private I sign for fat cats and politicians? Stan, that sucks even worse," Danny scolded.

The Silver Sidewinder's jaw clenched as he fought to keep from sinking his fangs into the kid, much to Trey's delight. *Awesome! Stan cracks the whip on a menagerie of Governors, Senators and Congressmen, but can't do shit with a surly teenager gettin' phat on Stan's payroll and drunk on his Bordeaux. Lemme show ya how it's done, Vanderprick.*

"You're right, it sucks," Trey told Danny. "But Stan made that offer, about you signing only for kids, because he's a nice guy. He didn't want to hit you with the truth of your situation. But I'm not nice, I'm your friend," Trey said with a sympathetic smirk. "Bro, you don't get to decide if you're a celebrity. The public does. Then they get to decide Danny Gold's a stuck-up cunt who won't give me an autograph, and maybe from then on they change the channel when they see your face, and maybe a lot of the work we did goes up in smoke. Or maybe not," Trey admitted, with a casual shrug. "But I can tell you this—if you can get with signing some autographs at this convention, we'll never ask you again. Right?" Trey asked Stan, who picked up his cue and confirmed the lie with a grave nod. Trey looked Danny in the eye.

Danny sank into the uniquely crowded silence of a conflicted adolescent.

Trey added an insurance lie. "The other thing is, we're good with whatever you decide, you won't get an argument, not a goddamn word."

Danny gazed at Trey, then downward and, with his eyes fixed on his lap, said, "But you think I should sign."

"Hey," Trey murmured, and waited for Danny to look at him. "I ever once give you shit advice?"

Danny thought. Took a deep breath. Somberly informed them, "No boobs. I'm not signing boobs."

Trey grinned. Stan chuckled, then guffawed. First time Trey ever heard the Sidewinder loud-laugh. The old tightass was deranged with relief.

"I'm serious," Danny protested, with a quart of *vino veritas* sincerity. "I'm speaking for the dead, there's no signing boobs."

Trey looked at Stan and deadpanned, "Can the AGA live with that?"

"If we have to," Stan joked, giving Trey a pleased, congratulatory look. Another first.

That's right, Vanderbitch—Trey shoots, Trey scores! 'Cause Trey owns *the star of this freakin' movie… I should rub that in.*

Trey stood, raised his glass to Danny and said, serious, no-fucking-around, "You're a good man, bro." Trey chugged the remainder of his Port and flung the Reidel crystal glass against a wall.

Danny blushed and his eyes went damp.

"Hey." Trey opened his arms.

Danny got up and hugged Trey, who was looking over Danny's shoulder at Stan, drilling Vanderfart with a triumphant smirk. *Booyah! No shit Jack, Trey's back on track, It's a mofo fact, My mojo's back—*

Makro Killer news alerts pealed on Trey and Danny's phones. They broke the hug and thumbed their screens.

Fuck! Did that asshole go ahead and kill... No. Wasn't that bad. But bad. The cops had replaced that lame sketch of Rudy with an old photo of a young cop named Guntars Markuss Rudzutaka. *That's his real name...? Screw that! Think! That photo isn't what Rudy now looks—Rudy's way older and his face is—Is it changed enough?*

"The police know who the MK is," Danny told Stan, handing him the phone so he could see.

"Only a matter of time till they find him," Trey assured Danny, trying to sound as if he were looking forward to that. "Meantime, cops got their work, we got ours. Need to show you guys my rough cut of the intro video for Danny's speech."

Trey cued it up on the suite's 70-inch, excused himself, locked himself in the suite's guest bathroom, sat on the closed toilet, woke his phone and stared at young goateed Rudy.

You're gone, right? Can't still be here. You're too smart to still be here. Gone to wherever the fuck it is you said they'd never find...

Text Rudy and make sure.

Trey reached for his burner—*No! No panic, no taking dimshit risks. Rudy's the dead opposite of suicidal. He's gone down his rabbit hole, and I'm running the table, bro. This all's playin' even better than I planned, the convention's gonna be a monster, ELE's gonna pass and the media's gonna kiss my dick 'cause I'm the eminence-fuckin'-grease who ran this show... If they catch Rudy, would he give me up?!?*

Trey took out his burner and texted:

U safe?

No answer.

C'mon cocksucker you broke silence to shake me down, so just fucking tell me you're gone.

No answer.

Wait, if Rudy went dark, he ain't gonna make a peep. Ever again. Calm the fuck down. Rudy's too smart to still be here... Is he that smart? "Rudy's" a shit alias for someone named Rudzutaka... SHIT HOW LONG I BEEN IN HERE!?!

Trey flushed, found a can of air freshener in the vanity and sprayed enough to fumigate an outhouse.

When Trey walked back into the suite Danny and Stan looked at him.

"You all right?" Stan inquired, hoping to hear Trey was going to be up all night squirting.

"I'm good." Trey glanced back at the guest bathroom. "But you don't wanna open that door, not until the maid's done in there tomorrow."

FORTY-THREE

I got a question," Doonie said as they were driving to Albany Park to drop in on Rudy's brother, John Roberts. "Why you think a guy so fuckin' careful smart as Rudzutaka would use 'Rudy' with yokels he didn't wanna give away his name to?"

"Maybe he wasn't killing a lot of people then, no need to be smart," Mark theorized.

"Yeah okay but why pick a name he doesn't like?"

"He's fine with Rudy. The Guntars thing—Rudy hated having to obey a straight-arrow training officer like Morgan Sheff. 'Call me Guntars' was 'Fuck you, Morgan.' Rudy's just that kind of guy." Mark glanced at Doonie. "Being his kid brother must've really sucked."

"Your lips, God's ears."

◆

The preliminary info on Ansis-John Rudzutaka-Roberts said thirty-nine, married, eleven-year-old daughter and eight-year-old son. Had a BA in Urban Admin and a city job in the Department of Planning & Development.

They lived in a classic brick bungalow, meticulously maintained, as were the others on his street in North Mayfair, an Albany Park district with a tradition of modest prosperity and major stability.

Roberts answered the door, looking glum and unsurprised. Roberts shared Rudy's beefy build and Arctic-adjacent coloring, but not Rudy's talent for radiating hostility. John radiated pained sincerity spiced with a whiff of dread.

"Detectives Bergman and Dunegan," Mark said, flashing the badge. "Are you the former Ansis Rudzutaka?"

"Yes," John Roberts confessed. He led them into the front room, where his wife Alice joined them. There was a flicker of That Look as Alice recognized Mark; a minor distraction, quickly dismissed. Alice sat next to her husband, gave his hand a squeeze and paid careful attention.

Mark was sure the couple had been expecting and rehearsing for this visit since the sketch and name Rudy went public three weeks ago. No need to warm them up with small talk.

"Thank you for your cooperation, Mr. Roberts. Do you know where your brother is?"

"No. Not at all," Roberts vowed. "Haven't seen or heard from him in fourteen, fifteen years."

Alice's lips twitched.

"Please," Mark urged, "whatever it is, we want to hear it."

"Seventeen years," Alice specified. "Two weeks after the Marion police fired Rudy, he hit the road and..." She shrugged.

"Did he usually go by Rudy, or Guntars?"

"Rudy," Roberts confirmed.

"Anyone else Rudy was close to, might've kept in touch with?"

Roberts shook his head. "No, not one of us has heard from him."

"He have friends, girlfriends?"

"Rudy didn't stay friends with guys very long. He was too... competitive."

"How about with women?" Mark inquired. Vanora Yard had been smitten enough to run off with Rudy.

"He, um... Certain women were attracted... but also not for long."

"Was there anyone who lasted longer than the others, anyone he lived with?"

Roberts' cheeks flushed. "There was one, but uh you can't—she died."

"How?"

"A car crash."

"A suicide," Alice corrected. "Melody drove straight into the only big tree on a long stretch of road... Six days after Rudy got kicked out by the Marion police."

"He was hell to be around when he was pissed off," Roberts said in an aggrieved near-whisper.

"More hell than usual," Alice clarified.

"Got it," Mark sympathized. Then, gently, "Melody's crash happened down there?"

Alice nodded. "But she was from here. Rudy moved in with Melody for a month, right before he moved to Marion. She followed him."

"So the two of you were friends?"

"I think we would've been—we only met Melody twice, with Rudy. It wasn't till he left town Melody was able to meet me for lunch. Rudy was that possessive—which Melody just laughed off, made some joke how she was lucky to find a guy so crazy about her. She was like that."

"Yeah she was..." Roberts murmured, his eyes widening; a buried memory flaring to life. "Once during dinner here, Melody teased Rudy that he liked her brother more than he liked her. Rudy says, 'Hell no. I just like your brother more than I like mine,' and gives me this grin. Meanest fucking... grin."

Alice squeezed Roberts' arm. "Rudy was always a shit to John, but it got even worse after John right out of college got a job at City Hall."

"Did you meet Melody's brother?"

Two heads shook in unison.

Mark asked, "Did she ever mention his name?"

"Yes, um... Casper?" Alice ventured.

"Corby," Roberts announced with bitter certainty. It was the one detail on which he'd corrected his wife, instead of the other way around. "The family name was Grundlich. Melody had an apartment near Lincoln Square, where they grew up. But she never said where Corby lived."

"Corby lived somewhere way southwest," Alice said, to Roberts' surprise. She guiltily confessed to him, "Melody told me, that time we had lunch," then told Mark and Doonie, "Said it was far, like an hour and a half, out in the sticks."

Mark and Doonie traded a quick look: Ninety minutes outside Chicago. Rural, isolated.

Mark asked Alice, "What else did Melody say about Corby?"

"Almost nothing. She didn't like to talk about her brother."

"Are Melody's parents alive?"

"They were, seventeen years ago."

"Their names?"

"She never said."

"When Rudy lived here did he have any special places?" Mark asked Roberts. "What did he like to do?"

Roberts glowered. "He liked being a son of a bitch."

"So how come," Doonie wondered, chiming in for the first time, "you didn't call us when we first put out the son of a bitch's face?"

"I wasn't… certain it was him. The first name was the same, but that sketch was… not exactly…"

"Why dintcha call today soon's you saw his exact photo and whole exact name?" Doonie wondered more forcefully.

Roberts swallowed. "I wish I had."

"Don't you judge," Alice scolded Doonie. "What happens when everyone finds out the Makro Killer is John's brother? Waddaya think John's bosses down at the Hall are gonna… *We have children.*"

"Me too," Doonie replied, empathizing. "But I gotta ask, seeing as how you two didn't come forward. John, look me in the eye, gimme it. For seventeen years did you really not once hear from your brother, do you really not know any place Rudy's been or what he's been doin'?"

"I swear." It was a low snarl packed with how much it sucked to be Rudy's kid brother.

Enough to satisfy Doonie. "Okay. You got any pictures of him?"

Roberts took it as an insult. Shook his head.

"One last question," Mark said. "That thing about how your brother hated it when you got hired at Development and Planning."

"Uh-huh."

"Do you think Rudy might be doing this in Chicago—doing it *to* Chicago—because he couldn't get a city job and you did?"

Roberts gave the possibility serious thought, for about two seconds. "No. Rudy wouldn't work this hard or run this kind of risk unless there was money. Only honest thing ever came out of his mouth was, *'I don't waste time on any shit that don't get me a buck or a fuck.'* And he's not gonna bother killing four people for a fuck."

FORTY-FOUR

3:38 AM, home and fried. Left it all out on the keyboard at work, cyberstalking Corby Grundlich. Who, for all Mark knew, could be in Paris using the name Didier Corsu and dating JaneDoe. No matter how many times and ways Mark asked the interwebs about Corby Grundlich, the interwebs shrugged and changed the topic.

Corby's deceased sister Melody was more accessible. Before making the mistake of becoming Guntars Rudzutaka's girlfriend, Melody lived her whole life with her parents, Patrick and Rhonda Grundlich.

But there was no record of Melody's parents having a second child.

So why did Melody introduce rural Corby as her brother? Maybe he was a half-brother; product of a previous, rural relationship of Daddy Patrick's or Mama Rhonda's. That relationship would've been unsanctified—Mark found no record of Patrick or Rhonda ever being married to anyone except each other. An out-of-wedlock Corby might not have been awarded the surname Grundlich.

Patrick and Rhonda's lips were sealed, inside coffins. Mark and Doonie's only option was to locate their relatives and ask if they'd ever met Corby The Theoretical Half-Brother.

Doonie researched Rhonda's family and Mark took Patrick's.

Mark hit the geography jackpot. Mama Rhonda was from Chicago. But Daddy Patrick was born in Leoville, Illinois. Population one hundred and ten. Ninety-nine percent white. Ninety-eight miles southwest of Chicago, in La Salle County, close to Starved Rock State Park, right off Interstate 80. You could get there in under ninety minutes with just regular speeding. Be a feasible area for Rudy to hole up, especially if he had a local helper named Corby.

There was no listing in Leoville for anybody with the first name Corby or Corbin. But there was a Grundlich—Ira, a barber, age eighty-four. But by the time Mark found Ira it was 2:27 AM, when you can't phone an eighty-four-year-old Grundlich to ask if he was related to Patrick, and did Patrick father a bastard named Corby. That would have to wait until well after sunrise.

First stop tomorrow morning would be in town. Doonie's research into the Mama Rhonda's family turned up a possible witness. Melody had a first cousin, courtesy of Rhonda's sister. Maybe Melody confided things to her cousin before she drove into that tree.

After interviewing the cousin, Mark and Doonie would drive down to Leoville so they could question old Ira Grundlich face to face. Cause that always works better. Always. It's gonna be a fantastic conversation. Ira's gonna tell us where to find Corby. Corby's gonna tell us where to find Rudy. We'll arrest Rudy before he murders anybody else. Rudy'll tell us the name, address and ten favorite songs of the person who paid him to massacre Makro drivers. We'll bust that sick sack of merde and the world will be a meadow of wildflowers.

Mark took off his shoes and fell asleep.

FORTY-FIVE

At 8 AM, powered by two-and-a-half hours of hibernation-level sleep and defibrillator-strength caffeination, Mark and Doonie showed up at the apartment of Rhonda Grundlich's niece, Kate Burke.

Burke was in her mid-thirties, dressed in a business suit and gave Mark an alert, unrattled That Look. Burke waved off Mark's apology for interrupting her breakfast, sat them down in the living room and asked, "How can I help you," aiming the question at both of them so Doonie wouldn't feel left out.

Mark asked, "Did your cousin Melody Grundlich have a brother, named Corby?"

"That was his name? I mean yes, but he was a half-brother."

"You never met him?"

"No... He didn't show up for Melody's funeral."

"And Patrick was the parent they had in common."

"Yes. My mother said it was something that happened when Uncle Pat was nineteen."

"Do you know anything about Corby's mother?"

"Nothing. This is the first I've heard his name, my mother wouldn't tell me," Burke said.

"What did she say about him?"

"Mom said Aunt Rhonda 'wasn't happy' when she found out about Corby. Aunt Rhonda told Mom she was 'uncomfortable' when Uncle Patrick would invite Corby to visit, though she put on a brave face because she didn't want to cheat Melody out of a chance to bond with her brother."

"Did Melody ever tell you about him?"

"Never. I was six years younger, it's not like Melody confided touchy personal stuff."

"Did the rest of the family know?"

"Absolutely not. Mom was the only one Aunt Rhonda told—they were sisters."

"Did your mother say what Corby did for a living?"

Burke shook her head.

"Take a moment… Was there anything else?"

"Mmm… yes. Aunt Rhonda thought he was the most awful thing she'd ever met—except for Melody's boyfriend Rudy. He didn't show up for Melody's funeral either… Men." Burke bit her lower lip. "That's all… I hope it helped."

Shit yeah. You confirmed Corby was Melody's half-brother and better yet, he was the result of a teen romance that ended with Romeo fleeing to Chicago, leaving Juliet to raise the kid on her own, in a town of one hundred and ten. If Corby's still there everybody knows him.

"Everything helps," Mark said. "Thank you."

FORTY-SIX

As they walked to the car Doonie asked, through a yawn, "Want me to drive?"

"Only if you're also gonna drink, text and fix your eye shadow while you fall asleep at the wheel."

Mark pointed the car toward Leoville and phoned Husak to let him know the promising new details about Rudy's girlfriend's brother.

Husak grunted. "If you locate Corby's residence be careful, in case this steaming pile of circumstantials turns out to be for real and Rudzutaka's inside."

"I'll make sure Doonie is first man through the door," Mark promised.

Mark called Agent Carlson to update him and ask how fast the FBI could get a warrant to search Corby's place if they got an address.

"Very fast, or not at all," Agent Carlson said, "Can't guarantee a judge is gonna bite unless we can show Corby and Rudzutaka have been in touch during the seventeen the years since Melody died."

"You're killing my fantasies about the FBI having the judiciary in their pocket."

"Sorry. I do have some new Rudzutaka bio. Five months after flunking out of the Marion PD he was back in law enforcement: Deputy Sheriff in Asotin County, Washington. Down in the southeast corner, shares borders with Idaho and Oregon. Militia-land."

"What was the Asotin Sheriff's excuse for not contacting you until now?"

"He said he didn't call after seeing the first sketch and the name Rudy because he didn't recognize the face, and at that point there was no last name or mention of a police background."

"How long did Rudy work for him?"

"Fifteen months. Sheriff claims Rudzutaka resigned and refused to give any explanation beyond 'personal reasons.' "

" 'Claims?' "

"Interesting fact: Turns out Rudy retired shortly after three combat AKs and a Mac-10 went missing from an evidence locker."

"The Sheriff confiscated Rudy's profits and kissed him goodbye," Mark said. "No wonder he wasn't in a hurry to remember Rudy."

"No wonder. All we have on Rudzutaka since then is a Washington state DL, a Toyota Trail Runner and no fixed abode—just a series of PO boxes across the Pacific northwest, then a final box in Kingman, Arizona."

"Where the stolen plates on the Cherokee came from."

"Uh-huh. Seventeen months ago Rudzutaka shut down the Kingman box, sold the Trail Runner and canceled his phone. Since then, no record of him buying a new ride or new phone."

"Makes himself invisible then puts in a year-and-a-half of prep before his first Makro hit."

"Yeah. Watch your ass."

Doonie tilted his seat back, closed his eyes and said, "Wake me when we get there."

"I'll try," Mark promised.

FORTY-SEVEN

It was the kind of tiny, not quite exhausted central Illinois town you drive through when you get lost on the way to someplace else. Leoville consisted of one T-shaped intersection, where Hickory Street dead-ended into E. 970th Road. Downtown was a cluster of forlorn 1920s brick storefronts loitering around the intersection. One was Ira Grundlich's home address, an apartment above a barber shop. Not bad; eighty-four and still living up a flight of stairs. Though not at the moment.

The two-chair barber shop, Ira's Haircuts, was also dark. But there was a sign propped in the window:

> **IF YOU NEED A HAIRCUT
> I MIGHT BE AT TOBY'S**

Toby's name wasn't on any of the four businesses on this side of Main or the two across the street. Mark and Doonie walked to the corner, looked up and down 970th and there it was, a pale green clapboard house that had gentrified into Toby's Tavern Grill.

At 11 AM roughly seven percent of the town's population was in Toby's. One bartender-waitress, two women in a booth having burgers and five men at the bar nursing beers. None were young. All fell silent when the place was invaded by two foreigners wearing topcoats, suits and ties. A moment later most of them were giving the younger foreigner That Look. Even here.

Seated on the prime stool at the end of the bar, maintaining a neutral expression, was the oldest of the locals. Medium height and build, average amount of wrinkles for his age, but a well above average amount of gleaming white hair. Just like in his driver's license photo.

Mark looked at him and said, "Hi. I need a haircut."

"No you don't, Detective Bergman," Ira Grundlich somberly informed Mark. "But Detective Dunegan sure as hell does," Ira added, enjoying the hell out of one-upping them.

◆

Ira skipped the barbershop and led them straight to his apartment without being asked. Soon as he locked the door, with the three of them standing in the hallway, Ira announced, "I don't know Guntars Rudzuwhatever," and waited for them to explain why they wanted to question him.

Doonie asked, "Are you related to Patrick Grundlich?"

"Second cousin. Patrick's not the Makro Killer. Died two years ago... But you know that."

"Yeah we do," Doonie agreed. "We also know he had a son, Corby."

"No he didn't," Ira declared.

"Corby's sister Melody told people he was her brother," Doonie countered.

"No she didn't."

"Because," Mark sighed, "his name was Casper."

Ira grinned. "With a K."

Mark and Doonie traded a weary look. The one detail on which John Roberts had corrected his wife Alice had, like everything else Alice told them, been accurate.

"You think Kasper's something to do with this Rudzu-zaza," Ira declared. He didn't sound upset about that.

"Has Kasper got a last name and an address?" Mark asked.

"Kasper Hollawell. Lives about eight miles southeast, I got the address."

"Thanks. Where does Kasper work?"

"Nowhere."

"Huh," Mark said. "How's that?"

"Kasper used to do this and that. Lousy mechanic, lousy hardware store clerk, and I may have once heard someone complain about him peddling lousy marijuana. But Kasper's third stepfather died and left a paid-off house and paid-up insurance to Kasper's mother, who died and left it to him. And then Patrick, after losing poor Melody and then Rhonda, had no one else to name except Kasper. Wasn't a fortune—from what I hear—but so far it's enough to keep Kasper from having to find some new job to be lousy at."

"Sounds like there's no love lost," Doonie observed, "but you still keep in touch."

"Almost never."

"Does Kasper have any connection to militias?" Doonie asked.

"Kasper's always had real strong dumb opinions and real poor taste in friends. But he's more mouth than action."

"Thank you, Mr. Grundlich, we appreciate your help," Mark said. "We have one more request, that you not warn Kasper we're—"

"No problem."

"And that you not tell anyone what we asked about."

"I don't know, Detective. I go back a ways with those fellas down at Toby's. They're gonna take it as an insult if I don't trust 'em."

"Buy them a couple of rounds and ask them to be patient," Mark suggested, and placed two twenties on the hall table.

Ira gave the cash a dubious glance. "If those boys turn on me, there goes my social life."

"Not if you treat 'em to a whiskey chaser," Doonie said, adding another forty to the pile.

Ira mulled the proposition. Said, "They're gonna need a burger to soak up that booze."

FORTY-EIGHT

They got in the car, buckled up and Doonie said, "That is a fucking competitive old man."

"I liked him too," Mark agreed, as he mapped Kasper's address. Satellite view showed a simple rectangular house large enough for two or three bedrooms. And a barn, small, but large enough to swallow a Cherokee.

Mark put the car in gear and Doonie got on the phone, updating Husak and Agent Carlson, who launched deep dives on Kasper Hollawell. Doonie spent the rest of the drive on the computer learning the basics on Hollawell.

"Kasper don't get his haircuts at cousin Ira's," Doonie said. He swiveled the screen toward Mark.

Driver's license photo of a long gaunt face. The bottom half was hidden beneath a massive scraggly fourth year of the Civil War beard. But from the ears up, three inches of bare-scalp fade, then his skull was topped with a deep layer of unruly curly hair in an unevenly receding widow's peak.

"I dunno," Mark disagreed, "Ira hates Kasper enough to say yes if Kasper asked for that haircut. What else?"

"Kasper's forty-three, five-eleven, one-sixty, single—how'd that happen—drives a new Explorer, red. Two handgun permits, a nine and a forty. He's got a sheet—two D&Ds, three DUIs and one peeping Tom, charge withdrawn. I Googled—local paper said the woman dropped the perv complaint when Kasper dropped an assault complaint against her husband, who busted Kasper's leg with a tire iron."

"Good marriage," Mark deadpanned. But he meant it. Being in it together, doing the stuff for each other that matters... Okay that's my maximum daily allowance of JaneDoe distraction. 'Cause look, there's the driveway to a house that might have a couple of heavily armed assholes inside, if we're lucky.

Mark pulled over. They popped the trunk, took off their coats and jackets, put on tactical vests, hung their badges, put their jackets back on, drove halfway up Kasper's driveway and stopped.

Kasper's house, like many in the area, was on a small square lot carved into the edge of an enormous field dotted with neat rows of brown stubble from harvested corn. From horizon to horizon it was flat Midwestern farmland, prime soil, divided by dead straight two-lane roads into a grid of gigantic rectangles. Kasper's house, like many in the area, was over a mile from the closest neighbor.

It was an old, uncared-for house, about one hard winter shy of being demoted from shabby to eyesore. Kasper's red Explorer wasn't out front and the house was dark. The Explorer—or Rudy's white Cherokee—could be in the barn, but its doors were shut.

Mark and Doonie went to the house. The doorbell was loud, and younger than the rest of the house. So was the front door, which was heavy and had three locks. The newest, impressively large lock was an armored steel cupcake mounted on a steel plate. Mark rang the loud doorbell again.

Nobody answered. Mark pounded. "Hello! Mr. Hollawell!? Anybody home!?"

"Let's peep in his windows," Doonie suggested.

"First the barn."

They started for the barn.

A truck entered the driveway. A red Explorer being driven by a huge brown beard. The SUV edged past their parked car and halted, with its engine idling.

The beard stared at the cops staring at him.

The beard came to a decision. The engine stopped and Kasper Hollawell got out. He had a backpack slung over one shoulder and was carrying a bright yellow plastic shopping bag pulled taut by heavy contents, which from the outlines straining against the plastic looked to be a half-dozen small brick-shaped boxes.

Kasper stood still and stared some more.

"Hello Mr. Hollawell, I'm Detective Bergman, this is Detective Dunegan, we're from the Chicago PD. We'd appreciate a few minutes of your time."

"Why you wearin' Kevlar?"

"That's just policy," Mark said. "Personnel operating outside city limits are required to wear ballistic vests when blah blah blah. You know, government regulations."

Kasper said, "I'm busy," and to prove it walked past them to the front door, yanked a set of keys out of his pocket and began opening the three locks. A little hurried, fumbling.

"Ah c'mon, Mr. Hollawell," Doonie implored, "if we could just stop in for a coupla min—"

"You may not empty my—I mean enter my house!" Kasper shouted, whirling to face them.

"We can talk out here," Mark offered.

"Get-off-my-prop-er-ty," Kasper growled, jabbing a key at Mark to emphasize each syllable. "I don't have a goddamn thing to say about any Makro."

"You gotta start wearin' a bag over your head," Doonie advised Mark.

"We don't suspect you of anything, Mr. Hollawell," Mark told him. "We're here to ask the same thing we're asking everyone who knew Guntars Rudzutaka. When was the last time you were in contact?"

The visible parts of Kasper's face and scalp flushed crimson. He hastily transferred his keys to his left hand, which was grasping the heavy plastic bag, and dropped the keys. The keys landed by Mark's foot. Mark picked them up and handed them back. Kasper pocketed the keys, pulled out his cell phone, selected Video and aimed it at Mark and Doonie.

"I am hereby exercising my right of free speech not to talk, I am exercising my right to refuse violation into my home and I hereby order you to remove yourselves forthwith from my property right now."

"Understood," Mark said. "Mind if we take a peek in the barn before we go?"

"GET THE FUCK OFF MY CITIZEN LAND RIGHT FUCKING NOW OR I WILL HAVE THE REAL LEGAL AUTHORITIES TRESPASS YOU!"

"We're gone," Mark said, amiable and accommodating.

He and Doonie strolled back to their car and got the fuck off Kasper's citizen land with him recording every second.

As they drove away, Mark asked, "You notice the logo on that bag full of cartridge boxes?"

"You notice me goin' blind lately?" Doonie wondered. He typed White Wolf Shooting Sports of Joliet, Illinois into the search box. "Got it. Small store, handles a lot of used guns, does a lot of customizing, fancy-ass camo coatings and shit like pirate-skull trigger guards."

"Joliet's what, sixty miles?" Mark asked.

"Mmm… sixty-six."

"How many gun stores are closer?"

Doonie tapped a few keys. "Nine gun shops and a Walmart."

"So why'd Kasper drive all that way to buy ammo?"

"I don't eat soon I'm gonna lose my shit and take an eight hour nap."

"We'll grab a sandwich on the highway."

"Fuckin' Rudzutaka."

FORTY-NINE

White Wolf's lair was in of one a dozen identical block-long two-story corrugated metal shoeboxes in a light-industry park on the outskirts of Joliet. The store's interior was no-nonsense utilitarian, well-stocked, impeccably clean. White Wolf's owner, Timothy Gray, was pushing sixty, had eaten himself portly but stood with the shoulders-squared verticality of a man who'd done more than a few tours in uniform.

Gray and an assistant were alone in the store when the two weary-eyed cops walked in. Gray and his assistant recognized Mark but didn't say anything.

Mark asked Gray if they could speak in private. Gray told his assistant to go to lunch. The assistant wasn't pleased about missing out on the serial killer gossip but limited his protest to a disappointed grimace.

Gray folded his arms and said, "So." Half-curious, half-wary.

"Did you have a customer this morning named Kasper Hollawell, purchased about a half-dozen boxes of ammunition?" Mark asked.

"Is he a skinny dude with a nasty beard and a worse haircut?"

"This one?" Doonie held up his phone to show him Kasper's DL photo.

Gray grunted in the affirmative.

"What kind of cartridges did he buy?" Mark asked.

Gray hesitated, as his belief in the sacred privacy of gun owners battled with his hunger to know if he'd sold bullets to the Makro Killer. "Nine mil. Paid cash."

"He buy anything else?" Mark asked.

"No."

"Is he a regular?"

"Never seen him before."

"Mind checking? It's Kasper with a K, H-o-l-l-a-w-e-l-l."

Gray consulted his computer. Shook his head. "If he was ever here, he paid cash and didn't buy anything that required paperwork."

"Did he look at something besides the ammo?" Doonie asked. "Didn't even maybe check out any of these weapons? Hell of a nice collection of new and used you got."

"No. Made his purchase and left."

"Huh," Mark mused. "Man drove sixty miles—a hundred-twenty, round-trip—to buy some bullets? Why would he do that?"

"No idea." Gray had a grade-A poker face but his poker voice topped out at B+. There was a worried belligerence in it.

Doonie played bad cop. Went dead still and grinned at Gray.

The old soldier stared right back, unintimidated.

"Mr. Gray," Mark said, "are you aware Makro has raised its reward to a million dollars?"

Gray lost interest in the staring contest with Doonie. "It was on TV."

"We're the detectives Makro will ask to confirm who provided relevant information, and what percent of the reward it deserves," Mark explained.

The old soldier and current businessman did a quick risk/reward assessment. Temptation won.

Gray said, quietly, "Hollawell asked—he didn't have the weapon with him—how much I'd pay for a .44 mag Ruger Redhawk in good condition."

Goddamn. "Which barrel?"

"Seven and a half inch."

Fuck yeah. "Did he like what you told him?"

"No. Before I talk price I ask the seller to show proof of purchase and a license for the weapon. He couldn't."

Mark and Doonie said nothing.

Gray asked, "So, does my information about that specific weapon… qualify?"

Mark replied, "How much did you offer Hollawell for the Redhawk?"

"Nothing," Gray insisted. Angry, insulted.

"It was lowball, but not zero. You would've told us up front Hollawell tried to sell you a hot gun, if you weren't worried we might find out from Hollawell you tried to buy it. Did he accept your offer? Is he coming back with the gun?"

Gray glowered at Mark. Exhaled. Gave his head one grudging microscopic shake, No.

"If you're lying you're gonna lose your license. But if you're not… You write and sign a statement about Hollawell asking what you'd pay for that specific unlicensed weapon, and we won't notice you left out the part where you named a price."

◆

When they got back in the car Doonie said, "Now I love that shot of Vanora's gun boob even more than before."

"Me too."

Kasper trying to sell an unregistered piece was no slam-dunk to get the FBI a search warrant. The piece being the same model Redhawk as the one on Vanora's breast, alongside a Rudy-size Rudy-blond hand fondling her other breast, improved the odds.

Doonie pulled out his phone to tell Agent Carlson to go grab a judge.

Mark's phone rang. Husak's voice erupted from the car speakers.

"We got another Makro hit. And he dialed it up a notch. Not a driver this time, he took out a Vice President. Get back here now."

Mark said, "We can't."

"Can't? What the fuck is can't?"

"Was the TOD last night?" Mark answered, and keyed the ignition.

"Yeah, body temp said between midnight and four."

Mark started driving. "If Rudzutaka was at Kasper's when we got there, he's gone now. But we might've come up with grounds for the FBI to get a search warrant."

Mark told Husak about the Redhawk.

Husak wasn't optimistic. "Kasper, who we don't know if he's talked to Rudy in seventeen years, talked this morning about selling a gun which is the same model as one on Vanora Yard's breast, but we don't know it's that exact same breast gun. Or if Vanora's breast and its gun ever were with Rudy. A judge is gonna whip out his pen for that?"

"Maybe one who just heard the MK notched murder number five. What else we got on that?"

"Samantha Barnes, female, thirty-four, divorced, lived alone. Prelim COD is small-caliber gunshot wounds for Barnes, and for her dog. The good news, Barnes and the dog both drew blood. The MK's hurt but we can't tell how bad."

"We'll sit on Kasper's house while the FBI works the warrant."

"Loo," Doonie said, "how about some backup. We're runnin' on two hours sleep."

"Sorry, Doon. Got no spare bodies to send out there on a circumstantial maybe. If your warrant happens there'll be FBI Swats to serve it."

Yeah. If. Mark asked, "You come up with anything on Kasper?"

A fistful of nothing. No spike in credit card use to show Kasper was buying groceries for two; if he was doing Rudy's shopping it was in cash. No unusual deposits in Kasper's accounts; if Rudy's paying him, Kasper's stashing it under the mattress. And no uptick in utility bills that'd indicate more than one person was showering and watching TV at Hotel Hollawell.

"Did the FBI check Kasper's phone and email to see if he's contacted any local real estate agents in the past year?" Mark wondered.

"They did, and he didn't," Husak said, dourly.

Doonie asked Mark, "You see Rudy trusting a dim nervous like Kasper to rent him a hideout?"

"No... Vanora! If Rudzutaka hasn't killed her yet—"

"—she could be the one rented a place and keeps the fridge filled," Doonie completed the thought.

"We'll survey the realtors again," Husak said without enthusiasm. "But we already put Vanora's name and picture on TV, if anyone recognized her they probably woulda called by now, especially with that million up for grabs."

"Only on arrest and conviction," Mark said, "and meantime this realtor or landlord has to worry about the downside if this serial killer figures out—" Mark yawned "—who snitched."

"You good to drive?" Husak asked.

"We're looking into that, we'll let you know."

FIFTY

Ookie knew Rudy was in there. The scraggly old mutt began growling when she and Samantha Barnes approached the front door. Barnes told Ookie to chill. The dog ignored her. "Hey I get it, you hear a mouse," Barnes teased, with pleasantly inebriated whimsy. "But Ook let's—just shut up a second, shh, shh... Oookieeeee. Let's be honest. You have never ever never caught anything. Mouse, squirrel, Frisbee. But I love you anyway."

Rudy, waiting in the darkened kitchen, grinned. It had been up to Rudy to pick which drivers to kill. But Trey had chosen this final target—said it had to be some kinda big sensational topper. Trey found his dream girl six months ago, so Rudy had plenty of time to study Samantha Barnes. Which is why Rudy knew Ookie growling and acting tough was so damn funny. She was a worn-out butt-ugly Schnauzer-Lab mix, dirty white muzzle, rheumy eyes, a fat stubby-legged waddler.

Soon as Samantha Barnes got inside and closed the door, Rudy'd swing out of the kitchen, fifteen feet away from the door, put a bullet in Barnes then quick put one in the geriatric mutt before it could get to him—if it even tried. Finish with a kill shot for Barnes, job's done inside a minute, he grabs the almost-full bottle of single malt that's sitting on the coffee table and he's out the door and off to Cleveland. Gateway to fucking Latvia.

Sound of the key, the first lock turning. The key, the second lock, the door opens, lights go on, the door closes, Ookie erupts in frenzied snarls leaping against the leash as Rudy steps out of the kitchen aims at Barnes' torso squeezes the tr—

Ookie lunges berserk tears the leash from Barnes' grip and Barnes stumbles—the .22 slug slashes her side—

Rudy fires at Ookie misses the fat fucker streaking at him in a murderous blur Rudy fires again but Ookie's teeth are in his calf she's whipping her head back and forth trying to tear the calf off Rudy's leg—

Rudy bends down grabs Ookie's hind leg shoves the gun into her gut and shoots, the dog screams once and—

Barnes snarling in wordless rage shatters the scotch bottle across the back of Rudy's skull he pitches forward onto his knees blood pouring from a gash on the back of his neck Barnes jabs the jagged remains of the bottle into Rudy's shoulder and he whips the arm across her ankles she falls hard, head slamming the floor Rudy's on her grabs her by the throat and drills her in the forehead, job done inside a minute.

But he's not out the door and on his way.

He rush-plods to the bathroom and with his good arm presses a towel against his neck. He tries to transfer the towel to his left hand— fuck! His stabbed left shoulder sizzles when he lifts it and his right calf's a motherfucking little mess.

Rudy chugs half a bottle of generic ibuprofen pills, rinses his wounds, yanks out shards of glass, pours in peroxide, slaps bandages on, then he's out the back door, up the alley to the cross street where his car's parked, gets in, starts the engine and strangles an urge to howl and pound on the steering wheel till it breaks off and he can go kick in someone's door and beat them to death with it.

Motherfuckingfuck! Cleveland? His clothes are soaked in blood and Scotch and stink like it. His wounds are seeping, stiffening, throbbing and gonna get nothing but worse until he treats them. Forget the fucking six-hour drive to Cleveland. Gonna take everything he has to get through ninety minutes back to the house, *right now* while it's still dark and people can't see what's driving this Civic so let's get fucking moving.

FIFTY-ONE

N ow don't take this wrong, bro, your new look, you totally rock the short beard thing… But—"

"I'm not shaving it off for the convention," Danny insisted, sending up a warning flare of teen indignation.

"Fuck no," Trey protested, amused, "that's not what I'm gonna say." Not now that he knew how Danny would take it. "During your speech there are gonna be lotsa tight close-ups. That beard's gotta be sharp. Like perfect sharp. But all you gotta do is nothing. From now on you stop trimming it. Don't touch the fucker. When we get backstage a pro will make that beard the best possible version of itself."

"Next you're gonna say you expect me to wear makeup," Danny warily accused.

Trey made a just-a-little gesture with his thumb and index finger. "Fuck no—no. No."

Trey grinned. "Right, you're good with baring your soul in video after video, but put on a touch of pancake to keep a hundred thousand watts of stage light from glaring off your forehead like it was the Bean on a sunny day… Really bro?" Trey stifled a cackle.

Danny scowled hard, then burst out laughing. Trey joined him. They clinked beer bottles. Alarms chimed on their phones. The alarm for a Makro hit.

Danny yanked his phone out of his back pocket.

Trey stared down at his phone on the coffee table. Steeled himself, slowly picked up the phone and gazed at it without registering what was on its screen. He knew what it'd say. Samantha Barnes, the target he'd selected as their crowning—

"Holy shit," Danny blurted, "it's not another driver—son of a bitch killed a Makro exec." He grabbed the remote and turned on the TV.

Rudy how fucking insane are you?!

"And he shot her dog," Danny muttered, poisonous, his eyes locked on the TV.

They know who you are you HAD to get the hell out why the fuck— But maybe now Rudy's running liked planned maybe the stupid crazy fuck is already out of the—

"Yeah!" Danny crowed, as the reporter said evidence at the scene showed Barnes and the dog had fought back and hurt the Makro Killer.

Jesus. JESUS.

"I'll make coffee while you start the research on Samantha Barnes," Danny said, glowing with grim enthusiasm. "We'll nail this video by tomorrow easy, this one so makes our point—Barnes wounded him without a gun, imagine if she'd had... Trey?"

Trey wondered why Danny was looking at him like—Trey realized a tear was dripping down his cheek and brusquely wiped it away.

"You okay man?"

"Yeah, yeah, I'm just..." Trey searched for a word, any word.

"Human," Danny said.

Trey gave a hapless embarrassed shrug, unable to prevent his eyes from puking more tears.

Danny went to Trey, gathered him into a hug. Trey stood with his arms dangling, then dutifully raised them and drooped them around Danny.

"Don't worry," Danny consoled Trey, "this time he's wounded, and they know who to look for."

Trey made a soft constricted noise, half sob, half burp, and hugged Danny so hard it hurt.

FIFTY-TWO

Kasper's red Explorer was in front of his house.

The cops parked on the shoulder of the road twenty feet from the mouth of the driveway, ready to follow Kasper if he left before the FBI scored a warrant.

Mark yawned. Doonie yawned. They unwrapped sandwiches they'd grabbed at a supermarket before leaving Joliet.

Kasper's Explorer pulled out of the driveway. Kasper recognized the car and the two monsters in it, did a U-turn and drove back to his house.

The monsters devoured their sandwiches.

A tractor drove by.

Mark yawned, looked at his watch then looked at Doonie, who grimaced.

It had been almost two hours. The judge the FBI approached must've said No. The silence meant Agent Carlson hadn't given up and was shopping for a judge who had a subtler understanding of the Constitution.

"Take a nap," Doonie instructed Mark.

Mark tilted his seat back and closed his eyes. *Kasper has nerves of jello, if we can bring him in for questioning he'll crack. If the Feebs don't get a warrant—or if they do but don't find the Redhawk—what else can we do to get at Kasper?...* Mark's body told his brain to shut up and sleep. Seconds later Mark was jolted awake by large vehicles screeching to a halt close to the car, their engines rumbling.

A pickup truck and an SUV were alongside the car, and a second SUV had pulled in behind it. There were two guys in the bed of the pickup staring down at Mark and Doonie. One had an AR-15 and the other a civilianized Kalash. They weren't pointing the rifles, just cradling them and staring hard.

Mark and Doonie stared back.

The driver of the pickup snickered, drove to Kasper's driveway and stopped. The guys in back jumped out and stood guard at the mouth of the driveway. The three vehicles drove up to Kasper's house and formed a barrier in front of it.

The driver of the pickup got out and was joined by two men from each of the SUVs; a total of seven, dressed in camo or cowboy or a combo. The driver of the pickup, the obvious Commanderissimo, was the only one who hadn't toted a rifle to the party but like most of the others he was wearing a sidearm. He and one other guy went into the house.

The two guards in the driveway kept their eyes glued on the cop car, in case Mark and Doonie decided this would be the moment to storm Kasper's domain.

Mark wondered if there was anyplace around here that would deliver coffee.

◆

Fifteen minutes later the driver of the pickup and three of his musketeers strode up to the car. The musketeers flanked the car so they had line of sight on both cops. The pickup driver—fiftyish, five-ten, powerfully built, shaved head, oversized thick gray eyebrows, and deep-set, small, vermin-shrewd eyes presiding over a bristling aggressive mustache the size of a car bumper—the guy looked like a cartoon version of himself—stood by the driver's side door and laid his nastiest rat-glower on Mark.

Mark lowered his window and said, "Hi."

The man sneered. "Well shit. You're the big badass cop?"

"I'm the nicest guy in the world."

The man rested his hand on the butt of his holstered gun. "I'm Kasper Holloway's legal advisor."

"You're an attorney?"

"You're illegally loitering on private property."

"We're legally parked on the shoulder of a public road."

"In La Salle County. Completely out of your jurisdiction."

"That one you got right. But the thing is, if confronted with a crime in progress—especially a violent one—we're empowered to make an arrest."

A derisive snort from one of the musketeers.

The legal advisor's hand closed on his pistol grip and he broke out a cold predatory grin. "I'd like to see that."

"They might," Mark said, indicating the musketeers. "You wouldn't."

The grin faded. The hatred behind it doubled. And… the shrewd eyes decided against testing the badass cop.

"Gonna be dark soon," the legal advisor seethed. "Gets pitch black out here. Never know what might happen."

"No," Mark agreed, "you don't."

Mark's text alert chimed.

The seething legal advisor turned and stomped back up the driveway. One by one the musketeers followed, reluctant, walking with a slow menacing swagger and tossing threatening looks over their shoulders at the cops to make it clear this retreat was purely tactical.

Mark pulled out his phone, read the text and held the phone up for Doonie to see.

FIFTY-THREE

The custom notification for a text from Kasper—a blaring car horn—went off. The ugly sound did its ugly job, ripping Rudy out of oblivion-level unconsciousness. He jerked awake, winced, gasped in pain. He reached for the phone, winced harder and gasped louder. The self-stitched gash on his neck hurt as bad as if he'd left a chunk of broken glass in it. Rudy sat up in slow motion and cautiously picked up the phone.

Hostile probe just now. Failed to breach perimeter. RU gone? RU OK?

Not as OK as Rudy would be if it were safe to go over there and kill that fucking moron before the cops came back—if they'd left—more likely they'd have eyes on Kasper's house. And it would also be nuts for Rudy to risk hitting the highway now, in broad daylight, in this much pain. Had to rest and recupe all he could, till it was late and dark enough to start the long grind to Cleveland.

Rudy texted Kasper:

Remain in place. Say nothing no matter what. GET A LAWYER RIGHT NOW.

Rudy checked the time—almost noon, what he'd set his alarm for anyway. He eased out of the bed and went to the john, taking the phone with him. While pissing he checked his offshore account... *Sonofabitch.* No deposit. That little prick Trey had thought he could break the contract, get away with ordering Rudy not to make the last kill, and now Trey thought he could get away with not paying up.

Rudy felt an urgent pressure in his bowels, sat on the can, stared at the phone, pinched out a log and texted Trey:

$. Now.

Rudy showered and changed the dressings on his wounds. His right calf, Ookie's chew toy, had swollen and stiffened into a block of wood, wood that burst into flame when Rudy put weight on it... Shit, gotta give the creaky old mutt credit, how she fucking launched at him and gave herself up... First thing when Rudy gets set in Latvia he hadda get a dog. Guarantee he'd have somebody who speaks English and is a friend.

Trey didn't reply to his text.

Rudy made some food and watched TV. His face was all over it. Fucking media going batshit how he'd "upped the stakes" by killing middle management. Like Makro drivers only counted as three-fifths human, even the white ones.

He gobbled Advil, iced his wounds, forced himself to stretch the shoulder and leg as much as he could take, and iced some more. Trey still hadn't replied to his text.

Rudy phoned Trey.

It went to voicemail. After the beep, Rudy held silent, then rasped three long slow harsh monster movie breaths, then in the middle of a fourth breath hung up. Grinned, imagining the arrogant shit interpreting that.

Rudy's grin collapsed, turning into a weight Rudy's lips were too weary to support. Eating lunch and changing his bandages left him totally whipped as if he'd run a marathon in brick shoes.

Good. More sleep he gets before tonight the better.

Couldn't sleep. Both wounds throbbing like they hated him. Rudy came this close to getting stupid and popping just one Vicodin. Staved it off by taking a few three four slugs of tequila.

Jerked off, thinking about Vanora, their last time, right before he finished her.

FIFTY-FOUR

Three County Sheriff cars showed up. Deputies got out and went to have a chat with the musketeers guarding Kasper's driveway. The Sheriff got out and went to have a chat with Mark and Doonie.

The Sheriff told them patrons at Toby's Tavern Inn had posted on Facebook that the Makro Killer detectives had been there, and left with Ira Grundlich.

"When Ira came back he refused to tell them what you asked about," the Sheriff said. "When I asked he wouldn't tell me, either."

"I bet old Ira enjoyed the shit out of that," Doonie said.

"He did."

Mark said, "Ira was honoring our request to keep quiet. But I'm guessing a few minutes ago someone reported seeing men with rifles out front of Kasper Hollawell's place, and two suits parked nearby, and you had a good idea who the suits were."

"Uh-huh. How is Hollawell connected to the Makro thing?"

"That's what we're trying to find out."

"You think Rudzutaka's in there?"

"If he was, he's probably gone by now," Mark said. He gave the Sheriff the bullet points, and stifled a yawn. "What are our chances of getting some food and coffee?"

◆

Lookie-loos began to arrive, along with media vans from Chicago TV stations. The journos had been in Leoville buying haircuts from Ira Grundlich and vying to treat him to dinner, vain attempts to pry Makro Killer gossip out of him.

The journos tried to pry some out of Mark and Doonie, who were every bit as stubborn as Ira Grundlich, though without the gloating.

Kasper Hollawell's legal advisor had lots to say. He strolled down the driveway, introduced himself—Downy Jepson—waited till all the cameras were ready, and began expounding on the Constitution.

The sun was setting and Jepson was explaining how Chicago police intruding on a sovereign citizen of La Salle County was the Constitutional definition of a foreign invasion which well-armed citizen militias were duty-bound to repel, when two FBI tactical vans arrived. The cameras deserted Jepson and rushed to the vans.

The Feds emerged; Agent Carlson backed by a dozen SWATs in black battle rattle, carrying fully automatic assault weapons.

Five SWATs, assisted by the Deputy Sheriffs, established a perimeter, herding the newsies and lookie-loos behind it, while the rest formed up in front of the Constitutional scholar and his two musketeers. The four musketeers guarding the house rushed down the driveway to reinforce their comrades. They scowled fiercely at the SWATs, though the effect was sabotaged by some nervous shifting of feet and mopping of suddenly sweaty brows.

Agent Carlson gave Mark and Doonie the good and bad news. The judge, based on the gun dealer's affidavit, had granted a warrant limited to a search of Kasper Hollawell's property for a Ruger Redhawk. Since the gun's connection to Vanora Yard and Yard's connection to Rudzutaka were pure conjecture, and Hollawell had no known contact with Rudzutaka for over a decade, no phones or digital devices could be searched or seized.

The three of them walked over to the driveway. When Downy Jepson saw Agent Carlson coming he stiffened drew himself up to his full height and glowered at the insultingly African-American FBI agent with even more venom than he'd beamed at Mark. Snarled, "As a sover—"

"We're serving a Federal warrant to search the property," Agent Carlson announced in a no-nonsense baritone. "You gentlemen will vacate the premises immediately and remain outside the perimeter."

"The Consti—"

"Requires me to inform you that any of you still inside the

perimeter thirty seconds from now will be arrested and charged with impeding a Federal investigation," Agent Carlson told him, sounding like someone who had an honors degree in Criminal Justice from Columbia.

Jepson, grumbling through clenched teeth, demanded, "Show me the warrant. I'm Mr. Hollawell's legal advisor."

"Are you a licensed attorney?"

Jepson's tiny eyes narrowed, his breath quickened and he began to tremble.

Mark couldn't tell if Jepson was about to leap on Agent Carlson or have a stroke or burst into tears or all three. Mark was certain getting schooled by a melanin-rich operative of the deep state, in front of his musketeers and a live worldwide TV audience, had never been a scene in any of Downy Jepson's heroic race war fantasies.

Jepson… Jepson… made a grudging, sullen *back off* gesture to his men. They turned to go to their trucks.

"Stop!" Agent Carlson bellowed.

Jepson whirled to face him—

By the time Jepson completed his whirl multiple SWAT weapons where aimed his way.

"Vehicles on the property are subject to the warrant," Agent Carlson growled. "Your thirty seconds are up."

Jepson treated Agent Carlson to a surly grunt but trudged away, trailed by his unhappy musketeers. As Jepson passed Mark he gave Mark a fang-baring sneer to let Mark know he was gonna make Mark pay for this.

Mark yawned.

FIFTY-FIVE

Since Danny came aboard he'd been helping Trey with the data dive on each new victim. Danny assembled the bio, which freed Trey to pick through more images than he'd been able to before.

Danny was awed by Trey's ability to devour stills and footage at near-blur speed, yet somehow catch the coolest. Even better was the joy with which Trey tore into the work and got off on beating his insanely tight deadline, slamming a video together in twenty-four to forty-eight hours. Trey's enthusiasm was contagious, an instant mood elevator and a deep distraction from dwelling on bad shit, a place Danny still visited too many times a day. So Danny was more than a little concerned when today, ever since the news of Samantha Barnes' murder, Trey's vibe had been more dawdle than slam.

Danny kept sneaking peeks at Trey, who was scrolling through images at what for Trey was a glacial pace. First time Trey had ever looked preoccupied. He was always high energy, super-confident, sharp, funny, unstoppable.

Danny pushed it aside and resumed reading Samantha Barnes' blog, *Samantha Barnestorming*.

Couldn't concentrate. Wondered what was it about Samantha that hit Trey so hard, so different than all the others? Did Trey know Samantha? If he did, why keep it a secret? Maybe Samantha reminded Trey of someone.

Trey caught Danny studying him. Danny blushed. Trey gave him a forgiving smirk, like he was reading Danny's mind and letting him know it was cool. Trey went back to work. Began scanning at normal velocity with normal manic absorption.

Danny's own concentration returned.

A text notification sounded on a phone in Trey's pocket. But the phone Trey pulled out wasn't one Danny had seen before. Trey stared down at the text like he was trying to incinerate it with his X-ray vision.

Trey took a deep breath and pocketed the mystery phone. Looked at Danny, explained, "Spam," and went back to work.

Almost. Trey scanned slower and slower. Stopped. Sat there thinking, one foot tapping.

"Trey…?" Danny ventured.

"Oh—it's nothin'—just hit on a concept for the script. How soon you gonna get me that bio?"

"An hour—maybe two. Samantha did a lot of cool stuff, she's—really interesting."

"Yeah. She is… So shut up and read, you lazy prick." Trey belched and dove back into the footage.

Trey being Trey again relaxed Danny. That "spam" was obviously something heavy, personal. But Trey was handling it, and it was none of Danny's business.

✦

Danny finished the bio and sent it to Trey. They ordered in Chinese and took a break to scarf it down.

"So," Danny asked, "what was the concept that hit you?"

"It's… gone. Brilliant, but didn't work. Got any ideas?"

"Well yeah, I still think we should go with how close Samantha was to saving herself with only that Scotch bottle—so imagine a gun."

"You're right, bro—it's all about the bottle! We open on a broken bottle and Samantha dead—then a gun and Samantha alive. We keep bouncing between bottle dead, gun alive—end with side-by-side broken bottle and gun: '*Which would you want?*' " Trey gave a triumphant smirk. "Fucker's gonna write itself."

"Yeah," Danny grinned, lit as shit Trey was gonna use his concept. "I got some ideas what my rant's gonna be in this one," Danny said.

"Don't tell me, I wanna hear it fresh when we shoot," Trey said, pleased.

Trey went to his computer, skimmed the bio and started writing a script—Trey's mystery phone rang. Trey stuck his hand in his pocket and silenced it.

Danny made a list of most important things about Samantha, and spent time perusing her photos and videos. Though Danny ad libbed his rants, he'd discovered the more homework he did on the victim the more true emotion he could put—

"*Fuck.*" A distressed whisper from Trey.

Trey was hunched over, with the mystery phone pressed to his ear, unable to resist checking out the voicemail.

Trey felt Danny's eyes on him. He pocketed the phone. "It's bullshit, just, ah… Someone trying to hit me up for a loan."

Danny gave a sympathetic grunt. Said, "I haven't been outside all day, I'm gonna go for a quick walk—anything I can get ya?"

"No, thanks," Trey said. In a quiet, sincere way that was unusual for him, signaling he appreciated Danny giving him some privacy to deal with the supposedly bullshit voicemail.

Danny strolled down to the lake and back up the riverwalk, feeling good. Though also a little concerned for his bro. This mystery mooch was really pressing Trey's buttons, and until now Trey's buttons seemed fucking invulnerable.

Must be an old girlfriend. Or family.

FIFTY-SIX

When Kasper Hollawell opened his door he was on the phone, narrating the invasion of the freedom-snatchers.

"The racially biased Federal agent is forcing me to take what he claims is a legal search warrant... I'm reading it..."

"And we're executing it," Agent Carlson informed Kasper as he strode into the house, followed by his team and their two guest snatchers from the Chicago PD, who stopped to share some quality time with Kasper.

Kasper gazed queasily at Mark and Doonie while he listened to instructions from whomever was the phone, then yelled in the direction of Agent Carlson, "You can't search till I finish reading!"

"Tell your legal advisor that's another thing he's wrong about," Mark advised.

Kasper's eyes widened. He told his caller, "Downy, they're tapping our phones!"

"Nah," Mark said, "just reading your minds. Was the Redhawk part of the original deal, or did Rudzutaka give it to you as a bonus?"

"I don't have no Redh—" the phone squawked an angry noise into Kasper's ear. He yelped at Mark, "No questions! No answering!" Kasper listened to another blast of legal advice, then shook the warrant at Mark and Doonie. "It's illegal for you to prevent me from reading this illegal warrant." Kasper stuffed the warrant in his back pocket and fled, resuming his narration. "Going into the kitchen now—the goddamn refrigerator! They're touching my food!"

The Feds proceeded to touch everything—except the phones and computers—in the house, the barn, Kasper's Explorer, Jepson's pickup and the musketeers' SUVs. Mark, Doonie and Kasper were only allowed to observe. Frustrating as hell for all three.

Frustrated Mark and Doonie because the FBI kept not finding the Redhawk, or any sign Rudzutaka had been here. And not a trace of the unsatisfactory marijuana Kasper's Uncle Ira alluded to, though a SWAT did find a bong which stank of bleach.

Frustrated Kasper because there kept being only one of him while there kept being multiple SWATs touching his stuff in multiple locations. He rushed from room to room trying to narrate every-thing—except any room Mark or Doonie was in, because they kept trying to talk to him.

Kasper's phone died. He fetched the charging cord and went from room to room plugging it in.

Mark pondered one mildly interesting thing. Kasper was a man of many locks. In addition to multiple locks on the front and rear doors, there were locks on some interior doors, closets, drawers, a gun cabi-net, desk and filing cabinet, plus hefty padlocks on an ammo locker, a freezer, three toolboxes, two footlockers, a duffel bag, the barn and an empty feed bin inside it. Which meant Kasper was also a man of many keys. He kept a spare set of keys in a locked kitchen drawer, which he was obliged to open so he could give them to the Feds. Fortunately each key was labeled.

Mark was watching a SWAT toss Kasper's bedroom when the SWAT unlocked a drawer in the bedside table and found a gallon-size baggie containing Kasper's stash of back-up keys. Three sets of house and car keys, two sets of cabinet keys, drawer keys and padlock keys, all labeled.

Two rooms away, Kasper heard the obscene jingling of a Federal thug pawing through his key treasury. Kasper rushed to the bedroom, saw Mark and made a U-turn.

The SWAT read the keyring labels, saw nothing new and began to seal the baggie.

"Nothing labeled Safe Deposit Box?" Mark asked.

"Uh-uh." The SWAT finished sealing the baggie and—

"You mind comparing all three sets to see if any ring has an extra key on it?"

The SWAT treated Mark to a hostile silence that said, *Fuck yeah I mind, got a whole room to toss and I didn't bust my hump acing special ops school so I could waste my life on street cop bullshit low-odds gruntwork.*

Out loud, the SWAT grumbled, "Got gloves?"

Mark held up a pair of the CPD's finest latex field gear.

The SWAT swung the bedroom door almost shut so nobody could see what he'd let fucking Bergman nag him into.

Fucking Bergman inspected every fucking keyring. Didn't find any anomalies. But didn't come away empty-handed.

FIFTY-SEVEN

By the time they finished searching every millimeter of the buildings and vehicles it was 7:40 PM, pitch dark and there was nothing left to do except use hand-held floodlights to search every millimeter of the half-acre lot for signs of a hastily dug Ruger Redhawk-sized grave.

The search was visible to the crowd on the side of the road.

TV news crews, who'd spent the last three hours with fuck-all to shoot, taped every inch of the ground search. Their camera lights helped illuminate the area.

The lookie-loos who spent three hours with fuck-all to gawk at were energized by the sight, live and up close, of a line of FBI SWATs at work.

Within ten minutes the reality sunk in that watching guys moving at a snail's pace staring at the ground was no substitute for the hoped-for shoot-out with the Makro Killer. There were murmurs of disappointment and derisive snickers, followed by the sound of departing vehicles.

Downy Jepson and his musketeers stayed. No choice, their trucks were FBI hostages. But they'd been joined by womenfolk and friends, and were having a high time booing, jeering, insulting and at one point serenading the FBI's slo-mo boring dumbass embarrassing public failure.

The slo-mo search ended at the back edge of Kasper's property, which abutted a vast barren cornfield settling in for its winter nap under a thin blanket of cornstalk debris. Mark, Doonie and Agent Carlson swept lights across the furrows, straining to spot a sign of digging that hadn't been done by a plow.

Doonie yawned. "I was hopin' a jittery fucker like Kasper wouldn't have the spine to flush all his weed."

"Yeah," Mark said. If they could come up with any shred of probable cause to scoop Kasper up and grill him, the jittery fucker would spill like Humpty Dumpty. Mark wondered if he could convince the Hague to designate Kasper's beard a crime against humanity.

❖

Mark and Doonie accompanied Agent Carlson when he went back to the house to inform Kasper the FBI had completed executing its warrant.

Kasper was still on the phone with Jepson, who heard Agent Carlson's admission of defeat, and let out a long whoop. Kasper invited Jepson and the boys to come on in, ended the call, gave Agent Carlson an aggrieved scowl and asked, "Where do I file my claim when I find all the damages you did?"

"We didn't," Agent Carlson informed him.

"Kasper, money doesn't matter any more," Mark said. "When we catch Rudzutaka—or maybe sooner—you're gonna get charged as a co-conspirator in multiple homicides for hire. Cooperating now is your only leverage for getting life with the possibility of parole, instead of life until you knot some sheets and hang yourself. Let's talk."

Kasper's beard trembled and deep inside it his lips pursed tight as he strained to keep from blurting a reply until he could come up with a satisfying but safe blurt.

Kasper settled for raising his arm and pointing at the door. Kept pointing until every last freedom-snatcher was gone.

❖

Mark, Doonie and Agent Carlson were in front of the house talking— their voices down and their backs to the news cameras—when Jepson, his musketeers and their posse began a raucous victory parade up the driveway. Every one of them put an arm in the air, giving the lawmen a middle-finger salute as they partied past and sashayed into Kasper's house.

Doonie assured Agent Carlson, "You and me are good. When the news runs close-ups of a cop gettin' the finger, it'll be Bergman."

FIFTY-EIGHT

The FBI wouldn't send a SWAT team to serve a search warrant unless they thought the Makro Killer might be there. So when the FBI SWATs and two Chicago detectives approached Kasper Hollawell's house, tens of millions of viewers were locked in tight.

Not as tight as Danny Gold and Trey Fister. Danny was desperate to see the cops kill the Makro Killer. Trey was desperate to see the cops kill Rudy.

The moment arrived. The FBI leader knocked. The door was opened by a gawky guy with a huge lopsided beard, talking on his cell phone. Commentators on cable news outlets across the world began speculating Hollawell was talking to Rudzutaka, hoping that would keep people from changing the channel now that the cops hadn't been greeted by a blast of gunfire.

No reason to worry about losing Danny and Trey. Dull as the next three hours were, they remained obedient screen zombies.

When the FBI began packing up, Trey did mute the sound. He and Danny had little interest in watching more but made no move to get back to work. Sat there buried in dismal silence. Danny, disappointed his Dad's killer was still alive. Trey, miserable the killer was still alive, available to get arrested and peddle Trey to the cops.

Danny, sensing his newfound older bro was taking it even harder than he was, said, "At least they didn't get to bust him. Still a chance they'll shoot the son of a bitch."

"A chance," Trey moped. "Not a guarantee."

Danny went someplace private for a moment. Confided, "I asked Detective Bergman to kill him for me."

Trey's gloom lightened into a sly hopeful smirk. "What did he say?"

"Nothing… Gave me his card and told me call if I ever blah blah blah."

"So he didn't say no. Emotionally, between the lines—how did Bergman seem to feel about it?"

"I couldn't tell," Danny said, and pointed to the TV.

There was a medium close-up of Bergman being given the finger by a rowdy posse of Second Amendment fans. Bergman watched them go by as if they were the third beer commercial in a row during a timeout in a basketball broadcast.

FIFTY-NINE

You hicks think waving your shit-stained fingers at Bergman hurts his little feelings? Lookit that face. Only thing on his mind is me. How he still got no clue where I am.

When the alarm woke Rudy at 9 PM he was still in pain, but feeling closer to human. Sleeping had been the smart move. If he'd run for it this afternoon he wouldn't have had the stamina for the six-and-a-half-hour drive to Cleveland.

Rudy's optimism took a hit when he turned on the tube and saw the SWAT circus at Kasper's. But the fact he hadn't woken up to a shotgun pointed at his nose meant they hadn't found anything. The FBI giving up and that cold blank face on Bergman meant they didn't expect to.

Either their warrant didn't cover Kasper's devices, or if it did Kasper had cleaned and encrypted everything as instructed. And so far they hadn't taken Kasper into custody. Even if they did, Rudy wasn't worried about Kasper talking, at least not until it was too late.

Last year, after Kasper took the deal Rudy offered, Rudy told Kasper he'd taken out a contract on him. Kasper was safe as long as Rudy got away clean. But if Rudy got arrested or killed—whether it was Kasper's fault or not—the hammer comes down.

Kasper nearly cried, and Rudy could tell he was going nuts trying to think of a way to weasel out. But Kasper kept his mouth shut, seeing as how he'd pocketed Rudy's front money and would rather shit nails than give it back. Plus, Kasper correctly suspected if he backed out, Rudy would kill him then and there.

Still, Rudy wondered maybe he shouldn't push his luck by trusting

Kasper to keep his chickenshit mouth shut. Might be safer to chow down, then hit the road right away.

No. Stick to the plan, wait until midnight. By then those limp-dick cops would be back in Chicago beating their wives. The highway would be dark and loose all the way, and dawn would be breaking when Rudy rolled up at the safe house in Cleveland.

SIXTY

A media scrum followed Downy Jepson and his middle-finger musketeers up the driveway and tried to follow them into Kasper's house.

Jepson ordered them off the property, promising, "Trespassers *will* be shot!"

Two armed musketeers herded the reporters back down to the road and stood guard at the mouth of the driveway, clench-jawed, ready to pounce on any Constitutional provocation to shoot and stuff a trophy journalist.

The journalists ignored them and peppered Mark, Doonie and Agent Carlson with questions.

The merciless cops answered with polite refusals to comment.

◆

The media, the last stubbornly hopeful lookie-loos and the County deputies went home. The SWATs were ready to do the same. Almost.

Agent Carlson was determined to salvage the operation by saving the lives of two raggedy exhausted cops. As he walked Mark and Doonie to their car he suggested, "How about you gentlemen ride with me. My guys can drive your car."

"Thanks," Mark said, "but we've seen what SWATs do to vehicles."

"Not always."

"Also," Mark said, "we're gonna spend the night down here,".

"Okay," Agent Carlson said, but his heart wasn't in it. "You're not gonna try anything especially stupid, right?"

"I make sure he don't go past regular stupid," Doonie assured him.

"Just gonna make nice with the locals tomorrow, see if we turn up any useful Kasper gossip," Mark explained.

They shook hands. Agent Carlson got in the lead tac van and drove away.

A noisy victory party spilled out of Kasper's front door and loaded itself into the pickup truck and SUVs parked out front. Engines roared to life and the motorized bacchanal rumbled down the driveway and onto the road, led by Downy Jepson's pickup.

Jepson saw Mark and Doonie standing by their car and braked, squealing to a halt as close to them as he could without risking a vehicular assault bust.

The bastard cops refused to flinch. Or speak. Just looked at Jepson, and the enormous beard next to him in the passenger seat.

Jepson leered down at them. "Hadda take this someplace else before we drank all Kasper's beer and trashed the place. Just wouldn't be considerate comin' on top of what you shits put him through, dontcha think? So we're gonna do it right, at a suitable commercial venue." Jepson indicated his passenger. "Kasper won't be touching a steering wheel, so any dream you got about grabbin' him on a DUI can go fuck itself."

" 'A suitable commercial venue?' " Mark asked.

"The Double Barrel. Road house out in the sticks. Kinda bar where a man can be a man... But you might like it."

"Yeah?"

"You and me could let our hair down. Hoist a few, loosen up, discuss the meaning of democracy in a civilized manner."

"In the parking lot?" Mark guessed.

Jepson's answer was a malevolent grin.

Mark thought it over. "I wouldn't get there until after midnight. If I came."

"Midnight this party'll just be hittin' its stride, so there goes that excuse. You gonna show?"

Mark's answer was a pleasant grin.

The musketeers and womenfolk in the back of Jepson's pickup, who'd been hanging on every word, took that as a Yes and broke out in whoops. Jepson winked at Mark, gunned the engine and tore on down the dark country road.

Doonie gave Mark a dour look. "For real?"

"Fuck no. Just jerking him around to get his hopes up, ruin his night."

SIXTY-ONE

They had to drive to Peru for dinner. It was the closest place where there was a restaurant open after 10 PM. It was also their best bet for finding last-minute lodging that wasn't a rural motel purgatory for their sins. Peru was a small city blessed with a long-established tourist trade, thanks to being located directly across the Illinois River from Starved Rock State Park. Situated on dramatic bluffs overlooking the river, with heavily forested trails leading to steep, narrow, rock-walled little glacial canyons, Starved Rock was the only thing anywhere near Chicago which did a passable imitation of scenic wilderness terrain.

This being a weeknight in late fall, when the weather usually runs the gamut from iffy to shitty, there was only a handful of customers in the restaurant, all of them at the bar. The dining room was empty. Beautiful; Mark and Doonie had a chance of getting through a meal in peace. Mark took a booth and Doonie headed for bladderland.

When Doonie returned there were double Makers on the table and Mark was on the phone completing a hotel reservation. They raised their glasses in a quick silent toast and dove into the bourbon.

"We got rooms on the top—the third—floor, facing away from the highway," Mark announced.

" 'Rooms?' " Doonie asked. The Department would only spring for a shared room.

"I'm treating myself to a private room," Mark explained. "I gotta sleep."

Doonie couldn't dispute the practicality of Mark's splurge. Phyl claimed she only married Doonie because his snoring sounded like her sexy cousin Jim's Harley, only louder.

Still, Doonie nailed Mark with a weary, skeptical look that said he wasn't exactly buying Mark's explanation.

"I'm not going to the Double Barrel," Mark vowed. "I swear, on a stack of hotel bedside bibles."

"You're a fuckin' atheist."

"If there was a God we would've caught Rudzutaka by now."

"If God didn't love me, I'd be stuck sharin' a room tonight with you wakin' me up every ten minutes to complain I was wakin' you up."

◆

They ate quickly, ignored the bar and went straight to the hotel. Good; a Doonie uninterested in a nightcap was a Doonie gripped by ditch-digger exhaustion.

They were given adjoining rooms on the third floor, as Mark requested.

Mark washed up, brewed coffee, took off his shoes, turned out the lights, sat upright in the bed, sipping caffeine and, courtesy of the thin hotel wall, listening to muffled fragments of Doonie's brief good-night call to Phyl. Doonie was going to be seriously pissed off at Mark tomorrow but it wouldn't last. Doon would understand there was no way Mark was gonna let him get near this, not with Doonie and Phyl having a mortgage, three kids in college and a herd of grandchildren lurking just over the horizon. Doonie wouldn't jeopardize all that for most of the cops he'd ridden with, but for Mark he'd insist.

Mark wondered if—when—he and JaneDoe got back together, had a family… Would he be taking this kind of risk to *maybe* clear a case? Or would he stay inside the law, and pass on making a move that might nail Rudzutaka before he killed again?

Mark heard Doonie begin to snore. Like a Harley with a faulty starter. When the blatting and backfiring relaxed into a sporadic soft sputter—the soundtrack of Doonie deep asleep—Mark put on his shoes and quietly left his room. Went to the parking lot, three stories down— the reason Mark booked a hotel instead of a motel, where the car would be parked right outside the room, and Doonie could've been jolted back to life by the car door slam, the ignition, the car driving away.

As Mark started the engine he glanced at the dashboard clock, which told Mark the same shit his watch had. It was already a little after midnight.

I'm counting on you, Downy Jepson. You better be waiting for me at the Double Barrel.

Mark drove back across the river, to Kasper's house.

SIXTY-TWO

When Rudy tried to put on the black wig it hurt so bad he nearly dropped the fucking thing, thanks to a red-flash-in-the-eyes punch-your-lungs-shut fireball that billowed from the gash on the back of Rudy's neck when he raised his hands above his head.

Goddamn motherfucking Trey. The one target Trey chooses cuts me, then Trey stiffs me... There should be a way, after I squeeze my money out of Trey, I get to kill him twice. Shit, gonna be stuck in Latvia long enough figure some way to do that.

A tight sadistic grin creased Rudy's face at the prospect of meeting that challenge.

Now all he had to do was meet the challenge of getting that fucking wig on his head. One Vicodin would do the trick, but he couldn't risk getting logy, he reminded himself for the fiftieth time.

But he also had to do the wig. No choice, now his picture was plastered all over the... Rudy glanced at the TV. Had it on with the sound off in case some new shit broke, but CNN was re-re-recycling footage from hours earlier at Kasper's. Specially shots of that smug prick Bergman makin' like it didn't bother him the search of Kasper's was a fail. Didn't even find something they could use to drag Kasper's sorry ass in for questioning. But there's Bergman telling the reporters, "No comment" and giving 'em this look, like he's on top of this, knows something we don't.

You don't know shit, Bergman. You got lucky and ID'd me too quick. But you're not gonna get me, CPD pinup boy. All you're gonna get is the whole world knowing Guntars Markuss Rudzutaka was the one kicked your ass, did five kills in your backyard and then's gone like a cool fuckin' breeze… *You're not gonna catch me you piece a shit cocksucker nobody catches me—**YAHGGGGGG**—*bellowing his way through the pain, Rudy hoisted the wig and yanked the itchy fucker down across his scalp.

When the panting, sweating and pain subsided, Rudy was able to adjust the wig until he got it to sit natural. Messed with the hair till it looked right. Put on a pair of black glasses with blank lenses. Checked himself out in the mirror.

Outstanding.

G'bye Rudy, hello Clark Kent.

SIXTY-THREE

Kasper's sovereign domain was dark, deserted. Downy Jepson's dream of stomping Mark, with his musketeers there to witness it—and if necessary save Jepson—was keeping Kasper and Jepson at that road house.

Unless they were on their way home.

Mark spent a few milliseconds considering the wisdom of returning to his hotel and sleeping his ass off. He drove past Kasper's sovereign domain and pulled onto a rutted dirt access road to the cornfield.

Mark put on gloves and walked to Kasper's house, moving fast. Pulled out the keyring he'd palmed from Kasper's bedside stash; truck key, house keys and a key to the drawers holding all the other keys. Mark let himself in and woke Kasper's computer, which the warrant had excluded.

The computer excluded Mark. It was passworded; no surprise, but had to be checked.

Mark exited the house, making sure all three front door locks were back in domain defense mode, and unlocked Kasper's red Explorer.

Mark switched on the GPS and selected Destination Memory.

The latest entry was Kasper's route to the gun store in Joliet that morning.

Kasper used the GPS to direct him to a store which was right next to a highway exit, as shown in a map on the store's website. Kasper was that uneasy about going anyplace unfamiliar.

This destination was also a place Kasper had gone in hopes of making a felony arms transaction, and yet he'd neglected to delete it.

Kasper's talent for getting rattled and sloppy was his most endearing quality.

Mark scrolled back through time. Two weeks ago Kasper mapped a route to Springfield, the state capital. Mark Googled the address. A strip club.

Mark scrolled through three months of even less exciting destinations before he found a hot one. A Walmart Supercenter outside Decatur, a hundred miles south. A place Kasper and his beard wouldn't bump into anyone who knew them. A place where Kasper could buy in bulk. One truckload would get Rudzutaka through multiple murders before he ran out of beer and toilet paper.

But Walmart was just the tease. The route had two legs.

The first went from Kasper's house south to the Walmart. The second returned north, but to an address eighteen miles west of Kasper's. Mark searched Destination Memory for other trips to that address; nothing.

Mark mapped it, satellite view, and zoomed in.

A house with an attached garage, on a small rise, tucked into a thick stand of trees. Out of view of the road. No other homes nearby.

SIXTY-FOUR

The satellite didn't lie. You couldn't see the house from the road. But when Mark drove past he saw light coming from between the trees. Someone was awake. Or just left a light on.

Mark drove a quarter-mile, eased to a halt on the shoulder of the two-lane road, silenced his phone, got out and closed the door gently as possible.

The sky was cloudy and moonless, which made Mark almost invisible as he walked along the blacktop, guided by the dull glow coming from between the trees. According to the satellite photo he'd be able to view the front of the house without leaving the cover of those trees.

A car engine started up—muffled, from inside a garage.

Mark froze. He was still twenty yards away.

A garage door clattered open and the engine noise got louder.

The sound of a moving vehicle and the flicker of headlights along the far side of the trees and down the driveway.

Mark pulled his gun and flattened himself in a shallow drainage ditch alongside the road. Held his breath, straining to hear which way the car turned when it reached the road—right, heading away from him—or left, which would take the driver past Mark, whom he probably wouldn't see, but then straight to Mark's car, which he couldn't miss.

The vehicle turned left. Tire noise hissed past Mark. Sounded smaller than an SUV. Mark slithered around to face the direction the vehicle had gone and lifted his head—

The vehicle braked and slowed almost to a stop by Mark's car—

At this distance and darkness the brake lights were two red blurs. Mark couldn't make out anything about the vehicle except it was a car. But Mark knew what was happening inside it. Rudzutaka's looking at the unmarked cop car, same model he'd seen on the tube today with Mark and Doonie sitting in it waiting for the FBI—

Rudzutaka punched the accelerator and tore ass—the car's bright red brake lights disappeared, replaced by dimmer, smaller tail lights.

Mark scrambled onto the road and ran, watching two dwindling red dots wink left and disappear before he got to his own damn car, gunned the engine and initiated pursuit of a vehicle with which he'd lost visual contact, a sedan or coupe whose color, make and model were Not A White Cherokee.

Had to stop Rudy before he reached the highway, where every sedan and coupe would fit that description.

SIXTY-FIVE

Rudy slowed to get a look at the parked—*It's THEIR fucking car—AND THEY'RE NOT IN IT*—Rudy twisted around, couldn't see shit—*GO!*—he stomped on it—the startled Civic burned rubber, fishtailed, centered itself and unleashed its inner Camaro.

Rudy checked the rearview—nothing there yet.

But soon! Gotta make it to the 80 before they—Goddamn cocksuckers how'd they find me—Fuck that!—My fucking tail lights!

Next intersection he got to Rudy heaved the Civic left onto a road that wouldn't put him on the 80 but did put him where the cops would lose sight of his tail li—

The CAR, did they see my CAR?! They coulda—if they were by the house they saw me pull out they know what I'm driving!—FUCK I need a new car before I get on the highway!... Calm down, break it down. Those Chicago pricks are calling for backup, I gotta shake 'em and get gone before the locals show up—A CHOPPER IF THEY GET A CHOPPER I'M THE ONLY THING MOVING OUT HERE!

Rudy doused his headlights but slowed only a fraction. The daytime running lights stayed on. At this speed the dim fuckers were nearly useless—*good,* hard for a chopper to spot—but threw just enough light for Rudy to keep heavy-footing it down the empty straight corn-country grid road.

He hit a cow.

SIXTY-SIX

Mark lit the siren and sparklers, floored it, pressed the inter-department preset on the scanner and raised a State Police dispatcher.

"Det. Mark Bergman Chicago PD I'm high-speed 10-80 on the Makro Killer, repeat Makro Killer, driving east from 121951 Jobaer Road, suspect turned north at first crossroad—WRONG—I just passed it, he turned at the next one—driving a sedan or other non-SUV passenger vehicle, make and color unknown. Request backup and a chopper fast—"

THUDSQUISH and a minor lurch then *thumpthumpthumpthump* as chunks of what he'd crushed spun off the tire, splattering inside the wheel-well. Mark braked and the car shimmied to screeching halt.

"Detective, you all right?" the dispatcher asked.

"Yes! Resuming pur—"

Mark gagged, loud convulsive throat-rippers, as a murderous eye-melting putridity incinerated the air and rotted Mark's innards—he shoved the door open leaned out and retched.

"Skunk," the dispatcher noted, for the record.

Mark wiped his mouth on his sleeve opened the windows slammed the door shut yelled "Get that bird in the air!" and resumed his high-speed 10-80.

SIXTY-SEVEN

Rudy only hit the cow's hindquarter but the goddamn thing was a meat wall. The impact flung the speeding Civic into a 360-spinout off the road, which ended with a sadistic jolt when its rear fender pinwheeled into a fencepost.

The airbag did its job, kept Rudy from fracturing his face on the windshield and his ribs on the steering wheel, but the stitches on the back of his neck tore loose. Warm wetness was oozing into the back of his shirt, though crash adrenalin was muting the pain from Rudy's re-opened wound, and from his right kneecap, which had bashed into the underside of the dashboard. The adrenalin did fuck-all to mute the agonized pleading of the shattered bovine thrashing on the road, unbelievably ugly and insanely loud cow screams, almost loud enough to drown out the distant shriek of a police siren.

Rudy limped over to the cow and shot it until it shut up, and instantly the siren sounded louder and closer. He hustled back to the Civic and saw, in the glow from the surviving running light, a crushed front right fender. Beneath it, the wheel was still attached to the axle, but bent at an ugly angle.

Now he could see headlights and flashers, distant but closing fast.

Rudy yanked open the passenger door, unzipped the athletic bag that was on the seat, pulled a weapon out of the bag and took cover.

Hadda wait till Bergman and Dunegan got close enough so he could kill them without killing their car.

SIXTY-EIGHT

Driving this speed with the windows open the car was a rolling freezer. Mark turned the heat on full blast then quickly shut it down as the heater began pumping warm skunk stench through the vents.

"Any visual?" the dispatcher asked.

"No." Mark was beginning to wonder if he'd hung a left onto the wrong—he spotted a faint glow up the road. "Maybe."

As Mark sped closer it became obvious the glow wasn't moving. A few seconds later he got near enough to see, hit his brakes, screeched to a halt and pulled his gun.

"What you got," the dispatcher asked.

Mark panned the car's spotlight across the scene. "Light blue Civic run off the left side the road, damaged. Dead cow in the northbound lane. No sign of the suspect but I'm not close enough to see inside the car." He swept the spotlight across the field behind the Civic.

"Do not approach. Remain in position until backup—"

Rudy raised up from behind the cow, firing a Mac-10 on full automatic.

Mark went flat a split second before his windshield disintegrated—slugs ricocheted around the cabin—Mark stayed low, threw the shift into reverse, pressed the accelerator, tried to hold the wheel steady and hoped the car stayed on the road long enough to get out of range—

Both front tires blew out and the engine stalled.

SIXTY-NINE

hit. Rudy could tell from the sound the sonsabitches didn't stop close enough for him to be sure he could spray only the front seat and hit nothing but cops. Hadda wait till they got out. Rudy stayed hunkered down behind the cow, listening for the sound of car doors opening. Rudy tensed…

No doors.

Then the rasp of a dispatcher's voice on the radio—too far away to make out words but Rudy didn't have to—dispatcher'd be giving ETA for the goddamn backup—*move!*

Rudy sprang up—the cop car was thirty feet away but there was enough dashboard light for him to see—*there's only one cop!* Rudy put a burst through the windshield, the cop went down but Rudy couldn't tell if he'd hit him—a second later the car jerked into reverse—Rudy emptied the clip—bullets hammered the grill, the tires burst, the car slewed to a halt.

Rudy popped the empty clip and slammed home a new 32-rounder. That cop behind the wheel wasn't fat, so it's Bergman—

The cop car's passenger door flew open, Rudy pulled the trigger and the piece of shit Mac did its famous trick of spitting three rounds and jamming—Rudy dropped it, pulled his nine and fired at the car as he rushed back to the Civic. The fuckin' indestructible Honda engine started first try and he eased it back onto the road, the front wheel wobbling, but it didn't snap off.

Bullets smacked into the trunk, Rudy floored it, a slug smashed his rear windshield, whistled by his head and went out the front wind-shield—the Civic wobbled and shuddered on down the road. The bent front wheel didn't come off, but was gonna, and the faster Rudy drove the worse the wobble got. Hadda slow down, now he's outta of range of that fuckin' deadeye—*nearly nailed me that distance in a moving car.*

Rudy reluctantly eased off on the gas. The car slowed, the front wheel wobble diminished and Rudy's shit tightened. It's not like Bergman's gonna catch up to him on foot. Rudy just needed the fuckin' Honda to hold together a little longer. He turned right, onto a road that became the east entrance to Starved Rock, near the park's campground, where there were cars parked next to tents containing the owners and keys—

A distant but horrible metallic screeching—Rudy looked in the rear view—the cop car was coming after him, driving on its two front rims, spraying sparks.

But not moving too fast. Rudy could outrun the bastard. Depending which car came apart first.

SEVENTY

Mark threw the car into reverse but bullets ruptured the front tires, the engine stalled and the car went into a backward S-shaped skid. Mark, flattened across the front seats, stabbed at the unseen brake with his left foot. The car jolted to a halt. So did the firing—a Mac empties in seconds. But reloads almost as fast.

*Rudy'll come here to make sure—can't sit up fast enough to spot him and shoot before he does—**Make him stop and waste ammo**—*Mark reached up and shoved the passenger door open—

Three bullets pinged the door—

A muffled curse then a clatter that might've been a weapon hitting the pavement—*Mac jammed and he tossed it?* Mark—

Two 9-mil gunshots ripped the quiet. One slug hit the car, one missed. Mark listened hard for approaching footsteps—two more shots hit the car—another pause, then more shots, but all went wide—

A car door slammed, an engine revved, Mark sat up. His one surviving headlight threw just enough light to make out the shape of a shuddering Civic driving away. Mark braced his hands on top of the steering wheel and pumped rounds at the gradually disappearing Civic. Didn't kill it or Rudy.

Mark turned his ignition—the starter went whupwhupwhup-whup, the engine stayed silent. He tried again. On the fourth try the engine coughed, started and quit. Sixth time was the charm. Mark accelerated cautiously to see how the car handled.

Like a drunk having a seizure.

Steering began to disintegrate if he took it past twenty-seven mph. Even at that speed the deflated tires shredded and sent fat hunks of rubber flubbing into the darkness, and the industrial shriek from the bare rims chewing pavement drilled Mark's eardrums. The rest of him was buffeted by a freezing gale blowing through emptiness where the windshield used to be. Mark concentrated on the distant glow of the Civic. He wasn't closing on it but wasn't losing ground.

Mark reached for the radio. Useless, a ricochet had shattered it. He reached into his pocket for his phone—gone—must've fallen out when he dove. Mark flicked the dome lights on. The phone was gone—under one of the seats? Wasn't gonna goddamn stop to search.

He noticed the siren and flashers weren't on. He hit the switch. Nothing happened.

Mark yawned, a long deep one, and nearly nodded. The adrenaline from the firefight was evaporating, Mark was leaking stamina, and his two days on two hours of sleep decided this was the moment to catch up with him, maybe faster than he was catching up with Rudy. Mark goosed the gas, the speedometer leapt to thirty-three and the front end began to buck.

Fighting to keep the car on the road would keep him awake.

SEVENTY-ONE

Rudy was into the state park and approaching the turnoff to the campground when his bent front wheel got the shudders. Rudy had to slow down even more. He checked the rearview—*Bergman's catching up*—Rudy hit the gas, the Civic shook like a paint mixer and skated sideways—Rudy braked, regained control but SHIT! He'd skidded past the campground turnoff and was headed up a winding road lined with dense forest, with the cop car getting bigger in his rearview... *Good. Sooner I kill that fuckshit sooner I can turn this heap around and go grab a real car.*

Okay. First thing was to position this heap so it blocks the road, with its passenger side between Bergman and him.

Rudy hesitated. The only time he'd shot anybody who could shoot back, it was a bipolar, ketamine-riddled, hallucinating 17-year old who was standing in the middle of a street firing wildly at a swarm of flying zombie orderlies.

BANG—a hard metallic **BANG,** coming from the road behind Rudy—he looked back—Bergman's front axle must've cracked, 'cause the steering died and Rudy saw the cop car heave itself into a guard rail.

Rudy continued up around the next curve to put himself out of sight and out of range in case the deadeye motherfucker was still functional. Rudy would take care of that when he drove by on his way back to the turnoff.

He eased the Civic to a halt. The two-lane road was too narrow for a U-turn. Had to make a Y-turn. He swung left then slowly angled right, not too sharply so as not to stress the bent wheel. Worked fine.

He put the car in reverse and began to back up, gently.

The bent wheel broke off. *Goddamn fuckin'—nevermind! Gotta start walkin' to the goddamn campground. Right after I finish Det. Famous-Ass Fool who put himself between me and my new ride.*

Rudy loaded a fresh clip into his Nine. Got out of the car gingerly, grimacing. The dog bite in Rudy's leg was wide awake, but wasn't shit compared to the bleeding trench across the back of his neck—*Fuck that! Think what's the safest way to do this. Not the road. Come up on Bergman through the trees—*

Rudy caught a faint whiff of skunk—looked around, saw a shadowy shape warily edging around the bend in the road, aiming a shotgun.

Rudy snapped into a crouch behind the fender, firing at Bergman as he went.

SEVENTY-TWO

The airbag saved Mark from any injury except an airbag burn on his nose.

He found his phone. It was under the passenger seat, had hit some hunk of metal down there and shattered. So much for telling the cavalry where to find him.

Mark popped the trunk, grabbed the shotgun and began jogging up the road. The Civic wasn't moving fast, and maybe its bent wheel would collapse before he did.

Ten yards from the starting line Mark was panting and the shotgun was weighing fifty pounds. He had to slow to a half-jog, then to an urgent trudge. He took long deep breaths and *ah shit*, finally noticed the skunk stench had taken up residence in his clothing—

There was a faint red glow of tail lights, from somewhere on the far side of an upcoming curve. The glow wasn't moving. Mark trudged faster.

He heard the Civic start to move, then stop. Mark paused, listened. He was close now, the Civic was just out of sight around the curve—he heard the car begin to roll again—there was an aggrieved **KRRRK!** followed by the dull crunch of the Civic's front bumper landing on the pavement.

Mark crept forward—might've heard a car door open, wasn't sure—he froze. Didn't hear a door close. He cautiously leaned his head out, trying to peek around the curve. Was still a little too far away. He shouldered the street sweeper and edged forward, following the fat black gun barrel around the curve—

Rudy was standing behind the car, staring in Mark's direction—the instant he saw Mark, Rudy fired and dropped.

Mark fired but Rudy was already down behind the rear fender—Rudy stuck his arm over the trunk and fired blind in Mark's direction.

Mark discouraged that with two quick loads of buckshot at the rear of the car—Rudy yanked his arm back—Mark went down on his stomach and fired his final two blasts at ground level, shooting under the car so the buckshot had a chance to get at Rudy.

Mark started to reload the shotgun. As he was about to insert the second shell he heard the harsh *crack* and *snap* of Rudy bashing his way through the dense weeds and bushes lining the far side of the road—

Mark jammed the shell home, jumped up and ran past the Civic—Rudy was into the trees now but still making a racket crashing through dense forest in the dark.

Mark hopped the guardrail and pulled out his flashlight. He spotted trampled weeds and damaged bushes where the big man had gone in. Once into the woods there was a sporadic debris trail with a few dots of blood. But it was rough going. In many places the oaks and hickories were crowded together, and the bastards had sprouted branches starting at knee level, on terrain serrated by a series of steep slopes down toward the riverside canyons. After a couple of minutes bulling and skidding downward through the tilted arboreal obstacle course, Mark was bruised and blown. He reached a more merciful patch where the ground leveled out and the trees were slightly farther apart. There was no more debris or blood trail, and Mark still hadn't caught sight of Rudy—but Rudy's noise said he was nearby and slowing.

The woods went silent.

Mark stopped and, keeping the flashlight pressed alongside the stock of the shotgun, panned it across the woods ahead. He began to hear a feeble wail of far-off sirens—then the judder of a chopper heading this way fast. But not a peep out of Rudy—*BUT RUDY CAN SEE MY*—Mark doused the flashlight—

Two bullets slammed into a tree next to Mark and a third kicked up dirt in front of him—Mark pumped two shotgun blasts in the direction of Rudy's muzzle flashes, and swung into a crouch behind the tree, which was just wide enough to be better than nothing. Mark dropped the empty shotgun and pulled his Sig. He and Rudy fired at each other's muzzle flashes—

From nearby, the eggbeater thwack of the chopper settling into a hover above the wrecked vehicles on the road—

Wasn't so loud Mark couldn't make out the steel slap of Rudy's gun dry-firing, an enraged grunt and a second later the sound of Rudy blindly fleeing—

Mark chased Rudy's noise—

The chopper began slowly cruising above the close-packed woods, probing with its spotlight. Almost useless. It was one of those years when the park's nearly opaque canopy of leaves was hanging on well into November.

But the leaves did fuck-all to block out the roar of the chopper as it approached Mark, obliterating Rudy's sound-trail.

The chopper waddled by without spotting either of them, the rotor thunder faded—

Mark heard Rudy rushing up behind him and turned—

Rudy barreled into him, grabbing Mark's throat and the wrist of his gun hand, yanking it upward as he slammed Mark into a tree, and the back of Mark's hand smashed against a branch and his gun arced away into the darkness.

Rudy had Mark's head pinned against the tree with his huge right hand clamped on Mark's throat, throttling him. Rudy let go of Mark's wrist and threw a roundhouse left at Mark's head at the same moment Mark kicked him in the balls. Rudy doubled over but didn't let go of Mark's throat, yanking Mark's head down so Rudy's left fist missed it and punched the tree so hard Mark heard the knuckles crunch.

Rudy straightened up roaring in pain but didn't let go. Mark grabbed Rudy's right arm and swiveled hard, trying a judo throw but he was exhausted and Rudy had too much size/weight/muscle, he wouldn't launch over Mark's shoulder. Rudy stumbled around Mark, pulling Mark with him. Mark didn't resist, he surged into Rudy's momentum and used it to whip Rudy around, but Rudy held tight and they stagger-whirled around each other in a tottering caveman waltz that spun them into a small clearing, where Rudy's foot swung down into something metal—Mark's gun, which went off with a startling blast as Rudy punted it away. Rudy tried to see where the gun went but that wasn't happening and Mark was trying to kick Rudy's leg— Rudy yanked Mark to him, clamped his left arm around Mark—didn't need his ruined hand for that—let go of Mark's throat, tightened his massive arms around Mark in a crushing bear hug, pinning Mark's arms, lifted him off his feet and began jerking sharply, trying to break Mark's ribs and spine—

Mark butted Rudy—the grip loosened for a moment, which was enough for Mark to free his left arm and grab at Rudy's eyes—Rudy turned his head away and pulled down sharply on Mark—Mark's hand slid to the base of Rudy's neck, Mark felt a bandage, dug his fingers into a wound and yanked.

Rudy howled, flung Mark to the ground.

A heavy rotor thump as the chopper banked into a turn.

Mark, exhausted and groaning in pain, rolled over and started to lever himself upright. Rudy kicked Mark in the gut and Mark collapsed face-down.

The rotor noise was deafening and—Rudy, exhausted and groaning in agony, gathered himself and pulled back his foot for a more vicious kick—the spotlight found the clearing—

Rudy looked—the spotlight was sweeping across the ground toward them, Rudy caught a glimpse of Mark's gun and started for it—

Mark flung his arm out and grabbed at Rudy's ankle—snagged just enough of it to throw Rudy off balance.

The spotlight followed Rudy as he staggered forward, fighting to stay upright, lost that fight and started to go down, but with a final crazed effort hurled himself into a headfirst dive at the suddenly well-lit gun. Rudy landed short of it, but, screaming, willed his right arm to stretch far enough to put fingertips on the grip. Rudy scrambled to his feet with the Sig in his hand but his back to Mark.

Rudy whirled around so he could shoot Mark but the ground

under Rudy's rear foot crumbled and Rudy lurched backward, arms flailing, eyes terror-wide and he disappeared.

A baritone infant shriek pierced the chopper thunder then cut off abruptly.

Mark wrenched himself upright, hobbled to the rim and looked down. It was one of the deeper canyons, a seventy-foot drop. Rudy was in the spotlight, flat on his back, a dark halo of blood spreading around his head.

Mark heard voices. Yelling his name. He stepped back from the rim, turned and saw two state troopers, whose arrival had been masked by the chopper's relentless hammering.

A trooper put his arm around Mark's shoulders, ushered him away from the precipice and solicitously yelled, "ARE YOU HURT?"

Mark shook his head, no.

"CAN YOU WALK?"

Mark nodded. The trooper radioed the good news to his CO, then escorted Mark back through the woods and up to the road.

As they were climbing over the guardrail and onto the road, a county police cruiser screeched to halt. Its back door flew open, Doonie got out, saw Mark and stomped over to him, glowering.

The trooper told Doonie, "He's okay."

"Good," Doonie muttered, and angrily hauled back his hand to slap Mark.

Doonie paused, hand raised. Mark waited to accept his due. The trooper watched, rapt, knowing he'd lucked into a lifetime anecdote.

Doonie wrinkled his nose in disgust. Said, "Get out of those fuckin' clothes and burn 'em," and gave Mark a gentle ceremonial slap upside the head.

SEVENTY-THREE

Tonty Canyon! Not only did the monomaniac motherfucker nearly get himself killed again, he did it at Tonty, JaneDoe's favorite Starved Rock canyon, and he dumped the Makro Killer in it, so now that sweet serene little canyon's gonna be infested with tourists flopping flat on their backs to take selfies laying in the, check it out dude, exact spot where the famous serial killer corpse landed, and then scratch their names in those beautiful rock walls, and also JaneDoe really wanted to call Mark to tell him she was glad that this time he didn't get shot or beaten into a Picasso. But also she was more pissed off at him than ever, for proving how right she was about him.

But… c'mon. She was an adult, she could manage to get through one phone call.

Yeah. Admit it, this total fatwa against any Mark communication was pathetic. There was nothing to be scared of.

Yes there was. A conversation, even a short, normal—it might lead to something. Reconciliation and heartshredding disaster. Mark wasn't gonna change, this was gonna keep happening and she'd keep being his collateral damage.

JaneDoe closed her laptop so she wouldn't watch that gushy BBC News video just one more time.

She turned her phone off.

She turned it back on.

Her phone gave her a blank innocent look, as if the condescending iShit wasn't enjoying this.

SEVENTY-FOUR

One of the keys to having a decent life is having a decent boss. When Mark got back to the bullpen late the next afternoon Lt. Husak gave him time to touch base with everybody, get some love for still being alive, before summoning Mark to his office to ask him the *What the fuck?* question. The one Mark had dodged last night by using the old two-days-without-sleep, firefight, hand-to-hand combat, three hours in the ER excuse.

No getting away with that one today. But when Mark walked in, Husak's expression wasn't angry or suspicious, it was maybe one percent more mournful than usual. The man was a rock.

Mark wasn't. He lowered himself into a chair slowly, in sections.

"Should you be here?" Husak asked.

"Broken skin but no fracture," Mark said, indicating where the back of his head hit a tree. "And no concussion, which kind of annoyed the doctor." He lifted his swollen, discolored right hand, which had slammed into a branch. "Ugly, but—" he wiggled his fingers, "—no broken bones." Mark pointed to the spot where a boot dug into his abdomen. "There's a museum-quality bruise, but no cracked ribs, no ruptured organs. Just wasn't Rudy's night. Heard about the gun?"

Husak shook his head.

"Turned out my gun was empty. Rudy killed himself getting his hands on a useless gun."

Husak stared across his desk at Mark. "Funny, the way some things happen... How'd you happen to be outside Rudy's house the moment he was leaving?"

"Deeply dumb luck. I couldn't sleep, too frustrated our search of

Kasper's place didn't turn up the Redhawk. The simplest possibility was Kasper gave the gun to his pal Downy Jepson—the guy whose truck Kasper was in when they went to celebrate. Jepson would be shitfaced by the time he drove Kasper home. I figured I'd wait for them there, pull 'em over, DUI Jepson and search his truck."

"Uh-huh," Husak grunted, not buying it.

"Yeah," Mark conceded, "I was stupid tired. Was halfway to Kasper's before it hit me, might not be a great idea to pull over two heavily armed drunks in the dead of night on an empty road. Or maybe I'd be looking at a whole convoy of heavily armed drunks. So I cranked the music and just drove around, not thinking about anything, which is sometimes how I manage to think of something."

"Like Rudzutaka's address?"

"Like stopping to take a leak, middle of nowhere. I'm standing behind the car watering a cornfield when a car pulls out of a driveway, starts to drive, then I hear it stop when it gets to me. I look over my shoulder, see the driver—Rudy's looking at me—he hits the gas, and it's on."

Husak gave Mark an unhappy wilted lettuce grin.

Mark said, "I know what you're thinking. Something like, during the search of Kasper's house, an FBI agent might've let me examine Kasper's bag of duplicate keys, and a set could've fallen into my pocket. Which would've made it possible to go back to Kasper's and take a peek at stuff the warrant forgot to authorize. Like his truck's trip computer."

Mark's turn to go silent and wait while Husak ran the variables.

If they told the truth about Mark's illegal search, any evidence against Kasper resulting from that search—say, Kasper's number in Rudy's phone, or a record of payments from Rudy to Kasper—would never see the light of court. But for sure it'd give Kasper grounds to sue the Department and the FBI. It'd also make Kasper this year's poster child for white male patriot victims of Deep State abuse; had to be some personal appearance fees in that.

Worse, the truth would embarrass the CPD and FBI. And damage the PR value of the CPD's star attraction, whose popularity had gone through a skyscraper roof in the twelve hours since the Makro Killer crash-landed at the bottom of Tonty Canyon.

So… Was there any kind of chance they could sell Mark's unlikely—fucking preposterous—story of catching a serial killer by taking history's luckiest leak?

Maybe. The Department could spin it as being the kind of inside baseball you only hear in cop bars. Tales of the coincidences, accidents and bolt-of-lightning luck that do happen on the job. Unbelievable shit that's totally somewhat true.

The public would love for that lucky leak story to be for real. If there's anyone they might buy it from it was Det. Bergman.

That went double for the media. Mark was good for business.

Sure, most people with an IQ anywhere in triple digits wouldn't buy Mark's story. But many wouldn't care. The niceties of how Mark located Rudy didn't weigh much compared to the fact he'd put the Makro Killer out of business. And done it in a way which spared tax-payers a lengthy expensive trial, and a long boring wait before they could enjoy the story's satisfying end.

On the other hand, the Department might see less risk and more upside in turning Mark into high-profile proof of how the bad old days were over, today's CPD is a clean, by-the-books outfit. Thanks for your service, Detective, now go fall on your sword.

Husak said, "The specifics of how you determined the suspect's whereabouts are confidential and will remain so until the investigation is complete."

"Understood."

Invoking the sacrament of procedural silence would buy the Superintendent time to decide where to place his bet.

SEVENTY-FIVE

Rudy had been carrying two phones. Both were passworded and so was his laptop. He also had a thumb drive, zipped into a concealed compartment in his belt. The drive was encrypted. The FBI's safecrackers were digital-twiddling their locks.

A fanatically thorough processing of Rudy's house was a bust. The closest thing to evidence was a raised middle finger Rudy left for them in the basement: a smashed and burned hard drive from his laptop.

In the garage they found an intact White Cherokee. Which did turn out to be Vanora Yard's. But there was no trace of her in the house, or anywhere on or under the property. Rudy had taken care to dispose of her elsewhere.

But there was one LaSalle County resident who'd seen Vanora. Spoken to her. Rented his house to her.

◆

Bo Nantz wasn't surprised when Mark and Doonie showed up at the modest apartment where Nantz and his wife lived, on the outskirts of Peru. When Nantz opened the door he said, "I understand why you're here. Can we talk in your car?" His wife had a degenerative nerve disease, was confined to a wheelchair and already terribly stressed by finding out she'd been the Makro Killer's landlady.

When they got in the car Nantz said, "Let me explain how this happened." He was a retired insurance broker whose nest egg got hammered in the 2008 crash. Nantz went back to work, but, being 67, part-time was all he could find. Between the mortgage and upkeep on the house, plus his wife's medical bills, they had to put their home up for sale. But it was old, needed work, and Nantz got no offers that wouldn't leave him underwater.

No one would lease the house long-term at the price Nantz needed. Which turned out to be a blessing. He looked into this Air B&B thing. Bingo. During Starved Rock's peak season tourists would pay insane nightly and weekly rates, enough to keep the Nantzes afloat.

"We went from can't afford to keep the house to can't afford to sell it, you know?"

"Uh-huh," Mark said. "So, Rudzutaka?"

"I never met him, never knew he existed, I swear."

"Who rented the house?"

"A woman. She said her name was Ann Smith. Told me, doing business stuff online made her nervous, asked if we could please meet in person. Really very sweet, you know?"

"This woman?" Doonie asked, showing him a picture of Vanora Yard.

Nantz nodded. "She wanted the house for three months—offered substantially more than I was asking—but didn't want to sign any papers. Offered cash up front plus a security deposit."

"She have any other conditions?" Mark asked.

"That, um—privacy. Complete—I was not to show up at all unless she requested it. Said she'd just been through something, and needed time alone."

"That didn't make you suspicious?" Doonie wondered. "Even a little?"

Nantz shrugged.

"Did you see our wanted bulletin on TV?" Mark asked. "The one with this picture in it?" Pointing to the Vanora Yard photo Nantz had just recognized.

Nantz nodded.

"So why didn't you do your civic duty, give us a jingle?" Doonie wanted to know.

"Didn't recognize her—I was mainly looking at Rudzutaka—and that woman in your picture is blonde, the woman I met was brunette…"

Doonie gave Nantz his best disappointed scowl.

"And… she was… provocatively dressed. I didn't… wasn't always looking at her face."

"Yeah," Mark sympathized, "impressive cleavage."

"Dear God," Nantz whispered.

"Which she shared with you," Mark said.

"N-no no."

"Y-yes yes. That's why you pretended to believe her 'I vant to be alone' bullshit."

Nantz bit his lower lip. "Only twice. The second time we met she showed me a video of us the first time. That's when she warned me I was never to come near the property, if I did my wife would see the video. Then she took off her blouse and we did it again… She promised we'd have a third go if I behaved right."

"So you fuckin' did recognize her in the wanted bulletin," Doonie sighed.

Nantz nodded. Then, deflated, "She was with *him*. I didn't want to die." Nantz looked back and forth between Doonie and Mark. "You think you'll find her?" he asked, hopefully. 'Cause if Vanora was alive, and if Nantz was still alive when Vanora got out of prison, maybe she and her cleavage would make good on their promise to reward him for behaving right.

❖

Mark called Kalinda Yard and gave her the tortuously inconclusive news about Vanora. Circumstances suggested Rudy killed Vanora. But there was no proof she was dead, no proof she was alive.

"That's my big sister," Kalinda replied, with a lifetime's worth of love and resentment.

SEVENTY-SIX

The Supe's risk/benefit analysis came out in favor of not smudging the Department's triumph. He decided to pretend Mark's cornfield piss meet-cute with the MK was plausible.

So did nearly everybody else. After seeing video of Mark's bullet-riddled cruiser and Rudy's bullet-riddled Civic, and dramatic shots peering down into Tonty Canyon, and even more dramatic shots starting at the canyon floor where Rudy went splat, then panning up the sheer rock walls to show the height from which Rudy flew, the media and their audiences were enormously less interested in the enormously coincidental way Mark found Rudy than in the chase, gunfire and fight that followed it.

The Supe did a presser at which he delivered a lengthy update, then invited Mark to the mic to take questions. Two questions were about the urinary coincidence, seventeen were about the violence. Mark was ready with dry, concise answers. The press enjoyed his camera-ready sound bites, and Mark enjoyed not being pressed for details.

But the final question had nothing to do with that night.

"Have you found anything that explains why Rudzutaka targeted Makro?"

Mark, for the first time, hesitated. "That part of the investigation is still ongoing."

◆

When they got offstage the Supe pulled Mark aside and asked, "Anything indicate Rudy wasn't just the usual sack of shit psycho following his bliss?"

"Money. This was some elaborate, expensive bliss. I don't think

Rudy could've financed it."

"His rich groupie?"

"One, Vanora's financials don't show a penny out of place. Two, her sister says Vanora's only core conviction was the man always picks up the tab."

"And the FBI hasn't cracked Rudy's thumb drive yet?"

Mark shook his head. His phone rang. He went to silence it—

The Supe gestured for Mark to go ahead and look at his phone, patted Mark on the shoulder and walked away.

Mark saw who the call was from and put the phone to his ear. "Hi. How you doing?"

"I'm… doing better," Danny Gold told him. "I, uh… I want to thank you for what you did."

Killing his father's murderer. "Well… no thanks necessary. And actually he killed himself by being in a big hurry to grab a gun and use it."

"Well—I also want to tell you I'm glad you didn't get hurt."

"Thank you."

"I mean it. Yeah I was really angry when you wouldn't promise to shoot him—and I know you didn't do this because I asked. I get that you'd rather arrest him. But, for me, it's better the bastard's dead. It does… help."

"For that I'm glad… But y'know, if we'd arrested him, we'd have a better chance of finding out why he did it."

"Would that bring Dad back?"

"No." Mark resisted the temptation to ask if Rudy being dead had brought Dad back. "I'm glad you called. I know it wasn't easy."

"Wasn't that hard. We don't agree on everything but… We're both aiming at the same thing, saving lives."

Mark took too long deciding how to reply.

Danny insisted, with tormented determination, "Universal concealed carry is going to save lives."

"Not nearly as many as it would get killed."

Danny's turn to go hunting for a way to not say what he wanted to. Settled on "Bye," and hung up.

SEVENTY-SEVEN

W hat's your response been to Rudzutaka being gone?" the therapist, Dr. Adrienne Bonfante, asked the Makro Killer contingent.

Clara Cahill, Nate Gold and Brooklyn McVay always sat together at the support group for the families of murder victims. Brooklyn, the 21-year-old fiancée of the MK's first kill, always sat in the middle, cocooned between the middle-aged Clara and Nate.

"I'm glad—relieved," Brooklyn corrected herself in a near-whisper. "So, so relieved there won't be any more…" Brooklyn teared up. Clara squeezed Brooklyn's hand. "Aren't you?" Brooklyn asked Clara.

"I went down on my knees," Clara confirmed. Didn't specify that in addition to offering thanks, she'd implored God to not let the AGA use Roz in any more of their vile gun peddling videos, to not let them desecrate Roz ever again. To not place temptation in Clara's path.

"But," Clara continued, "Rudzutaka's death wasn't what I wanted. I wanted that man arrested and tried. Forced to confront what he'd done—and me. In court, face to face, every day."

"No," Brooklyn moaned, "not me. I was dreading being in a room with him—but I wouldn't have been able to stay away. So I'm glad—relieved—he's dead."

Brooklyn and Clara looked at Nate.

Nate gave a philosophical grunt. "I feel both ways. Six different ways. Glad he's dead and pleased it was a terrifying painful one, God help me. And grateful he'll never hurt anyone else, and I won't have to relive it all in court, in public. Yet, I also feel cheated I won't get—what you were saying Clara—to be face to face, watching him go through it… But at the same time I'm relieved there *won't* be a trial… Had so many fantasies what I'd do to him… This way there's no chance I could sneak a ceramic knife or one of those 3-D printed guns into the courtroom, and… " Nate gave a guilty shrug.

Brooklyn touched Nate's shoulder and flashed a shy grin. "Thank you. Helps to know I'm not the only one who thought, a lot, about doing… that kind of stuff."

"Aw Hon, there's nobody here who hasn't," said a woman seated across the circle, whose sister and nephews had been bludgeoned to death by her brother-in-law.

"Not just that," said a young man whose grandfather had been sitting in his living room when his throat exploded thanks to a stray bullet from a drive-by. "I'm bettin' we all got some down and dirty fantasies, lot nastier than regular shooting or stabbing. Right?" He looked at Clara and repeated, "Right?" making it a good-humored, sympathetic tease.

The group was riveted as Clara considered her response. Since joining the group she'd been the quietest and angriest one in the room.

Clara, for the first time, showed them something resembling a grin. "Wanna have a contest to see who wins for Most Gruesome Revenge Fantasy?"

"Oh yeeeeaaah," the young man crooned, and burst out in delighted cackles, as did most of the group. Two people managed only wan, wary smiles.

The group looked to their therapist, a tall woman with the wide almond eyes, long nose, plush lips and indecipherable empathy of an oracle painted by one of her Etruscan ancestors.

"Dr. Bonfante," Brooklyn asked, "can we—a Most Gruesome contest is all right, isn't it—would you be the judge?"

"No I will not. If you do this, all of you have to vote on the winner. And nobody's obliged to be a contestant," Dr. Bonfante assured the wan smilers. "In fact, if anyone's uncomfortable with this, we won't even—"

"No no please I really want to hear," a wan smiler protested. The other wan smiler seconded that emotion.

"Okay." Dr. Bonfante looked at Clara. "This was your suggestion. Would you care to go first?"

Clara said, "Um… I think we should put our names in a hat, and you should draw one at a time."

"Everyone good with that?" Dr. Bonfante asked.

Everyone was.

Clara went around the circle and contestants dropped folded pieces of paper into her hat, a stylish black-on-black Sox cap Roz had given her last March, with opening day Sox tickets and a card that read, *Greater love hath no Cubs fan than this, that a woman might lay down her credit card for a heathen Sox fan, and here's the goddamn proof.*

Clara walked over to Dr. Bonfante, held out the hat and instructed her, "Close your eyes and don't you dare pick me first."

"I'll do my best." Dr. Bonfante closed her eyes. Dramatically covered her closed eyes with her hand. Turned her head away. Blindly extended a lengthy elegant arm in the direction of the hat, and missed.

Everyone laughed, even Clara.

Nate and Brooklyn gave each other a check-in glance: *Yeah me too, I'm lump in the throat happy. Clara's gonna be okay.*

Clara guided Dr. Bonfante's hand into the Sox cap. The therapist stirred the folded scraps of paper. She chose one.

Clara's and Nate's phones vibrated. Nate silenced his. Clara took hers out, read the alert, unlocked the phone and thumbed a link. A video began to play.

Nate murmured, "Shit." Brooklyn dug her fingers into Nate's wrist.

Only Clara could see the screen but the sound was clear enough. It was Danny Gold's voice, saying the Makro Killer being gone was a good thing, but nothing had changed. "Our need and our right to have a way to protect ourselves and our loved ones hasn't changed. Our need to honor the Makro victims hasn't changed. Kody Wallace. David Gold. Roz—" Clara shut off her phone.

"Clara…" Dr. Bonfante said.

Clara turned her hat upside down and dumped the contestants' names into the doctor's hands. She put the hat on, went back to her chair, put on her coat and picked up her purse.

"Please stay," Brooklyn urged. "Talk to us."

Clara blessed Brooklyn's forehead with a kiss, and walked out.

SEVENTY-EIGHT

The Deputy Minority Leader of the Illinois General Assembly was in Chicago and Trey Fister was in the Deputy Minority Leader, thrumming like an industrial sewing machine on speed. Or in this case four bumps of coke.

Trey gushed and spasmed, Evie Burnett gushed and groaned. Trey collapsed, slid off and they lay side by side, panting, sweating, oozing and evaluating.

"You're in," Evie rasped, between gulps of air, "an enthusiastic… mood, even… for you."

"That's how excited I am to see you."

"Gallant," Evie deadpanned.

Her cynicism wasn't misplaced. What Trey was so stoked about was Rudy being dead, for five whole days, and no cop had knocked on Trey's door. When the news broke Bergman had changed Rudy from a nightmare into a corpse, Trey's response was exultation at being saved from spending his life waiting for Rudy to show up with a cleaver. Trey's second response was a 24/7 mini-migraine throb from wondering if the cops were busy uncovering a connection between him and Rudy. But this morning Trey's paranoia gave up and went home after it watched the CPD's latest update: There was no evidence Rudy had any accomplice other than Vanora Yard. And, despite intensive investigation by the CPD and FBI, the Makro Killer's motive remained a mystery. *It always will, 'cause look who wrote-produced-directed this sick OG master-fucking-piece. Trey shoots, Trey scores!*

"Evie, I was so excited to see you I walked in and tore your clothes off without asking about the Senate," Trey protested. "Where we at with the vote count?"

"One. My Senate colleagues flip one more Dem and we're there."

Trey complimented Evie with a deep appreciative suck on her nipple. She said, "The problem is, all the remaining the Dems are hardcore libs."

"Some of them have gotta be getting enough calls from constituents demanding ELE to make 'em worry about re-election."

"Not yet. In their districts the anti-ELE numbers are still solid. And, while your Danny Gold campaign has been brilliant... It may have plateaued. All the super-blue voters who could be flipped by Danny Gold, have been. We need more converts, or there won't be enough to scare their Senator into voting ELE... You wouldn't happen to have any ideas?"

Trey smirked.

Evie raised an eyebrow.

Trey said, "Danny called Det. Bergman to thank him. I asked Danny to call Bergman again and invite him to come hear his speech at the convention. Danny refused."

"Smart boy. Bergman, like most cops, hates concealed carry—he hasn't been shy about it. He's not gonna be a set decoration for your tent show."

"But I had to try. I made the call, invited Bergman to Danny's speech—not as a political statement, but to show personal support that'd mean a ton to Danny. The kid looks up to Bergman more than Bergman knew."

"And Bergman politely told you to go fuck yourself. He didn't fall for your touchy-feely line about Danny, or that crock about him attending Danny's speech wouldn't be taken as an endorsement."

"Not entirely."

"Yes entirely. Which is a shame. Bergman would be a quantum influencer."

"That's why I went after him," Trey murmured, staring blankly, as he wracked his brain, trying to think of a way...

"I have to be at a fundraiser in forty-three minutes," Evie said, and fondled Trey's balls.

Trey's erectile tissue began to rise and so did his determination. He went down on Evie, lost in thought… *I can do this, I'm the man getting away with five murders right under Bergman's nose, I can get him to a goddamn convention… How? What would trick him into showing up?… Nothing. Nothing would do that. Accept it… Fucking right! Accept it. WE DON'T NEED HIM IN PERSON.* Trey moved up and into Evie, humping slowly, contemplatively, as he gnawed on the problem… *AN AWARD! We give him an award for stopping the Makro Killer! Bergman won't show up to accept it. But I'll put the trophy on a pedestal downstage center, pinned in three spotlights, while I plaster a video of Detective Bergman's Greatest Hits on a sixty-foot screen, with the VO message, "Here's what a good guy with a gun does, what every one of you good guys with a gun can do if you practice enough."*

After a minute of Trey distractedly kneading Evie's lady-dough while gazing at the headboard, she said, "Trey."

Trey remembered Evie was there, offered an apologetic grin and began humping with slightly less disinterest, but he was staring into her eyes with a stricken puppy neediness, a wordless plea for permission to leave and get to work on the awesome brainstorm he was having.

Evie gripped Trey's ass, clamped him in and said, "Keep going. I'll think about him too."

SEVENTY-NINE

The FBI cracked Rudy's phones and laptop.

The laptop was useless; its hard drive was a virgin. The good stuff must've been on the demolished drive Rudy left in the basement.

Rudy's phones were slightly more fun. Their GPS had never been turned on. The call logs were deleted but easy to recover.

Phone One had made five calls in the last year to a burner—now disconnected—that had a Miami area code. But all five calls had pinged a tower in Cleveland. The most recent Cleveland call was made minutes before Rudy got into his Civic and drove past Mark.

◆

"There's no record connecting Rudy to either city. Rudy's brother says they had no family or friends in Cleveland or Miami, and far as he knew Rudy had never been either place," Mark told Husak.

"But we figure from the timing, right before he hit the road, it mighta been Rudy lettin' someone know he was on his way," Doonie said. "Like maybe Cleveland was his escape hatch. He was carryin' that fake passport."

"Was the passport name booked on any flights?" Husak asked.

Mark shook his head. "Not out of Cleveland, or anywhere else. We don't know where Rudy and his passport were heading, or how he planned to get there."

"And Phone Two?"

"There was one call—also to a disconnected burner—that pinged a tower near Kasper's house, the day before Kasper made that trip to Walmart and then to Rudy's house," Mark said.

"That trip to Walmart we don't know about because you didn't break into Kasper's truck and read his GPS," Husak said.

"But there are also repeated calls over the last few weeks, to yet another defunct burner, that pinged a tower in Streeterville."

"Who the hell Rudy know there?" Husak wondered. Streeterville, occupying a magical space bordered by Michigan Avenue, and the lakefront, and the riverfront, was one of Chicago's busiest, shiniest, priciest neighborhoods.

"Good question," Mark said. "The calls to that number were made right before and after Rudy's two final hits."

"Like he was checkin' in with somebody," Doonie said. "Sure as shit looks like Rudy had some kinda upscale accomplice."

"Or maybe just a pricey girlfriend, or a cousin who parks upscale cars," Husak noted, with the expectation-free precision of a man who long ago matured from world-weary to universe-weary. "Our Federal friends make any predictions how much longer it'll take 'em to decrypt Rudy's thumb drive?"

"Nope," Mark said, "but they promise we'll be the first to know."

EIGHTY

Trey pitched his Bergman award idea to Stan Vanderman.

The Silver Sidewinder spent a half-second considering it. "Don't bill me for the time it took you to fill that diaper."

"Wait—"

"Shut up. Your genius plan gives the most visible cop on the planet a gigantic platform—ours—to tell the world he won't accept the award because ELE sucks. That'll be the main media takeaway from our triumphant rally, a week before the Senate votes. How fucking high were you?"

"We still need to flip one more Dem. Building an even bigger, a fucking irresistible tidal wave of demand for ELE, is the only way to make that happen."

Vanderman gave Trey a pleased, condescending sneer. "No it's not."

Trey favored Vanderman with an inquisitive smirk.

"Maybe someone had a heart to heart with a Democrat Senator," Vanderman explained, "maybe showed him certain documents from when he was an Alderman in Chicago. Documents that would end his career and likely send him to a state institution less cushy than the Senate."

"And this devout socialist caved?"

"Said he needed to 'think it over.' Someone gave him twenty-four hours."

"Ah, the dude's squirming tonight. He's gotta go for the deal, because jail. But he's messed up about how if he votes for ELE, his libtard voters gonna kick his sorry ass to the curb."

"Maybe not, if he keeps voting 100% left on everything else, and ELE turns out to be as popular as I'm sure it will be." The Sidewinder, throwing Trey a magnanimous crumb, acknowledged, "Danny's speech is an asskicker. Your video to introduce him isn't bad either."

"True... Just one thought: Det. Bergman's an even bigger star than Danny. Danny's got almost as many haters as fans, he polls 53% favorable. Bergman's at 72."

"Bergman's not our friend."

"He wants to be Danny's friend, told Danny to call him any time."

"Touching."

"I called Bergman, invited him to come to Danny's speech, told him it'd mean a lot to the kid."

"And Bergman told you to go fuck yourself. Me too. Stay in your lane you fucking moron. Don't go near him again."

"We could use some insurance. Your dirty Senator isn't a done deal, he'll say yes, but then he's got weeks to find a way to weasel out. I get *one* photo of Bergman with Danny and I can turn that into—"

Vanderman sloshed a tumbler of single barrel single malt in Trey's face. "Contact Bergman again and you're *over*. Get the fuck out."

❖

While waiting for the hotel elevator, whisky fumes coming off his clammy shirt and steam coming out of his rage-red ears, Trey pulled out his phone and wrote to Bergman:

In case you reconsider.

Trey attached a pair of backstage passes to the text, and hit Send.

EIGHTY-ONE

Mark was in the shower thinking about his last shower with JaneDoe. And trying to stop thinking about it. Just turn off the shower and get out before you depress yourself again. But the pummeling hot water felt better than anything else that happened to him lately. But the longer he stayed in it the more vividly he imagined how much better it would feel sharing it with her. Dilemma.

The dilemma was resolved by the muffled sound of Mark's new phone ringing in the bedroom. This early in the morning it wouldn't be spam.

◆

It was a two-word voicemail, from Agent Carlson. "Call me."

Mark did. Agent Carlson picked up on the first ring. "Good morning, we cracked the thumb drive. You were right, looks like someone was financing Rudy."

"Looks like?"

"It's complicated. But the NSA is working on it."

"The NSA."

"You and Dunegan should come to my office, I'll order in breakfast."

◆

A conference table, scrambled eggs and Powerpoint.

"Rudy kept his data light and tight," Agent Carlson said. "All he saved were these three photos and a one-page document."

The three pictures appeared on the screen. Standard souvenir shots of himself. Nothing real useful at first glance.

"We're analyzing them to see if we can determine where and when they were taken, and ID the other men in that third shot." Agent Carlson closed the photos. "The good stuff's in the document."

It was a list of numbers. The shortest was four digits, the longest was thirteen. Most were all numerals, but a couple of the longer ones included numerals, letters and punctuation marks.

"This one," Agent Carlson said, highlighting an eleven-digit string, "is a phone number. 371 is the country code for Latvia."

"So that's probably where our Latvian-American pal was headed until that cow got in his way," Mark said. "And that 371 phone's a burner?"

Agent Carlson nodded. "Purchased in Riga two months ago and never been used. Now it never will be, unless the owner's a complete moron."

"So we got a fifty-fifty chance," Doonie noted. "Account numbers and passwords?" he asked, indicating the rest of the list.

"This one's a bank account, at the Bogenschild Privatbank, in Liechtenstein."

"But none of those other numbers is the password," Mark said, "or you'd be into the account instead of asking the NSA for help."

"And the NSA ain't been able to hack it, or you woulda said right off," Doonie said.

"Uh-huh," Agent Carlson confirmed. "What the NSA could get at is the record of internet traffic to the bank's website. One recent recurring visitor logged in through a cell tower in LaSalle County—the one closest to Rudy's house. Recognize these dates?"

A list appeared on the screen.

Oh hell yeah. "Each of the first four comes a day after Rudy's first four hits," Mark said. "Checking to make sure he'd been paid. But then, after he kills Samantha Barnes, Rudy logs in seven times—last one's about a half-hour before he smashes his laptop's hard drive, then hits the road."

"Like maybe a guy who keeps checking 'cause his client's stiffin' him on the last hit," Doonie wondered.

"Or maybe he's just shifting funds, or, who knows," Agent Carlson shrugged.

"Wait a minute," Doonie said, "this bank knows it's Rudzutaka's account, and how he was this fuckin' serial killer. So why ain't they cooperating?"

"Forget it, Jake, it's Liechtenstein," Mark told Doonie. "That's German for Bank Secrecy R Us. These guys hide cash for warlords who top Rudy's body count before breakfast on a slow Thursday."

"Exactly," Agent Carlson murmured, mildly impressed.

"He reads," Doonie explained. "But, ah, what if we tell this bank we're gonna go public, let everybody know they're protecting the fuck who paid a fuckin' serial killer?"

"They'd love that," Mark said. "Be great for their brand, reassure the world's dictators and oligarchs Bogenschild Privatbank is the place their money wants to be." He turned to Agent Carlson. "Do you have any back-channel leverage that'd convince Bogenschild Privatbank to sneak us a peek?"

"There's usually some kind of play CIA or State can make. But not always. And, even if the spooks or diplomats do have a play, no guarantee they'd be willing to make it."

"Tell them Rudy was Muslim," Mark suggested.

EIGHTY-TWO

S o," Mark summarized for Husak, "we're sure the account belonged to Rudy, but can't prove it. And the routing number of whoever was paying Rudy is behind a firewall we may never get through without regime change in Liechtenstein."

"You gonna work on that?"

"No. I'm gonna go look at pictures."

◆

Mark opened Rudy's three snapshots.

The first was of Specialist Guntars Rudzutaka, US Army military police. Rudy was slouched on a folding chair, and resting his feet on the back of a hunched-over prisoner he was using as a hassock. The prisoner was dark, fat, hairy and naked except for the black bag tied over his head. Rudy at Fort Lewis, Washington, playing make-believe Abu Graihb.

The second was a shot of Rudy holding his Mac-10 and posing with one foot planted on a bullet-riddled moose with a medium-size rack.

The final photo was of five armed men wearing camo, their faces hidden under ski masks. The man in the center was bigger and burlier than the others—same size and build as the man who'd tried to snap Mark's spine the other day. Rudy was also wearing spiffier camo, a black/white/gray digital print. The guys on either side of Rudy were waving their weapons in the air as if they'd just liberated Paris. Three of them were pudgy. The fourth was thin, and what you could see of his eyes and mouth looked young. He was standing next to Rudy, who was casually resting an arm on the young man's shoulder. Only photo of Rudy where he wasn't stepping on somebody. Did that mean something?

Yeah. Rudy hadn't yet found the most enjoyable moment to stomp the kid.

Mark gave each of the pictures one last due diligence perusal, then closed them.

Wait.

Mark reopened the third shot. That spiffy black/white/gray digital camo Rudy was wearing—Mark had seen that...where?... *Shit!* On the Sovereign Swords website, back when he was researching Vanora Yard.

Mark went to the militia's site, clicked on the merch page.

Bingo. The cover photo on one of the Combat-Ready Militiaman training videos was of the masked Rudy-sized man, dressed in that digital camo.

Mark ordered the DVD. Paid an extra $14.99 for 24-hour delivery. Probably wasn't anything useful in it, but you never know. And it wasn't like Mark had anything else to look at.

Yes there was.

Tony Mower, leader-owner-marketer of the Sovereign Swords. Mower might have deep enough pockets to fund five hits. Mark couldn't think of a reason why Mower would want to massacre Makros. But motive could wait. First the money.

Mark looked at Mower's financials.

The commanding officer of the Sovereign Swords was a 21st Century George Armstrong Custer. Charged his way into two bankruptcies and his credit cards were galloping straight at number three. Mark was closer to being able to bankroll a Makro Killer than Mower was.

◆

The FBI examined the financials of Makro's business rivals to see if those companies, or any of their major executives and investors, had done business with Rudy's favorite Liechtenstein bank.

Mark and Doonie did the same, with every wealthy Chicago-area Makro passenger who'd ever sued Makro, or sent a threatening message, or written an especially bonkers driver review.

The FBI found eleven people, and Mark and Doonie found three, who'd done bank transactions in Liechtenstein.

But none were with Bogenschild Privatbank.

EIGHTY-THREE

The Sovereign Sons combat training DVD landed on Mark's desk four days later. The DVD for which Mark had paid for overnight delivery.

Made sense. With a wife, three kids and a bankruptcy lawyer to support, Tony Mower needed Mark's $14.99 more than Fedex did.

Besides, the timing worked out in Mark's favor. Watching Rudy's Infantry For Dummies DVD would be better than what Mark and Doonie had been watching on the bullpen TV.

It was coverage from McCormick Place, a vast convention center set in a venerable swath of lakefront, whose other occupants were museums and Soldier Field.

McCormick was it's own mini-neighborhood, a behemoth complex of four semi-behemoth buildings. The AGA convention was at the West Building, into which Second Amendment maximalists were thronging, while being heckled by crowd of Second Amendment minimalists across the street, penned into McCormick Square plaza by sawhorses and a line of bored but wary cops.

Outside the West Building's main entrance, ace political reporter Marina Karrel was interviewing three young women wearing ELE hats and Danny Gold T-shirts. Each was holding up a sign that had one word on it, forming: DANNY MARRY US.

"People," Doonie sighed. Then got enthused. Said, "Lookit that," referring to the number and passion of Danny's fans. "The AGA saw real benefit outta the Makro Killer. And they got the means. The AGA could bankroll a hundred Rudzutakas and still afford an open bar at their fuckin' convention."

"Which is why they don't want a Rudzutaka," Mark said, while doing a quick excavation of his file trays and desk drawers. He looked at Kazurinski, seated two desks away. "Kaz, who stole my disc drive?"

"Husak," Kaz said, then fished Mark's drive out of a drawer. "I stole it back for you." Kaz tossed the drive to Mark—

Doonie intercepted it and held it hostage. "The Makro Killer comes along right in time for the AGA's big sales push but they ain't worth even a look?"

"The Makro Killer did goose the AGA's argument. But even without him, there were plenty enough regular murders to make the AGA's videos popular."

"But not as much," Doonie grunted, and handed over the drive.

"True. But the AGA doesn't need to get violent—they get what they want by buying and bullying politicians," Mark said, as he plugged the drive into his computer. "I don't see AGA management risking a multiple homicide bust. Too much to lose—hundreds of millions in gun sales, thousands of housebroken legislators, life in prison." Mark opened the drive and inserted the DVD. "My money's on the AGA doesn't greenlight a pile of murders, a PR stunt that's almost impossible to get away with."

A video file icon appeared on Mark's screen: *The Art Of The Ambush.* Mark opened it.

Doonie scowled. "This stunt's so fuckin' impossible, how come we ain't cracked it?"

"I'm an idiot," Mark murmured.

"Prove it," Doonie urged, getting a contact high off Mark, who was peering at his monitor with the feral serenity of a cop who can see the blood at the end of the tunnel.

Mark swiveled the monitor toward Doonie. The video was paused on a list of credits:

Directed by
T-Knuckles

Camera
T-Knuckles

Editor
T-Knuckles

Took Doonie a few seconds before the grin hit. "Trey Fister."
A few more seconds. "Fister and Rudy's asshole buddies from way
back—and Fister's got the smarts to dream this shit up."

"And motive," Mark said. "ELE videos about random murders,
that's just politics—but give 'em a serial killer attacking a global
empire and you got the whole world munching popcorn. Now if ELE
passes, Trey Fister's the whiz who made it inevitable. Payoff's fame,
fortune, political player status—enough to convince him mass murder's the way to go."

"Fuck yeah," Doonie ruled. "All we gotta do is prove it."

EIGHTY-FOUR

Mark reexamined the photo of Rudy and his Sovereign Swords chorus line. The guy Rudy was leaning on was skinny and tall. So was Trey Fister.

Only the skinny guy's eyes and mouth were visible. Facial recog rated them a probable match to Fister's. Probable's a hot tease, doesn't prove shit.

◆

Mark and Agent Carlson agreed the FBI shouldn't ask the Sovereign Swords to confirm T-Knuckles was Trey Fister. Too big a chance they'd alert him.

"What about your paranoid hermit snitch who described Rudy?" Mark asked. "Fister was there when Rudy was."

"Worth a try. I'll tell his handler to flash the Batshit Signal. And then we wait."

Right. Mr. Paranoid's standard reply window was two hours to two weeks.

◆

Took two minutes for the FBI to download Fister's financials.

Same for Mark to get in touch with a contact at the Southern Poverty Law Center, a civil rights organization that tracks hate groups. They of course had a dossier on Fister.

Fister's financials and dossier paired like sugary Zinfandel and stinky cheese.

◆

As a high school kid in Portland, Fister churned out precocious anti-gun-control, anti-abortion, pro-voter-suppression videos featuring crude teenage snark and sophisticated editing. His YouTube channel made a lot of fans and a little money.

Fister graduated to ambush videos.

Posing as a wealthy young idealist eager to donate his inheritance, Fister talked his way into meetings with executives of social service non-profits, which he taped with a hidden camera. He'd confide his most socialist globalist abortionist dreams, trying to tempt his targets into doing the same. Then Fister edited the conversations to sound as if the libtards were confessing to serious crimes, in the service of their transsexual Soviet agenda.

A couple of Fister's smears went viral, infected the mainstream media, induced poisonous ideological meme wars, and won top-of-the-monolog position on late night comedy. Fister got fifteen minutes of notoriety, a trickle of donations, and some quiet offers to make real money producing tame conventional campaign videos for tame conventional politicians—as long as Trey signed non-disclosure agreements forbidding him to reveal these upright public servants were getting their images polished by a gleefully sleazy millennial attention junkie. The pols didn't hire Trey Fister, they hired The Truth Factory, a corporation registered in the Caymans.

The anonymous campaign spots led to far more lucrative gigs, producing attack ads for right-wing PACs funded by billionaires who wanted full-on Fister snark—along with full disclosure of Fister's involvement. Gleeful sleaze is heavy cred with the 18-to-34 demo. A usually too-lazy-to-vote demo.

Fister added the word Consultant to his business card and doubled his fee.

Two years ago the AGA became Trey's major client. Eighteen months ago they put him on retainer, blessed with a signing bonus, in exchange for exclusive use of his talents. Substantial monthly payments went to Fister's new company, The Cosmic Revelations Factory, registered in Zug, Switzerland.

Yet the salary Fister paid himself was modest. Fister was living below his means and leaving the bulk of the income in the Cosmic Revelations account. Enough to finance the Makro Killer.

But to prove that's what Trey had done with his money, Mark needed access to Cosmic Revelations' account, in Switzerland, whose bank secrecy armor was only a millimeter thinner than Liechtenstein's.

◆

Miracles happen. Agent Carlson called back, less than an hour after their previous conversation.

Mr. Paranoid Snitch had come in from the cold and come through: Rudy was the surly shit who starred in *The Art Of The Ambush,* and Trey Fister was the full of himself snot who directed it.

Mark hung up the phone and looked at the TV. Marina Karrel was interviewing protesters, outside the building Trey Fister was in.

Okay, quit staring at that convention center like you're a dog and it's an unattended roast beef you can't quite get at, yet.

◆

"We got Fister, if there's payments from his Cosmic Swiss account to Rudy's numbered account in Liechtwhatever," Doonie told Husak.

"Only if we can prove that numbered account was Rudy's," Mark cautioned.

Husak asked, "Can we?"

Doonie shot Mark a *Better you than me* look.

Mark took a breath and dove in.

"Fister's bank in Zug won't let us at the Cosmic Revelations account. The Swiss federal police do have the power to examine bank records—but only if we show them 'compelling evidence' of criminal activity. We're waiting to find out if the fact Makro Killer murders coincide with activity in what we think is Rudy's account, plus the word of a whack-job snitch that Fister and Rudy are old friends, will fit the Swiss definition of 'compelling.' "

"How long's it been?" Husak asked.

"That's the hopeful part," Mark said. "The FBI says usually when you hand the Swiss evidence slim as ours, they wait ten minutes for the sake of politeness, then say no. But it's been forty minutes, and not a peep."

"Tough call for those guys," Husak sympathized.

"Uh-huh," Mark nodded. Somewhere in Switzerland senior

police and pols were calculating, *Is the worldwide credit we'd get for busting the boss Makro Killer valuable enough to justify breaking God's bank secrecy commandment?* A question that profound doesn't get answered until it works its way up to someone who's got the weight to survive if he gets it wrong.

Mark looked at Husak's TV. The broadcast was showing the crowd inside the hall where Trey Fister would be introducing Danny Gold, about an hour and a half from now. Mark wanted to bust Fister before that happened. Which Mark could do, if he got his hands on the account data soon enough to get an arrest warrant.

Crickets.

EIGHTY-FIVE

An hour later Mark was staring at the AGA's live-stream of their save-the-gun telethon and trying not to think about the silence from Switzerland.

The venue was louder than Switzerland and almost as large. The Skyline Ballroom was an indoor prairie that'd been tamed with wall-to-wall carpeting, beneath a sky-sized ceiling twinkling with a Milky Way's worth of recessed lights.

A temporary stage made of black risers filled the ballroom's rear wall. The sleek spare set consisted of a lectern downstage center and a backdrop of three mammoth screens that could display a single vast wall-to-wall video or three separate ones. At the moment the center screen was filled with a mammoth AGA logo. The left screen was showing testimonials from gun owners telling tales of how they'd be dead today if not for concealed carry. The right screen showed live views of the ballroom so the crowd could watch themselves.

Forty rows of chairs were set up across the back half of the ballroom for the old, infirm and insufficiently effusive. The acreage between the chairs and the stage was open, so most of the two thousand attendees were on their feet, with the truest believers packed dry-humping tight in front of the stage, trying to generate a passable facsimile of rock concert buzz. The energy, enthusiasm and cheerfulness were high. But, in the signature style of hard-right crowds, it was a rage-based energy, a sullen enthusiasm, an angry cheerfulness.

Doonie strolled up from wherever he'd been killing time and said, "Wastin' pizza is a mortal fuckin' sin," indicating a forlorn half-eaten slice congealing on Mark's desk.

Mark handed Doonie the plate. "I think the dentist said my gum disease isn't contagious."

"I got three kids who been nothin' but."

Doonie took a bite, made a face, dumped the dying pizza fragment in a wastebasket and changed the topic. "Bigass room," he commented re the Skyline Ballroom. "You could fit two Irish weddings in there at once."

"Nah," Mark disagreed, "only holds five thousand."

The feed cut to Marina Karrel, who was backstage interviewing a silver-haired gent named AGA Executive Vice President Stan Vanderman, who sneered only a little when Karrel's first question was the one Vanderman least wanted to hear.

"Why is this the first event at which the AGA is allowing attendees with concealed carry permits to bring their weapons?"

Mark blew Marina a kiss.

Despite its holy mission to legalize the toting of guns everywhere—churches, hospitals, kindergartens, bars—the AGA never allowed open or concealed carry at its events, and never responded to questions about why.

When this convention was scheduled the American Gun Association's no-guns restriction applied. Then the Danny Gold pro-ELE videos stoked the political pressure to a fever pitch beyond the AGA's wildest dreams, but also whipped up a tsunami of tweet-scorn about the AGA's refusal to allow legal weapons at its own convention. The scorn wasn't only from liberals. Fervent true-believer AGA members began calling out the AGA. The media kept showing those true believers, and showing them, and showing them.

With a history-changing victory on the line and the vote in the Illinois Senate still teetering, the gun liberation gurus swallowed hard and pushed all their chips into the middle of the table.

"The fact is," Vanderman lied, indignantly, "the unconstitutional restriction on licensed weapons has been imposed on the AGA by the venues where our functions were held. This facility is the first willing to listen to reason."

Vast sums of reason.

The AGA had ponied up a premium over the contracted rental fee, and taken out extravagant liability coverage, and placed bonds in escrow against damage the hall might suffer. Convention attendees were required to sign a waiver forfeiting all rights to sue the landlord, on top of which the AGA agreed to indemnify said landlord if anyone found an attorney who found a way to invalidate the waiver.

"To answer your next question," Vanderman continued, mildly miffed at being obliged to calm this hysterical female, "no, there is no security issue. Attendees wishing to bring their gun had to pre-register a valid ID and permit. There are metal detectors at the entrance, and anyone whose ID and permit don't match the one in our database is turned away. There are uniformed and plainclothes guards throughout the venue and our video surveillance would do a Vegas casino proud."

"Was all that required by the venue," Karrel asked, "or was it inspired by your—the AGA's—safety concerns?"

Vanderman gave her a pitying grin. "Don't worry, Marina, being surrounded by responsible gun owners is the safest place you'll ever be."

Mark's phone rang. He looked at it. Nodded to Doonie, yeah, it's Agent Carlson.

Mark pressed *Answer* and said, "Hi."

Agent Carlson said, "There's been some movement in Zurich."

"Some?"

"The Swiss are willing to bend the bank secrecy and grab the Makro Killer glory."

"But only if we pay an account service fee?"

"Good guess."

EIGHTY-SIX

The Swiss will play ball if their Foreign Ministry is a granted 'a certain favor' from the State Department," Mark told Husak.

"Which is?" Husak asked.

"Above our pay grade," Mark shrugged. "But the FBI says State says this mystery favor is do-able. State thinks they can close the deal inside an hour. Or two."

"And how we know Fister's account activity says what we think it will?" Husak asked.

"An FBI agent in Zurich was shown a list of cash transfers, matching the Makro kill dates, all to our favorite account in Liechtenstein."

"Which we still can't prove was Rudy's."

"That's a sweetener State is demanding: the Swiss guarantee their banking cousins next door will, in the name of justice and whatever the fuck Zurich's leveraging them with, reveal the account holder's identity."

"And State's pretty sure they'll get it?"

"Carlson says yeah," Doonie nodded. "So any hour now the diplomats get through hand-jobbin' each other, we get a warrant and go bust Fister."

Mark looked at his watch. If those diplomats had any sense of decency they'd finish their handjobs in the next ten minutes. Any longer than that and Mark wouldn't get to the convention in time.

Mark's phone rang. Marina Karrel, calling to confirm a rumor.

"I'm hearing whispers you've identified a new possible accomplice of Rudzutaka's. This for real?"

Shit. "No, Marina, it's not," Mark lied. "We're still looking for the old possible accomplice, Vanora Yard."

Doonie and Husak stiffened when they heard Mark say that.

"Is there any indication Yard is or isn't still alive?" Karrel asked.

"Can't comment on that. Sorry." Both those statements were true.

As Mark hung up, Doonie growled, "Somebody leaked."

"Karrel buy this is about Vanora?" Husak asked.

"Yeah," Mark said, "but when she reports 'A reliable police source insists the leaker was wrong'..."

"This leaker asshole maybe decides he's gotta prove he's right, so he blabs Fister's name," Doonie muttered. "This leak ain't from one of ours. Some attention whore in lederhosen."

"Whoever," Husak sighed. "Nothin' we can do 'cept hope we get our warrant before the leaker runs his mouth and tips Fister."

"Yes there is," Mark said. "Doonie and I are gonna go down there, stick close to Fister until we hear from you. When you get the warrant, we bust him. If Fister's name gets leaked before we get a warrant, we grab him for questioning."

"Stick close?" Husak scoffed. "Waddayou think Fister's gonna think about you walking in?"

"He'll be glad to see me," Mark said. "I'm his favorite cop, I got rid of the one man who could've dimed him."

"So what," Husak said, brow slightly furrowed, studying Mark for signs of a recent lobotomy. "He's still gonna wonder why the fuck you needed to come say Hi in the middle of him doin' his goddamn show."

"Nope. He sent me backstage passes." Mark gave Husak and Doonie a moment to process that. And for him to enjoy their faces. "Fister called right after Starved Rock and told me it'd mean a lot to Danny if I was there for his speech."

Husak and Doonie remained silent. Mark watched them do the math: Fister's arrogant enough to invite the lead detective on the Makro murders to come watch him cash in on those murders. Does that mean Fister's arrogant enough to see Mark's surprise visit as nothing but proof of his genius?

◆

Mark lit the siren and went NASCAR until they were a block away from McCormick, where he killed the siren and slowed to a less conspicuous speed.

Doonie eyed Mark. Said, "You're tryin' ta get there in time to bust Fister in front of Danny, before Danny can make his speech, so the kid won't have to live with that."

"It's what the fat old fuck who taught me the job would do."

EIGHTY-SEVEN

Quickest way into the West Building would be its front doors, but those were surrounded by TV news crews and a crowd of Instagramming protesters who knew a famously lethal Det. Bergman when they saw one. Mark and Doonie preferred to show up backstage without everyone from here to Bangladesh wondering why the Makro Killer detectives were attending Gunsapalooza.

Mark drove down a service alley that descended below street level, and parked by a basement loading dock.

As they walked to the entrance, a security guard so young he had to be somebody's nephew gave Mark That Look and blurted, "You here to bust somebody?"

"Not unless you got something to confess. Where's the elevator to the Skyline Ballroom?"

"Take a left and go, it's uh, at the other end of the building."

They hustled down a basement passage that was slightly shorter than the highway to Starved Rock. At the end of their journey they found two elevators, one passenger and one freight. Mark pressed both buttons and checked his watch. Danny's speech was scheduled to begin six minutes ago. But these things never start on time. Mark figured they had a ten, maybe fifteen minute cushion. Or at least five. Not that it'd matter, unless Husak called before then with good news from the Alps.

The freight elevator arrived first. Mark pressed Four and the elevator, large enough to accommodate a Jetta, moseyed upward, as if Mark and Doonie weighed as much as a car. *If Husak calls now, is there cell service inside this thing?...* Mark accepted the relaxing Zen advice offered by a sign on the wall: CENTER ALL LOADS. Wise elevator.

The wise elevator's doors opened and Danny Gold's amplified voice blew in. But there was a musical score underneath it. Fister's introductory video was still playing, Danny hadn't gone on stage yet.

Mark and Doonie emerged into a wide service corridor that led to a backstage area which had been set up behind the giant video screens on the temporary stage at the north end of the hall.

Access to the backstage was blocked by two weightlifters wearing dark suits and overdone scowls; a Secret Service tribute band that was trying too hard. They both recognized Mark but only the younger one gave him That Scowl.

"This is a restricted area," the senior weightlifter warned.

"This is our invitation from Mr. Fister," Mark said, raising his phone.

The senior weightlifter glared at the uppity QR code, then threw a grudging look at the junior weightlifter, who pulled out a scanner. The scanner laser-kissed Mark's phone and burped its approval.

The senior weightlifter gestured for Mark and Doonie to wait, held his wrist to his mouth and had a brief conversation with his shirt cuff. He lowered his arm and informed them, "The Assistant Stage Manager will take you."

The music track on the Danny Gold video swelled to a heart-wrenching yet rousing conclusion, triggering a Vesuvius of angry applause and threatening cheers from the crowd.

The Assistant Stage Manager, a gangly woman in a t-shirt, jeans, a headset and a relaxed hurry strode up to Mark and Doonie. She recognized them both and frittered away a half-second on That Look before instructing: "Set your phones to vibrate. Don't talk. When you do, whisper."

Trey Fister's live voice came booming over the PA, offering gloating thanks for the ovation and whipping up the crowd for Danny's entrance—"The toughest, most dedicated, fearless, ferociously honest son any father ever had."

"Walk where I do, there are cables everywhere," the ASM cautioned as she led Mark and Doonie past three long tables at which video, audio and lighting techs were communing with laptops, toward a short flight of steps which led up to the stage. The steps and the corner of the stage were hidden from the audience by masking. Danny Gold was standing behind the masking, looking out at the stage—

The ASM halted and flung her arms out like a school crossing guard to keep Mark and Doonie back where there was no chance they'd mess up Danny's entrance.

"My friend, my *brother*," Fister's voice crooned, "and—he's gonna hate me for saying this—America's conscience! *DAN-EE GOLD!*" Fister exulted.

Danny took a deep breath, walked onstage and the crowd erupted in an ecstatic storm of cheers, applause, stomping feet and tear-stained cheeks.

The ASM gestured for the cops to go stand where Danny had been, and marched off to ace her next task.

The sustained roar from the crowd evolved into a massive chant, "DAN-NEE! DAN-NEE! DAN-NEE!"

Doonie gave Mark a watcha-gonna-do shrug.

Yeah. Busting Fister was the main event, busting Fister in time to stop Danny from giving his speech was not. But, shit.

Mark and Doonie went up the stairs and stood behind the masking. They had a good view of the stage. As the crowd roared DAN-NEE DAN-NEE, Trey was giving Danny a bro hug and whispering something in his ear, a pro move that never fails to drive fans and rookie reporters crazy with curiosity.

From their perch in the stage left wing the cops could also see hundreds of adoring fans crowding against the right side of the stage. The three girls with the DANNY MARRY US signs were near the front. Mark saw a fortyish woman, head down, ruthlessly squirming through the crowd, determined to get closer. Mark caught a glimpse of part of the woman's face—there was something familiar—she disappeared into a grove of taller people—

Mark and Doonie's phones vibrated. A text from Husak:

GO

All fucking right. Mark and Doonie's radar locked on Fister and they savored that moment where you know what's coming next, but the murderous turd out there styling like he's got the world by the balls doesn't.

Fister had one arm clamped around Danny's shoulder and with the other was grandly waving to the crowd. Danny gave a few uncomfortable waves then gestured for the room to settle—

Mark saw MARRY and US jerk apart as the fortyish woman shoved between the adoring girls and stared up at Fister, who still had his arm around Danny—Clara Cahill! The look on her face wasn't adoration—

Fister let go of Danny and began to exit toward Mark and Doonie—

Soon as Fister moved clear of Danny, Clara pulled something from her pocket—

Mark bellowed "GUN" ran onstage tackled Fister landed on top of him to prot—

Clara fired—

EIGHTY-EIGHT

The bullet blew a hole through Mark's flapping coattail, then through the giant center screen, hit steel bracing and ricocheted into an electrical junction box that gave a harsh outraged sizzle and blew open, geysering acrid yellow-gray smoke, hot metal and sparks—

Onstage, Danny dashed in front of Mark and Fister to shield them from Clara, who screamed "MOVE MOVE!!!" waving for Danny to step aside—

Half the stage lighting shorted out and the huge screens suffered jagged flickerflash video seizures—

"CLARA NO!!!" Doonie bellowed, rushing onto the stage reluctantly pointing his gun—

Multiple overlapping terrified shouts of "GUNGUNGUN!" chain-reacted through the ballroom, security guards with weapons drawn struggled to get at Clara through an hysterical 2,000-deep crowd that kept changing its mind about the safest direction to stampede, because in every direction there were licensed concealed carry civilians pulling their pieces, and one near the stage leveled his weapon at Clara—

Doonie did a 230-pound stage dive onto the guy, pancaking him—

The air boiled with ear-shredding screams and gunfire provoking more screams and gunfire provoking more screams and gunfire—

Clara recognized Doonie and froze, stricken with guilt as Doonie pistol-whipped the still struggling pancake beneath him then began looking around for where the pancake's gun had gone.

Mark yanked Danny down flat and sprang to his feet as the senior weightlifter ran onstage and snapped into a shooter's stance aiming at Clara.

Mark knocked the senior weightlifter's arms upward as he fired, rammed an elbow into the weightlifter's throat, twisted the gun out of his grip and threw him flat on his back.

Sparks from the gut-shot junction box had ignited fires backstage—flames swelled, smoke metastasized into a noxious breath-killing cloud that sent smoke detectors into shrieking fits—a fire alarm blared, battalions of sprinklers doused the ballroom, bright white emergency lights bleached the place and an authoritative pre-recorded voice commanded, "Fire emergency evacuate in an orderly fashion, Fire emergency evacuate in an orderly fash—"

The wet and terrified crowd kept panicking in a disorderly fashion, some of the armed ones firing into the air or at anyone else who had a gun, but most were rushing to and jamming the exits, trampling those who'd gone prone to avoid the gunfire or been hit by it, trampling those who'd tripped over the wounded or lost their footing on blood-soaked carpet dotted with slippery viscera, and trampling the brave few who'd knelt to assist writhing groaning gunshot victims, trying to protect them from the stampede while compressing wounds and yelling "Wounded! Wounded! Medic!" The girl who'd been carrying the MARRY sign took a bullet in the back and fell against a husky woman who caught her, slung the bleeding girl over her shoulder and began bashing her way toward an exit, unaware the girl she was carrying was dead, as two security guards who'd been shooting at civilian shooters whirled around frantically scanning for new threats and opened fire on each other—

Doonie found and pocketed the pancake's gun and was levering himself to his feet as Clara watched, gun in hand and eyes brimming—

"DROP THE GUN DROP THE FUCKING GUN" three twitchy security guards screamed as they edged toward Clara, who was oblivious, gazing forlornly at Doonie.

"DROP THE FUCKING GUN NOW OR YOU'RE DE—"

Mark leapt off the stage, landed on his feet alongside Clara waving his badge and roaring, "POLICE! POLICE! STAY BACK LOWER YOUR WEAPONS!"

That Look flashed across the guards' faces and they froze.

Doonie took Clara's gun from her. Mark cuffed Clara's hands, picked her up and put her on the stage

Mark looked around the stage—Fister and Danny were gone. *Good, still alive.* Mark scrambled up beside Clara, leaned down and helped Doonie clamber up. They hurried to the deserted backstage, three soggy people slogging through a soaked but smoldering terrain of debris that stank of melted rubber cables, incinerated plastic chairs and charbroiled laptops. But no corpses. The sprinkler system was top of the line and the stage crew hadn't stopped to shoot at each other.

Mark, Doonie and Clara headed down a service staircase that was wide, sturdy and empty, until they ran into a posse of cops, firefighters and EMTs pounding their way up. An EMT stopped and asked if any of them needed attention. They didn't.

As they resumed hurrying down to the basement Mark phoned Danny.

Danny's phone sent Mark to voicemail. Mark told it, "Call me right back, I need to if know you guys are okay, and to send over some security—we don't know if there's more than one shooter targeting Fister."

Clara snorted.

Mark asked her, "Is there?"

"I hope so."

Mark texted Danny; no reply. Mark tried Fister. Same silence.

They reached the basement and began squishing down the endless corridor to the loading dock, Doonie gripping Clara, Mark gripping his phone and deciding what next. Maybe Fister had grabbed the first cop he saw outside the building and asked for protection. In that case *we got him.* But Mark's money was on the vicious shit getting himself the hell away from here, away from cops who'd have a million questions for the target of the assassination attempt that set off this AGA bloodbath.

Danny's uncle Nate said Danny moved into a downtown building where Fister was staying. That would be the closest haven they could run to.

Mark called Nate. Voicemail again. "Nate, Mark Bergman. Last I saw Danny he was unharmed, but I wanna make sure, and I can't get him on the phone. Call me right away, I need to know where he lives."

Mark had to update Husak, but didn't want Clara to find out Trey Fister was a suspect. Mark sped up, getting far enough ahead so Clara couldn't hear, then phoned Husak. Voicemail streak intact. "Fister's in the wind," Mark said, "we don't know the building where he and Danny live, and Danny's uncle isn't answering."

◆

The loading dock was surrounded by a herd of twinkling emergency vehicles. A uniformed Captain was running the show. Mark and Doonie told him they were in pursuit of a suspect, handed over Clara and the guns they'd confiscated, accepted towels from an EMT, rushed to their car and yanked open its doors—

"Detective Dunegan!" Clara shouted. Both cops stopped. In a flat, devastated, but firm voice Clara said, "I'm sorry. Thank you."

Doonie absolved Clara with a small sad knowing nod packed with ten centuries of Celtic fatalism. Then he slid behind the wheel, put the car in gear and began zigging through the emergency vehicle scrum, while Mark got Husak on the radio.

"Nate's wife Cheryl is unlisted," Husak told Mark. "Unis are on the way over to bang on their door."

"The AGA?" Mark asked.

"Their head of security's too busy to talk, his assistant gave me the good-news, crap-news. Fister and Danny ain't answering the AGA's calls, but Fister texted—'We're alive, no thanks to you.' I asked the assistant did he send people to check on them and this fuckwad says he'll get to it soon's he can, every man they got who ain't dead or in surgery is busy. I asked for Fister and Danny's address, the fuckwad says he can't give it without their permission and they ain't talking. Told him I was gonna bust him myself for impeding, the fuckwad says good luck with our lawyers—"

Mark's phone rang. Unlisted number. He took the call. "Bergm—"

"This is Nate Gold, I'm using Cheryl's phone mine's dead, sorry to bother you but Danny's not answering so we jumped in the car to go down there but everything's gridlocked, we're—"

"Gimme Danny's address."

EIGHTY-NINE

The sprinklers began to gush—Trey began to rise—
Danny grabbed Trey's arm—"Stay down!"
"Fuck that!" Trey yelped, and scrambled into the wings and down off the stage. Danny rushed after him.

The backstage fire was outgunned by the sprinklers and dying fast, but the water/flame battlefront was boiling off clouds of opaque smoke spiked with scorched particulates. Trey paused for a microsecond and plunged into it, in the general direction of the service corridor. Danny followed. The toxic smoke seared their eyes and sawed their throats—Trey staggered into the sizzling hot edge of a metal table, jerked away and fell. Danny, fighting a razor-tooth coughing fit, pulled Trey upright. They escaped into the service corridor that ran along the west side of the ballroom.

The freight elevator and human elevator were both gone. The far end of the service corridor was clogged with conventioneers who'd fled through the ballroom's emergency exits and were now fighting to get through the service corridor doors to the central concourse.

Danny and Trey found a service stairway at their end of the corridor. It was empty—the stage crew had fled down it soon as the gunfire and brimstone hellmouth blew open. Trey and Danny did the same, gulping the relatively clean air. As they raced down the stairs Trey phoned Vanderman—if Vanderman's limo hadn't left yet they could hitch a ride, and if the limo was gone, Vanderman could send a security team to get them.

The Silver Sidewinder didn't pick up. Or reply to a text.

Danny and Trey exited at the far end of the building, around the corner from where a few thousand desperate convention-goers were spilling out of the main entrance. Danny and Trey blended into a damp hectic throng fleeing down Cermak Road. They surged into the already crowded Cermak el stop and squeezed onto the last train before the CTA froze service in the area.

Danny and Trey were two of many wet, bedraggled convention-eers packed in the car, pressed against dry but sympathetic riders who'd been on the train when it arrived. Nobody recognized Danny. Partly thanks to his brand new beard, but mainly because he was one of the boring wet people, silent, head down, no eye contact. All the attention was on the interesting wet people who were venting about what they'd just escaped—"No no I'm not exaggerating, people dying in there, for all I know they still are—it's a massacre, check your phone, how's it not on Twitter yet?"

No lie, Danny confirmed, staring down, communing with his sodden shoes. *People died.*

When they got off at their stop, Danny checked his phone—

"No!" Trey barked, "No calls, no messages!"

"My uncle wants to know I'm okay."

"*Nobody*. Not yet."

"You think Uncle Nate's in a plot with Clara Cahill to kill you?"

"Who's Clara—you saw who shot at me—you *know* her?"

"She's—was—married to Roz Espinosa… Clara tried to talk me out of working for ELE."

"Does your uncle know her?"

Danny blushed. "Clara… said she was in a support group with him," Danny admitted.

He pocketed his phone. Not that Uncle Nate's gonna kill Trey, or anybody. But Trey's the one got shot at, not me. Whatever he needs, I'm there.

As they entered Trey's apartment Trey said, "I get towels, you pour whisky—big ones, no ice," and headed for the linen closet.

Danny didn't move. Decided booze wasn't first thing he wanted.

"I'm gonna go change, be right b—"

"No!" Trey yelled, returning with towels and tossing one to Danny. "We stick together till we find out what's going on," Trey declared, taking off his suit jacket and tossing it on the kitchen floor. "I'll grab us some clothes. You—" Trey pointed at a bottle of Whistle Pig 15 Year that was on an end table by the couch, and hustled into his bedroom.

Danny hung his jacket on a stool by the kitchen dining counter, shucked shirt, shoes and socks, and went to the living room, toweling himself. He laid his phone on the coffee table, went to the end table, picked up the bottle, and yelled, "What do you think's going on?" as he began pouring luxury rye.

"No idea," Trey said, arriving with socks, underpants, jeans and sweatshirts. "Like, we don't know if they got her, or if there are others, or if they're after you too." Trey dropped the clothes on the coffee table. Which revealed the gun in his hand. Trey waggled the gun. "Till then I'm your bodyguard, not letting you out of my sight. Unless," Trey smirked, "you're shy and have to change in the john."

"Fuck you."

"No, fuck Vanderman and those AGA bitches, ran away and left us," Trey snarled, teeth clenched. Then he gave a dismissive grunt, put his phone and gun down on the coffee table and stuck out his hand, demanding that triple shot of Pig.

Danny'd never seen Trey so emotional—rattled, flipping from mood to mood... *Trey's scared. Yeah he wants to make sure I'm safe, but also, maybe mainly, he doesn't wanna be alone... Yeah well, me too.* Suddenly Danny was back on that stage, locking eyes with Clara Cahill yelling and waving her gun while around them the world smeared into a screaming shooting burning blur... *Have I got PTSD?*

Danny picked up the glasses and handed one to Trey, who raised it in a toast. "The future."

They clinked and Trey drank.

Danny gazed into his glass like he wanted to disappear into it. *People died.* He murmured a halfhearted, "Future's almost gotta be better than tonight."

Trey did an expensive spit take, gasped, "Y-yeah, you think?" and cracked up.

After a moment, Danny grinned. Then laughed. Guiltily, then gratefully.

They finished their drinks and Trey gestured for a refill. Danny poured him one, put the bottle down and began changing into the dry clothes.

Trey took a sip and turned on the TV. It was showing jerky phone video taken from the middle of the primal panic mêlée fighting to squeeze through the ballroom's exits, drenched by the industrial downpour from the sprinklers and dying from random bullets blasting from any and every direction.

"Can you turn off the sound," Danny requested.

"Sure." Trey muted it, then saw Danny was keeping his eyes averted from the screen. Trey turned off the TV, and Danny gave him a grateful nod.

Okay, now's the moment. Trey looked Danny in the eye. "Know what, bro? We're gonna finish this drink, grab our toothbrushes and take a nice relaxing drive to my place in Alexandria."

"Huh?"

"It's safer. In every way. Soon's the media gets tired of that clusterfuck," Trey indicated the blank TV, "they're comin' after us, whole army of drooling dogs, no escape. You wanna spend the next part of your life trapped in this building?"

"Trey, the cops are gonna wanna, have to talk to us—"

"We will. From my lawyer's office in DC."

"Why?"

"So we don't say anything that gets us in trouble—not with the cops—but they're gonna ask about your relationship with Clara Cahill, and her defense attorney's gonna use your answers to make out like we drove her to it, which'll also be the argument the shysters for everybody in that ballroom who got killed or broke a fingernail is gonna use to sue the AGA—*and us.* Danny, we're consultants, not employees. You think Vanderman's gonna hand out six-, seven-figure legal fees to protect us? Fucker who left us to die?"

Danny frowned, torn. Trey was his big brother-guru, knew the world and had his back. But running away and lawyering up didn't feel like what good guys did.

"Trey, the shit you've just been through, it's normal that maybe you're a little freaked out, y'know?"

"I'm not freaked out, I'm dialed in," Trey stated, definitively. He forced himself to stop there; selling too hard might backfire. Trey had to have Danny. Scumbag Vanderman was gonna try to make Trey the scapegoat, tell the world how allowing weapons in the room had been all Trey's idea. Which there was no paper trail to prove, but the lamestream media would pound Trey anyway. But with Danny vouching for his innocence Trey could dry-clean this mess. Danny Gold's word would now be magic with a way broader demo than just the AGA base. *Danny's going superstar, thanks to his fucking heroic move putting himself between me and that cunt Cahill's gun. All of it on camera. Multiple angles. That's gift from God shit. Yazzzz! It's not only me, God-bro also knows Trey should be President. Danny's gonna front all my videos, not just the gun shit. Twerp still has libtard illusions about everything except guns, but I can lead Danny any fucking place I want.* Trey stared at Danny and let the silence weigh on the kid.

Danny sighed. "Okay… But before we go—Det. Bergman also left messages, just wants to know we're okay." Danny pointed to his phone, on the coffee table. "I won't call—just text him and Uncle Nate, won't say where we are or that we're leaving."

"I'm sorry, but, bro, for real, we can't trust anybody."

A brief silence. "Bergman saved your life."

"So did you, bro. And you didn't do it 'cause it's your union salary pension government job to do it."

"I, I didn't, you were already down, I just—"

"Put yourself between me and a screaming bitch with a gun. Willing to take a bullet." Trey gave him a warm, affectionate smirk. "You, I trust."

Danny couldn't find words. Spent a few moments staring down at Trey's phone and gun on the coffee table before he managed to say, softly, "After Dad was… When I had no… You…" Danny steeled himself, lifted his head, met Trey's gaze. "You're not my bro. You're my brother."

"Yeah." Trey opened his arms, inviting Danny to come around that damn coffee table for a hug—

An alert sounded on their phones. Makro Killer news. Danny scooped his phone off the table. Trey finished his drink, reached down and picked up his phone—

According to an anonymous source, an unnamed European law enforcement agency has evidence the target of the gun convention assassination attempt, video whiz Trey Fister, was in fact "the mastermind and money behind the Makro Killer."

Trey looked up—

Danny, glaring, bewildered, enraged but not quite certain—

Trey threw his phone at Danny and reached down for the gun on the coffee table—

Danny backhanded the flying phone and lunged for the gun—

Danny and Trey banged heads hard and recoiled but Trey grabbed Danny's shoulder, yanked him down and impaled him on an uppercut to the chest, then shoved Danny away—

As Danny lurched backward onto the couch he grabbed at Trey's face, fingernails ripping skin—

Trey shrieked, jerking away and covering the bloody lacerations with his right hand, but reversed direction and went for the gun with his left—

Danny, splayed on the couch, kicked the coffee table over—

Trey spotted the gun on the floor, bent down to pick it up—

Danny hurled himself into Trey.

NINETY

They came in five-ten minutes ago. Same as you," the doorman said, indicating Mark and Doonie's clothing. "Get you some towels?"

"Just Mr. Fister's apartment number."

"2817."

Mark said, "Thanks," and gestured at the heavy glass door separating the outer lobby from the elevators.

The doorman glanced at the phone he was supposed to use to notify tenants before admitting visitors, then looked at Mark.

Mark shook his head.

The doorman buzzed the door open.

Mark told him, "More cops'll be here soon—"

"I'll tell 'em where you went. Nobody else."

"Good man."

There was an elevator waiting. Doonie pressed 28, the car whooshed, the whooshing dropped an octave and the car came to a satiny halt at the Seventh floor. Site of the fitness center and swimming pool. The doors opened and four boisterously unsober twentysome-things in damp bathing suits and towels fell silent at the sight of two large men in damp business suits—the swimmers' eyes widened into That Look.

"Next car," That Bergman instructed.

Doonie jabbed the Close Doors button. The doors obeyed, the whooshing resumed and Doonie shrugged. "We'll have cuffs on Fister before those punks can finish typing how they just saw you in their elev—"

They got a text from Husak. Read it fast.

"*According to an anonymous source*—fucking Swiss," Doonie snarled.

Mark pulled his jacket back and rested his hand on his gun.

Doonie too.

Twenty-Eighth floor. The doors opened. An arrow on the hallway wall indicated 2811-20 were to the left—

Crashing furniture and sounds of fighting.

Mark and Doonie drew their weapons and ran.

A man screamed "NO!!"—a gunshot followed by a sobbing howl—

They got to 2817—another gunshot.

Mark kicked the door once, twice, third one smashed it—he rushed in, gun raised, Doonie right behind—

Mark stopped aimed yelled "DANNY DON'T! DANNY!"

Doonie growled, "Danny put the fuckin' gun down, put it the fuck down now."

Ten feet away in the living room Danny was standing, arm extended, pointing a gun at Fister, who was seated on the floor slumped against a wall, groaning, a bloody wounded hand pressed to his chest and his other hand clutching his leg just above a gory knee.

Danny, keeping his gun on Trey, turned his head toward the two cops in the vestibule pointing guns at him. A whole side of Danny's face was bruised, an eye swelling shut, a lip split and bleeding, and he was staring at Mark as if Mark were insane.

"Danny," Mark coaxed, "It's okay—"

"Shoot him! I'm bleeding out shoot him!" Fister shrieked.

"Shut the fuck up," Doonie snapped.

"Just fucking shoot himmmmm," Fister whined.

"You nailed him," Mark said. "Don't be him. Please, Danny, just lay it down." Danny stared at Mark. Mark lowered his gun, took one step forward holding out his left hand, palm up. "Put it in my hand. I'll come to you nice and sl—"

Danny turned his head and resumed glaring at Trey—

"Don't!" Doonie yelled.

"Danny," Mark said, edging closer. "Danny, look at me… C'mon.

Look at me."

Danny kept glaring at Trey. Trey whimpered.

"*Wait*," Mark pleaded, raising his gun. "Just wait."

Danny kept glaring at Trey and slowly shifted to a two-handed grip, steadying—

"Tell me what your Dad would want you to do," Mark demanded.

Danny's hands trembled and his eyes moistened but remained fixed on Trey. Danny muttered, "He killed Dad. And got me to shit on Dad's grave. Over and over and over."

"Don't let him kill you too," Mark said. "Don't let him shit on you."

"Anything for my bro," Danny whispered, smirking at Trey—Trey screamed—

Mark launched himself at Danny—

Doonie couldn't risk a shot—

Danny's gun went off cannon-blast loud an instant before Mark crashed into him, took him to the floor and raised up fast to see where Danny's gun was.

Danny was flat on his back, arms outstretched, the gun gripped in his right hand. But he wasn't resisting, just laying there looking at Mark.

Danny opened his right hand and slowly raised it, offering the gun. Mark took it, tucked it away.

Doonie went to check on Danny's target.

Mark rolled Danny over, placed Danny's arms behind his back and cuffed him.

Doonie pressed two fingers against Fister's neck and searched for a pulse, in case Fister was the first guy to still have one after taking a round through the middle of the forehead.

Doonie straightened up, saw Mark and Danny were watching him.

Doonie glanced at the corpse, then gave Mark an impressed look.

Yeah. The hand, the knee and a 40-caliber Bhoddivista dot between the eyes.

"They bought me shooting lessons," Danny explained.

NINETY-ONE

You find this amusing, Detective?"

"This is the first time IA's called me in because I didn't shoot someone."

"You allowed an unarmed suspect to be shot to death."

"I believed I could disarm the shooter without anyone getting hurt."

"You believed wrong."

"Yes. I was a split-second late tackling the shooter. Just like I might've been late pulling a trigger. Then we would've had two people shot to death."

"You chose to risk the life of an unarmed man rather than risk the life of the man threatening him with a gun."

"I tried to keep both men alive. Only saved one. Was it the wrong one?"

Mark got the answer he was hoping for: stony silence followed by a swift end to the interview. IA had no intention of ripping him for choosing to risk the life of a piece of shit serial killer instead of a distraught teenager. IA had requisitioned Mark to use him as an irrefutable statistical chart in their live PowerPoint presentation. *This graphic illustrates how no cop, not even one with higher name recognition and favorables than all fifty Aldermen, is outside the range of IA's swinging dick.*

Just in case there was a cop somewhere in the world who didn't already know that.

◆

Next stop, top floor, corner office. Mark had been told to report to the Superintendent after he finished his IA waltz.

When he walked in the Supe greeted him with, "Still got your badge?"

"And all my teeth and fingernails."

"Lucky me." The Supe gestured for Mark to sit. "Every news network's got a hard-on for time with you and Doonie. Not a presser with a scrum shouting questions, they want face-to-face sit-downs. Raye thinks that's the way to go, and so do I."

Interesting. Raye Stills, the civilian head of PR, usually would be in this kind of meeting. In fact, usually Raye would be handling this herself, and the Supe would be off running the Department. Must be some reason the Supe didn't want Raye in the room.

"Raye's other good idea: Instead of you and Doonie running studio to studio doing the same interview over and over, y'know like some actor plugging his crap movie, you're going to do just one. The opening segment of this Sunday's *60 Minutes*."

"Doonie should be the focus."

"You'll both get your props. But we can't control how they edit the thing."

"Doonie saved Clara Cahill's life, and saved that responsible gun owner who was about to shoot her from getting busted for manslaughter. I failed at both."

The Supe grinned. "That's good. Say that to Lara Logan. Without the 'responsible gun owner' snark."

"Yes sir."

"From now on you're going to be doing more press, and representing the Department at more events, public and private. Pain in the ass I know, but you'll be doing a lot of good for the Department."

Mark nodded.

"Also... You'd come across even better if you were a Lieutenant."

"Sir, I can do what's needed at those events, but in between, I'd be a lot more useful working homicides than working a desk."

"Yeah? Whole city knows your face, you can't walk down the street or go on meal break without drawing a crowd—and that's only gonna get worse, now you and Doonie cleared the Makro Killer case, *twice*. And this time with video of you saving Fister's life."

"A half-hour later I failed to save his life."

"A better outcome than crippling or killing Danny Gold. Quit changing the topic. And quit yankin' my chain about how being Det. Rock Star isn't getting in the way of the job."

"Sir... I'm fried. Putting in for some serious leave. By the time I get back, it'll be somebody else's fifteen minutes."

"Ah son, you got it bad. Trying to duck promotion, bullshitting how a couple of months off and nobody's gonna remember your name... Just 'cause you think you can't give up the street. Look, we've all been there. Some of us are too sensible to stay stuck there."

Great. My sixty-three-year-old boss agrees with my permanently stoned twenty-four-year-old lover who hates me: I'm addicted to the badge, the gun, the action.

"That's another reason I need time away," Mark said. "Slow down enough to figure out what's sensible. "

The Supe gave him an understanding nod. "Speaking of which... I imagine you've been getting book and movie offers."

"Yeah."

When Mark didn't add any detail to that, the Supe asked, "You allergic to money?"

"Hope not. Haven't had time to listen to pitches, or look at the written version they send when you won't talk... Also, I'm bushed. Not ready to sign a deal and spend a month re-living every second of this year for some writer."

"Uh-huh," the Supe commented. He studied Mark for a moment. "Well, the sensible way to deal with those offers is to get someone who can sort 'em out for you... I got a nephew who's a literary agent. He also does film deals, just made partner at a hot shit New York firm."

Okay, there's the reason the Supe didn't want Raye Stills in the room.

◆

Down in the garage Mark almost made it to his car when he got intercepted by a couple of probies, a boy and a girl still sporting that eager first-day-of-school glow, who hurried over to introduce themselves.

Before they could say it Mark stuck his hand out and said, "Mark

Bergman and I'm honored to meet you, too."

He asked Officers Jackson and Haneesh how long they'd been on the job, what their assignments were, and wished them well.

They thanked him.

Then Jackson hesitantly asked, "Can I, um, get an autograph—for my 12-year-old brother—he'd go, he'd be over the moon."

Mark looked at Haneesh. "He really got a 12-year-old brother?"

"Yes," she said. Then grinned. "And I have a 17-year-old sister."

Three other cops saw Mark signing, came over and requested the same. He couldn't be the dick who signed for this one but not for that.

Two veteran detectives walked by, saw Mark doling out autographs to fellow cops, and nailed Det. Rock Star with sour, disgusted, massively pleased smirks. As they walked away one of them muttered something, and they snickered.

❖

It was a dark and stormy afternoon. Late autumn nasty. Thirty-three degrees, gusting winds, barrages of fat ice-water raindrops thumping the car. And the traffic sucked. Mark was inching along, trapped in a hellacious jam, killing time by imagining his career as Lt. Bergman, commander of the one-man Publicity & Fundraising Squad. Hey, know what'd bring in some real money? Make the take from that bachelor auction look like chump change? We raffle off the chance for one lucky fan to win Lt. Mark Bergman's private, personal, just-between-us guided tour of the holy grail.

What's it like to kill four men?

Relief. The first thing is, relief. I survived. I'm still here. Compared to that, everything is footnotes. And all four shoots were righteous; three self-defense, one to save somebody. But. Turns out, sometimes taking a life can come with no more than trace amounts of guilt, but always comes with a certain... heft. A responsibility. Like, there's something I have to—not atone for—to prove. Shooting people isn't all I am. It's not gonna be the most important thing I'll ever do. Though, yeah, going four-for-four does, like nothing else, build you some hardcore self-confidence. And some nightmares. Ones where you don't survive. Where the panic you were too busy to mess with at the time shows up, plays kickball with your heart, pours Drano through your nervous system, melts you into a whimpering puddle, and you wake up on soaked sheets, glad it's only from sweat.

That's what it's like to kill four men.

Hard.

Not as hard as being snickered at by your brother cops.

I know; killing serious, snickering trivial, no comparison.

But, killing guys who were trying to kill me didn't make me wonder about what I'm doing. The snickering makes me wonder.

NINETY-TWO

T hey have to give Dad a commendation for this, right," seventeen-year-old Patty Dunegan deadpanned, showing Mark her phone. It was playing a gif of Doonie repeatedly diving off the stage and squishing the guy aiming at Clara Cahill. "Right?"

"And also a spot on the US diving team at the next Olympics," Mark informed Patty.

"That was supposed to be a surprise," Doonie complained.

Dinner at Doonie and Phyl's, where the whole family were CPD veterans. Mark was the lucky adult they'd adopted.

Patty's older brothers Kieran and Tom were away at college, but both phoned to say Hi and give Mark shit about making sure to keep his will updated, because they were calling dibs on his car and TV. Mark advised them they needed to stop stealing their Dad's material and come up with some of their own.

After dinner, Doonie retired to the john, and Patty got Facetimed by her best friend, who immediately asked, "Is he still there?"

"Tell her he's clearing the table, so you're free to go dissect him in private," Mark said.

"Vivisect," Patty corrected, blew Mark a kiss and sashayed to her room.

Mark took plates into the kitchen, scraped them and handed them to Phyl, who was loading the dishwasher.

As Mark handed Phyl the final plate, he asked, quietly, "How you doing?"

The strapping, sturdy woman gave him a delicately wry look. "The both of you came home without first spending a week in the hospital, and neither of you came home in a box, so hey," Phyl said, took the plate from Mark and put it in the dishwasher.

And there's the reason JaneDoe's four thousand miles away from being in this room. JaneDoe would love Phyl, but would hate having to be Phyl.

"Why you lookin' at me funny?" Phyl wondered.

"Trying to figure the safest way to tell you the pork loin was over-done. I only had a second helping to make you feel better."

"Bastard." Then, serious, "Mark, how come I'm the only girl you flirt with any more?"

"Talk about vanity."

"About six months ago—since Rockford—you went from sleep-ing with too many women to none at all," Phyl declared, and shut the dishwasher door.

"None?"

"None."

"How would you know?"

"You've been—low. So low even you can't hide it… And, if you have been getting laid, it ain't working… Who is she, and is she still there, or she gone for good?"

NINETY-THREE

Mark was sipping Blanton's in an exclusive lounge, where the other exclusives respected Mark's privacy semaphore: He was sitting at a small table with his back to the room and wearing ear buds, despite how wrong it felt to sit with his back to the room and Warren Zevon impairing his hearing. But this way fewer people would see Mark's face.

So far, so good. Been allowed to sit there drinking and thinking, like any normal anonymous loner pondering his abnormal love life.

JaneDoe was anything but flimsy. She wouldn't have issued her total ban on all things Mark unless she really needed it.

But it had been over six months. Enough time for someone as non-flimsy as JaneDoe to get it together. But her Mark embargo remained seamless, impervious. JaneDoe had not checked in to see how Mark was after the thing with Rudy, or after him being in the middle of that AGA bulletfest.

Which, c'mon, were exactly the kinds of things JaneDoe wanted/needed to stay away from. She wasn't up for moving in with Mark Bergman and waking up one morning next to Roland The Headless Thompson Gunner.

But the fact JaneDoe still required that absolute, no exceptions blackout kept hope alive. The fact she couldn't risk one email, one word… JaneDoe still loved him.

Or maybe Mark was kidding himself. JaneDoe was dead silent because she's just plain done with him.

Six months. More like seven now.

"Another?" Mark's waitress discreetly inquired, sympathizing with his empty, lonesome glass.

Mark shook his head. "Gotta go." He paid cash, emerged from the VIP cocoon into a teeming O'Hare corridor. Went to Gate H23 and boarded a 757.

He wasn't carrying. He could bring his gun on domestic flights. Not on one to Paris.

Hadda admit, felt kind of naked without it.

ACKNOWLEDGMENTS

I'll thank but not identify the smart, sweet, supportive people who read early drafts and responded with annoyingly accurate notes. Notes requiring cuts and rewrites, which, I'm obliged to admit, did result in some tiny improvements.

And I'll thank but not identify the friendly, generous folks who provided access to and advice about some of the locations in this story.

I acknowledge what the topic of this book entails. I acknowledge this is 2019, and none of these good people deserve to be troll fodder.

LENNY KLEINFELD's first novel, *Shooters And Chasers*, was called "A spellbinding debut" by Kirkus Reviews.

His second novel, *Some Dead Genius*, was one of National Public Radio's Best Books Of 2014, and named Thriller Of The Month by e-Thriller.com.

Back before he was spellbinding, he was a playwright in Chicago and a columnist for *Chicago* magazine. His fiction, articles, humor and reviews have appeared in *Playboy*, *Galaxy*, *Oui*, *The Reader*, the *Chicago Tribune*, *New York Times* and *Los Angeles Times*. According to a reliable rumor he also spent fifteen years writing screenplays.

JENNIFER CAWLEY